JUDGE ROSA SOMBERLY

The Caiman v Tau al-Gorz

Colly Campbell

Sooty Publishing

JUDGE ROSA SOMBERLY

First published in Australia in 2024 by Sooty Publishing, Canberra, Australia.

www.collycampbell.com.au

Cover design: Red Tally Studios
Typeset: Liquorice Light Publishing

A catalogue record for this book is available from the National Library of Australia.
ISBN: 9-780645-1967-26

The most powerful force on Planet Earth is nature.
The second most powerful is the human imagination.

Ciara Somberly

For Emma and Lachie

GREEN PADLOCKS

Seven padlocks hang from a row of green shutters along the outside wall of an attic room. I crouch in this strange roof garden. Being night, and cloudy, the padlocks are just visible in the thin bright beam of my pin torch. Old-fashioned, each shaped like the number 8, with a steel locking loop above, dull green.

Between shuttered doors and along the rooftop terrace are garden plants: creepers and climbers. Shadows of two small trees are visible in the back corner and I hear the rustle of a bird in the foliage. The pungent smell of jasmine and magnolia linger in the overgrowth. An intoxicating smell. I feel a little dizzy as I sit on a wrought-iron seat by a round garden table.

Don't know why I stay. Don't know why I sit pondering my chances in this hidden roof-garden, with its walls. But I know after the hot summer's day, a storm is almost come – I can hear rumbles above – and the rain is thickening. Cold pelts start to hit my face and shoulders, and they mute the scent of jasmine. Clouds are low, catching the dull glow of the city. Behind the shutters it's soundless and dark.

I decide to break into the attic and get out of the rain. Question is, which of the old-timey padlocks to pick?

*

Earlier, I'd stood on top of the attic room, on the roof ridge-caps, and looked over the wall to the streets below. This house is the highest in a line of old sandstone townhouses, with a long view over every other building in the vicinity, so I have an excellent vantage point, the highest in this 'hood.

I stood there for a while and watched the stars blink in and out behind gathering clouds. I meditated on the blending sounds in the city canyons: busses, cars, trams, jostling pedestrians, music from bars, people talking beside open windows, lonely birds. Then I'd slid down the slate roof on my bum and landed quietly in the roof garden. Again I listened. Below, the city hummed its hum.

I didn't run off. My urban explorer friends Yusif and Sukki had jumped earlier, but I still hoped to bust into this attic and find a temporary shelter for my urbex crew.

*

It's now cold and raining. I hold the tiny pin torch with its bright needle beam between my teeth and pull the pick tool from my leg pocket, and bend to the end door aiming the light-beam at the hole in the padlock, which I lift. The heavy green lock fits the palm of my gloved hand, and with a twist or two of the pick, the mechanism clicks open. The lock feels too heavy for its size. Lead? Its dark-green paint is peeling. I slide it from the latch and then hook a finger under the long wooden shutter and gently pull. Behind, a closed French door, frame painted dark green. Through the glass I see almost nothing, but a soft glow down the end of the room through a slit in the thick curtains.

My heart beats hard and fast when I break into the unknown. Tonight, it *thumps* in my chest. I stick a loop of packing tape through the gap where the doors meet and gently hook the upper and lower inner latches to slip them out of their holes. I slide behind the velvet drapes, drawing the shutters and the French doors shut behind me. Silently.

Then I peek through the dusty drapes. First impression, the attic is a long single room with rafters. A bit musty, mingled with other strange smells: the sour tang of swamp, and wet on the nose. How odd. I peek through the drapes. Further down the room two figures slouch in large chairs. Big figures that cast giant shadows on the wall. A standard lamp throws light onto a table they both contemplate. As my eyes adjust I see the table has a chess set upon it, a game in progress.

Now, being a man of action I'm not one for chess, but I see the game is three-quarters finished with captured pieces lined up at either end of the board.

The board, and those glittering gold and silver chessmen, is not my focus though. The two players are a strange sight. When my eyes fully adjust and I see what I see, I almost retreat through the doors, the garden, and jump over the wall, but decide: *This must be some fancy dress thing*. One figure has a shock of black unruly hair, lank around his shoulders. A cruel-looking face. Thin lips. Blotchy red skin and a massive hand, with huge dirty nails, sitting flat on a huge knee. His brown robe is open and I see movement on his chest – a blinking face poking through the robe's gap, small, but not that of a child. Two beady little eyes gaze at the board. Apart from the blinking chest face that comes and goes from my line of sight, the hairy ogre (or what I imagine is an ogre) remains implacably still, thinking through his game with a crooked eyebrow and furrowed forehead.

Closest to me is the back of the other chair. I can't see the opponent's face, but I gasp when I see a thick reptilian tail, looping from under the sitting creature. The tail has a jagged top ridge of armored scales which shine dull gold. I can also see a green scaly claw on the chair's arm. The reptile thing is hunched over the board, its toothy snout casting a long shadow on the wall.

"Well Tau al-Gorz?" the scaly figure says in a low rumble. But the ogre remains immobile.

"Patience, Caiman," says a voice, not from the ogre's mouth, but from the ugly little face in the ogre's chest.

I start to breath. Very quietly. Time passes and I have to stay still – something I always find difficult. My t-shirt label starts itching my neck for the hell of it. The scaly hand reaches forward and picks up a glass and drinks some pale-brown liquid. That's all that happens in the space of half an hour, and I feel terribly trapped. Can they possibly hear me in the room? I try to make no sound.

Then a door opens. A bright hall behind it with a vivid red light. A small girl ambles into the room. Maybe 10? She's dressed in cotton pajamas. The light illumines the two figures even further, and makes them even more frightening – cast in a crimson glow – but neither move a muscle as the child enters, so fixated are they on the board.

The girl walks up to the board and stares at it with the same fixity. She tilts her head slightly toward her right shoulder. Two smart little black-pupiled eyes, and black hair in bedtime plaits. Why isn't she terrified of these monstrous creatures? I can see a floating head on Tau al-Gorz's chest look inquiringly at the child, but the ogre himself is as still as a mountain.

The child reaches out with a quick little hand and moves the remaining gold rook on the board and takes it forward three squares. The ogre lurches forward and looks where the rook now squats. The ogre roars. The ogre's face becomes thunderous and he stands, almost bashing his head on the rafter above. The robe opens down to the waist and I can see two figures almost carved on its chest, enveloped in saggy skin, locked in a furious fight with each other. The tattoos (are they tattoos?) hold each other around the head. They seem to be planted there, but they yell and punch.

Then the ogre pulls a long dagger from his robe belt.

"No...no..." says the Caiman, who starts to stand, reaching out a claw to stop the ogre's savage intent. I gasp in horror. I can now see the huge crocodile trying to calm its opponent, but the ogre roars one word, *Sabotage!*, and in a flash the dagger is thrust into the chest of the little girl who yelps once and is lifted like a leaf on a spike in the ogre's hand and dropped limp against the third chair.

I feel sick, but frozen to the spot.

At this moment a tall man rushes into the room like a storm, an old guy, grey hair, glasses, wearing what appears to be a dressing gown over a business suit. He sees the crumpled form on the observer's chair.

"Rosa, no!" he shouts. "No!"

He inspects the dead child pinned to the chair and there is a long pause, as the ogre and its chest creatures stands frozen. The ogre, though, looks defiant.

Then the tall man yowls an anguished howl. He slaps Tau al-Gorz's face hard with an open hand, and the ogre starts to burn with a yellow-blue glow, all over. Flames rise, growing hotter and hotter. His robe catches fire. Flames lick up his neck and I can just see the two creatures on his chest move in panic. The fire grows bigger and a sudden searing heat almost burns my face as the flames turn white and I smell burning cloth and flesh, but it doesn't last long. A *whump* noise, and the ogre becomes a tornado of fire stretching from floor to rafter that implodes on itself with a hiss and disappears. Then dark again, apart from the red hall light and the dim standard lamp. When my eyes adjust moments later, I see the crocodile creature tipped back in its chair, the small child impaled by the ogre's cruel knife on the third seat, and a mound on a rug on the floor beside her.

The mound, I assume, is the tall man, her father, buried under his dressing gown.

Finally, I exhale, too noisily. The Caiman's face turns for a moment toward me, I see the glint of a golden reptilian eye with its black vertical slit. The creature's breath is a stink of river mud and fish. Our eyes meet and somehow I know that the Caiman was accorded the chess game victory – pyrrhic, but a victory nonetheless – on behalf of the rivers and jungles, the home for which she is fighting.

The Caiman is fighting the ogre, Tau al-Gorz, who is colonizing her lands. I somehow know – perhaps through the fish-breath – that the child's father was mediating this dispute through a game of chess, as agreed by the parties, which is an almost eternal game in a continuum of the likes of the Caiman and Tau al-Gorz. As my eyes meet the crocodile's, this knowledge breaks into my head, like I'd broken into this strange room. Furtive, but definitive.

The Caiman knows she owes the child her victory and knows the father has not the Caiman's powers over life and death. The Caiman growls as if making up her mind. I watch the creature's long armored tail uncurl from beneath the chair as the crocodile moves toward the dead girl. The tip of the reptile's tail touches the girl on her slack foot, on the sole, while at the same time, a claw reaches across and pulls the knife from the child's chest.

The girl's body doesn't fall, just seems to sit there. Somehow I know that the power of the Caiman's world and its creatures – the anaconda and jaguar, birds and monkeys, trees and vines, the shamans of the great watershed, the winding streams and rivers – will send their energies like a mighty defibrillator, through the Caiman's tail, into the child's foot, and up through her inert body. The blood caking the small girl's chest starts to dissolve. The green currents of life mend her heart and restart the bioelectrics of her brain, and the wound knits, while a reptilian shadow enters her at the same time. Color comes back to her pallid lifeless face, and finally, finally, her eyes open. And like the gold chess pieces, like the Caiman's eyes, they are now golden.

The girl inhales – a short sharp breath.

The Caiman then, after her life-restoring act, slides from the chair with a soft thud, and maneuvers her massive head and sizable bulk out of the attic, through the red-lit door and away, past the girl's lifeless father on the red Chinese rug. The last thing I see is her spiky tail disappearing through the door.

And I exhale again, very noisily.

The girl's golden eyes turn toward me. She jumps from the chair, oblivious to the mound that is her father.

She walks over, lifts her hand and I hold it. It's small and cold.

The child says: "Are you hungry? I'm very hungry." Cautious voice.

"I'm hungry, too," I hear myself say. And I am! I haven't eaten all day. The child's question is almost normal. I look at this troubled girl.

Her mysterious eyes gaze at me, and yes, they have the crocodile's black pupil, a vertical line in the gold. They are beautiful in themselves, but the child appears dazed after her ordeal.

The girl leads me in silence past the chess game, not looking at the slumped shape of her father, into the red-lit corridor and down a short flight of steps and we get into a small lift that descends two floors and opens directly into a vast kitchen, but I'm still stunned and can't think of anything to say. Two great lights, like white flying saucers, hang from the ceiling on thick brass chains. I see marble benchtops, brass edgings, a large silver fridge in the corner which she walks over to.

"Here," she says, and opens the fridge. "Can I have a toasted sandwich?"

Being brought back to life by some giant Crocodile firing up all your organs like a machine clearly makes you starving hungry.

"I will, if you tell me your name," I start uncertainly. I'm not used to children. "I'm Benji."

"Rosa," she says quietly. "You are a Benjamin?"

"I'm a Benjamin."

"I'm a Rosa."

I can't help myself – I smile at her and she smiles an uncertain smile back. I cannot fathom what she's thinking, asking a random found in her attic to make a sandwich, after her father has collapsed, but here we are. I feel I should be back there, tending to the father, but I don't want to leave the girl alone.

Rosa sits motionless, watching. I scramble to find a sandwich press, some bread, cheese and ham, and make four toasted sandwiches. Rosa munches through three, daintily, holding each edge with thumb and forefingers. I eat one.

"Where is your mother?" I ask.

"In heaven," says Rosa, and I can tell she knows it is just a sad euphemism for something else. I feel the urge to check on her father even more, but also feel bound to stay.

"I'm really tired," she says, slurping some milk. She is so small. She is also, if I am correct – (and I am) – alone.

"How old are you, Rosa?" I ask.

"Ten."

We look at each other. She hasn't asked about anything that happened. The monsters, the chess game, her dad, anything. Rosa looked pale and exhausted. I wondered what to say next, then thought – what would my Mum have done?

"Rosa, maybe you should pop to bed. You've just been through … a lot. It's very, very late."

She slowly nodded.

"Do you want to sleep?" I add.

"I think I do," she says. The child's golden eyes are half closed with tiredness.

We find her snug bedroom with a little single bed, which she shuffles into with a bit of fuss. She doesn't ask what happened to her father. She probably already knows, as I, when in the attic, suddenly knew things without knowing or understanding them. I read half a page, very quickly, from a bedtime story she picks called *The Bone that Rapped*, but she's fallen asleep at the first sentence, exhausted by the effort of dying and then coming back to life, head and black pigtail resting on a soft pillow.

I turn out her light and hurry back upstairs.

Still the same. There is the chess game, the huddled heap that is Rosa's dad on a huge Chinese rug, the standard lamp, the bloodstain on the back of the third chair. I pull the lamp closer to the father and turn him over and lift the dressing gown. The man is curled, almost fetal, not breathing, eyes open, but fixed. I look for signs of life and, with an achingly slow movement, one of his pupils slides toward me and seems to focus.

Just alive, then. There is a long slow moment and then a voice comes to me. The sound is freakish, in my head. Goosebumps run riot up my arms and neck.

"Rosa?" he asks, but his mouth doesn't move. I just hear the voice like a creak in the wall.

"She's alive," I say aloud.

He sighs without breathing. A strange, happy sigh from a man in so much pain. A mixed sigh. All there, so expressive. I begin to relax.

"I'll call an ambulance."

"No, no, I am gone. I am dead. My heart failed instantly when I saw her pinned on the chair ... with the knife ... how is Rosa alive?"

"The crocodile thing. The Caiman, somehow ... brought her back. Don't know how."

"Ah. Caiman. Caiman." His creaky voice I hear, but the lips don't move on his corpse. "Queen of the rivers, empress of the forest. Her bastion is the living jungle and its waters and all its creatures. So powerful."

The man stops and there's a sound like the wind in trees, but again, no sigh is exhaled from his still mouth.

Then he speaks once more. "Caiman is now Rosa's godmother ... which may be a problem ... but still. She is alive. And you. You are now Rosa's protector, for I am gone."

Protector? All I did was break into the house, make her a sandwich and read a bedtime story.

"Who are you?" I hesitantly ask the corpse.

"I was ... The Judge. I should have ruled on their case, Caiman and Tau al-Gorz. I should have heard them in court and ruled, but I was a coward and ordered them to Vindication by Chess. I let them battle it out on the board. I was a ... fool. And Rosa was attacked because of my idiotic, foolish, cowardly decision.

"Usually, usually ..." the voice in my head vagues out and returns like crappy mobile reception, "Usually, the Judge rules. The Judge is the last resort of all disputes between the Elementals ... and many others. I am gone now, and Rosa is my heir. This house ... Rosa's house, is the safe place for all who are in dispute. They can come to the Hall of Justice with a complaint, and their case can be heard, with the rule that justice will be meted out. In the end, one side will not prevail, but justice must be served, and I failed on that. I let my love for Rosa cloud my thinking and the house became a place of danger. Then my temper was roused ... I struck out. For The Judge, this is forbidden. I cannot cause harm."

There was a choking noise, a pause, and then the wavering voice in my head continued.

"You will find this place strange, my boy. But in our continuum you will eventually make sense of things. In my study are the books, the precedents." His voice withers like a gust of wind had ended. Then, again it returns like scratching paper: "... the links and chains. She knows much already. You must read too, to understand, help her."

I hear the man swallow without anything on his body moving. Clearly he is making a mighty, mighty effort post his death, to stay and instruct, to tell me about stuff that's way past my ken, my understanding.

"The law will become clear to you," he says, as if reading my mind. "She will be the next Judge ... ha! ... already, she IS the next Judge. You will henceforth protect her from the folly of the human world, and the cruelties of the Elementals. Protect her, keep her safe. The house is yours, my boy. Yours and Rosa's."

No, I am thinking, I already have a place and life with my crew. The sliding eyeball regards me, but how can he be so sure?

The Judge's voice sounds so sad. He says softly: "I am glad she lives, but I don't know what it means."

"Who was the creature that burned?" I ask.

"Tau al-Gorz, sweeper of change. The invader. The bull. He lost because Rosa intervened." Pause. "Like she was some pawn." Long pause. "And then she became a queen as pawns sometimes do."

"And who are you. What is your name?"

"My name was Somberly." I note he talks of himself in the past tense. Finality there. "But I was best known as The Judge."

And with that the voice blows away for the last time, and the man remains curled around, stark and stiff, with his open eyes like whelks on a rock, staring at me. I close his eyes, like I'd seen in movies, and pull the skew-whiff glasses from his face, lay him out on the rug as if he was asleep, and cover the body. Then I push the bloodstained chair into a dark corner and cover the stain with a large cushion.

What do I do? My head is filled with horror and anxiety about this dead judge basically sentencing me to look after his strange daughter. Why hadn't the Caiman revived Rosa's dad also? What did he mean: *protect her from the cruelties of the Elementals*? This chills me. Elementals like Tau al-Gorz? Were there more ogres? The books in the study should tell.

I stand over The Judge's body for a moment, and then collapse on a chair and stare at the chessboard to see what Rosa did with that rook. The rook had clearly been Tau al-Gorz's piece. I'm a man of action, not much of a chess player, but even I could see the game had only a few pieces left standing. Pieces protecting pieces. An intricate network of threats and bluffs that were beyond me. The Elementals were both deep thinkers and plotters, clearly a long and complicated battle. Moving the rook had exposed the ogre's queen to the danger of a pawn and the queen would have been bottlenecked in the next move. The silver king was still vertical, but the gold king lay across its square, taken. I hadn't seen anyone move the king in a final abdication during the earlier melee. Curious. Why hadn't the ogre laughed the child off and moved his rook back three squares and then kept going? Why had he roared and murdered her? What was significant about the chess set?

I reach out to shift the rook back but can't lift it from the board or slide it with my finger. I try with all my strength but it is set like a golden stone. As soon as Rosa had shifted the rook, the game was over. Somehow Tau al-Gorz had lost. I sit in the ogre's chair surveying the battlefield, conjuring question after question.

*

Finally, after many ponders, and my decision to stick by Rosa until other arrangements are made, I creep down the staircase with its oil paintings on the walls. Looking up, right above me is the wide skylight which I'd seen earlier, while standing high on the roof capping. Framed in the white ceiling I see a hint of grey dawn lick the glass. Rain is still washing across its outer surface. I stop to listen at the slightly ajar door of Rosa's room and hear her breath softly, a nightlight catching the lump of living child under a quilt.

Looking after a kid is a big ask! Never have I thought of caring for children, because I've only stopped being a kid myself, and sometimes, if I'm honest, I still am a kid! Nineteen's not old. I'm tired too and the thought of being a carer exhausts me more.

The house is apparently Rosa's and mine, though I don't know how that happens without lots of lawyers and kerfuffle. I shower, and in a chest of drawers in Judge Somberly's simple bedroom find some cotton pajamas. I decide not to sleep in a dead man's bed and settle in a guest bedroom next to Rosa's, leaving my door open and a side-light on so Rosa can find me if she wakes up. I don't want her to be frightened.

I wasn't to know then that "being frightened" was never a trait of Rosa's after the Caiman's touch.

ROSA

"Hello? Hello?" says the girl, standing by my bed, shaking my shoulder.

For a moment I don't know where I am, then I see her spooky eyes, and jolt awake.

When I'd first seen Rosa in the attic room with her pale face and eyes of coal black she'd seemed just a normal little girl. Small straight nose. Black hair, still in tidy night-time plaits. Now her gaze was golden, flecked. Her pupils are not small round points, but black reptilian slits.

"Rosa," I say, gathering my wits. "I must show you something. You might not like it."

I slip out of bed and motion her over to a wide wardrobe mirror.

She looks into the mirror.

"The color of your eyes changed," I say. "After the Caiman … revived you last night."

She stared impassively at her reflection. I thought she'd be upset, but nothing seemed to surprise her. Head tilted one side, then the other. I gazed at the reflection in front of me – two people in a bright bedroom. The child in her pajamas. Me in mine, standing to one side with a shock of mussed black hair. I seemed a little more hazy in the reflected image, almost a grey oblong blur, but perhaps it was a trick of the light.

"It's okay," she says finally. A simple statement.

"Breakfast?" I ask and she nods.

I am filled with dread.

I filled with dread when she woke me and the dread was not about those golden eyes. I dreaded telling her that her father was dead. How do you tell a little kid? Still, I follow her down the stairs, through the cavernous house, 'til we reach the kitchen.

*

I've been a street kid from the age of 13, so I've seen rough things and often felt hard times and hunger. I had a healthy fear of adults: been beaten by oldies before, and escaped worse at their hands by using my wits and running legs. I wasn't much older than Rosa when my stepdad chased me out after he'd found a new girlfriend. Living on the streets, my schooling was patchy, but I learned to think my way through life - read, write, and do numbers with the help of many kind people. I learned very quickly about kindness v. bad people's ways and I thrived with good ones. I grew tall, my shoulders broadened and I learned to fight to protect me and mine and be kind and loyal in return.

Now I'm a survivor who doesn't live on the streets anymore, because I know all the tricks, and as urbex – an urban explorer – I'm one of the best. I survive on my smarts and work together with friends in the same sitch. Strength in numbers, we say.

I do small, sometimes illegal, jobs for people to make a little money here and there, move with my crew to empty flats or abandoned apartments or offices, which we bust into and use to sleep for a while, then move on. All move, move, move. We sometimes find work and share resources, or eat food from restaurant skips, and cafes, or simply steal from shops.

Me, Elodie, Chaz, Yusif, Sukki, and a few others on the margins, who come and go depending on chance meetings, romances, or are newbs who turn up and receive my crew's generosity. So, we hang together in various permutations of people.

The core five of us have been a crew for a long time. In this city, everywhere is owned by someone, but many flats and apartments are unused and empty. They are well-appointed holes waiting to be filled; vacancies crying out for life. When we find a property with water, electricity, even wifi, we enjoy our good luck, but also know that the rich folk's sensors will detect us if we stay more than a couple of days. Rich folk may not use all their possessions, but they can always tell when someone's messing with their stuff.

Last night on Rosa's roof garden, my urbex friends, Yusif the Greek and Sukki Tokyo girl, were with me, but they'd jumped. When we'd climbed up and over to the intriguing garden ledge with the rickety-looking shutters we'd thought: looks empty, this could be a new hangout with a great view, all quiet and dark. Then a sudden red flash behind the shutter slats had half blinded us. Yusif and Sukki looked at each other (they're very close) and made a silent decision to retreat. Their call.

Like mountain goats skipping across ledges, Sukki and Yusif had jumped, using a vertical row of awnings and a fire escape further down to break their fall. Sukki thinks she's a little ninja. Perhaps she is – she's small and fast. Yusif is slim and strong too, but much, much bigger. If some handhold – gutter or rail – were to go, it would break under Yusif's weight, not Sukki's. I watched over the ledge, and they made it without crashout. I'd looked down to the gloom of the back garden and saw them land, crouching, scuttling into the shadows like the city crabs we urbex are. Then there was no movement. A silent garden plot, a back lane. An emptiness.

I knew we'd meet the following day at the elbow park further downtown that was our afternoon hang. The park formed where a big boulevard split into a Y junction. Green space for the surrounding (rich) residents in the cleft of the Y. And some trees. A park where the locals take their desperate dogs for a pee, and birds land on their way through to a better forest.

I stayed on that roof because something had made me curious – the strange old-fashioned feel of the padlocks, the shutters and the little garden.

Urbex are everywhere: roofs, cellars, sewers, schools, spires, telco towers, factories, offices, riverboats. We have balance, ropes, helmets, pro-cams. We prowl and we know our world. Our parents have died or forgotten us, let us down or made us flee. We are the abandoned.

*

So, I look at Rosa and know about loss and aloneness. I know why Judge Somberly made his judgment that I was not to abandon his daughter: I was abandoned once, and it hurt so deeply. I already take the Judge's request seriously, but Rosa must agree to it too. I don't want to force the issue on her.

Anyway, what would the state do with a child with golden eyes? Children's Services and all that? A girl who is some sort of judge herself, but too young to have the old-person presence, and legal knowledge to unravel the big games of life? My heart aches for her, like it ached for me those years back when I was thrown out. Until my heart grew a tough crust.

I pour cereal into Rosa's bowl and sit and I started off with: "You know how you told me that your mother is in heaven?"

"Yes."

"Well, your dad's there too, now, with your mum. He died last night and I'm very, very sorry."

She nods.

Rosa looks miserable and I reach out and hold her small hand. I want to hug her, but I don't really know her. Her nod confirms she already sensed her father was gone. In fact, I had an inkling she'd known last night when she turned to me for help. Walked over to me in that gloomy room and reached out to the interloper, the soft touch, trying to be bright and friendly, reaching out for an ally. This girl is not a stupid unit.

Now she is crying, because of the truth that had been spoken. The truth of her father's death.

"Rosa," I say gently, "after you went to bed, and before he went to heaven, I spoke to him."

I tell her of the strange conversation, when he'd talked to me when he was dead (this fact doesn't surprise her) and that her father had asked me to look after her.

She finished her cereal. I made us some tea. We sit on stools at the big brass kitchen island which could fit 12 people.

And then we talk and talk. She is ten years old, both small and hyper-smart for her age. She was taught at home by her father, and a series of tutors who schooled her in music and maths on Mondays, Tuesdays, and Thursdays. Somberly the Judge taught her writing, history, philosophy and law. Especially law. Imagine a 10 year old doing legal studies?

Most days she shopped for the household, sometimes went swimming at the beach or the municipal pool, because she loves swimming. Sometimes she and her father caught a train to other cities where he would preside over trials, or they'd travel just for fun, for holidays. She'd climbed in the mountains and looked for lakes – more swimming. All these things she tells me that morning while I make cups of tea for us, and we warm to one another.

After starting the morning sad and subdued, she becomes more animated as she speaks about things she liked.

Rosa talks about her mother, who died when she was six, how warm and loving the woman was. Died in spring when the crocuses were emerging, giving Rosa a loathing for crocuses.

"I learned many things from Mum. Things Dad could never have taught me," she says in a steady voice.

"Girl things?" I ask. "Or science things?" Her mum was apparently a chemist.

Rosa shrugs. "Things that Dad didn't know."

When we stop talking, the grief again floods into her.

"I'm very sad," she says.

"Your father seemed a wise man."

"He was a judge. I will miss him a lot."

Then she weeps for some time, and her face looks like a crushed flower. I hold her hand and pass her a tissue. Soon the crying becomes mizzle, then a few sniffs, and then she jumps off the chair and clings to me for a minute. She wipes her face with a greasy napkin.

"What do you think?" I then ask. "About what your dad said about me?"

"My father said you are to protect me. That is your sentence by The Judge for breaking and entering. To look after me. I don't think it is a harsh sentence," she says.

"I don't think it's a sentence at all. Your father asked me to be responsible because you are on your own. But it must be your decision too. Is this your wish? That I look after you?"

She stares steadfastly at the floor.

"It is," she says.

"Can I see my father?" asks Rosa finally. I know she's been preparing herself for this all morning, becoming truly animated when talking about life with her parents. "I want to say goodbye and prepare him for his journey."

She slides off her stool.

Still in our pajamas, we walk up two flights of stairs and up the smaller set of steps that lead to the attic room, which she terms the Hall of Justice.

"Wait here, kid," I say and open the drapes. I go out the same French door I'd entered last night and to my disbelief find all the locks gone. No time to ponder. I open the shutters and let the sun flow in. In daylight, the room looks clean and bright. Rosa stands at the doorway.

"He's over here, Rosa."

She walks over to where her father lies under the dressing gown and we both crouch beside him and I pull the gown from his body. The corpse appears old, craggy and serene.

Rosa has the saddest little face I've ever seen.

"Why did he die?" she asks, perplexed.

"Well, I think it's because he saw you were dead and his heart broke. And remember, you were indeed dead at the time. He must have loved you totally and forever." Rosa is silent. Then she nods.

"Goodbye, Father," she says. "I love you too." Tears trickle from her eyes.

I cover him up again. I should be crying along with her because it's so sad, but instead my head floods with practical questions.

"When your mother died, where was the funeral? Where was she buried?" I ask.

"She wasn't," Rosa says. "It's not the way of our family. Come with me."

We go onto the sunny terrace, a beautiful roof garden that I could smell last night. Pruned shrubs and a couple of small trees, perfumed flowers creeping on the wall of the attic room, some twine through the shutter louvres, even a patch of grass under the wrought iron chair where I'd sat last night. There's a hint of damp on the leaves after the rain. We walk up the side and round the corner, and here there was a higher wall along the edge, and a green-slate slab, almost like some sort of altar.

"We laid Mum there, and in two days she was gone."

"What?" I ask, shocked. Laid bare to the elements? The weather? The birds, insects and rodents? I thought of crows eating the corpse. The very thought made me feel queasy. I remember hearing a bird in the tree last night.

"Our family is made differently. The elements took my mother away. That's what Dad said. He said this is where we must be laid, on our deaths. All our family members."

I examine the slate. It's flat and hard, washed clean by the rain over time. Dark shapes – flecks of something – can be seen in the rock. Fossils, perhaps?

"Can you help me lay Papa here?" she asks.

"Don't we have to tell the authorities?"

"We are the original authority," says Rosa miserably. "That is our burden."

"Did your dad say that?"

She nods.

"He didn't let the city authorities know when your mother died?"

"I don't think so."

Go with the flow, I think. Do what the kid says. My urbex crew survive because we keep things neat and simple. Let's see what happens.

So we lift her father onto a small rug and gently slide him onto the terrace, and round to the slab of slate. I lift his slack body with the limp swinging arms and lolling head onto the slab with as much respect as I can. There we carefully undress him and lay him so his sightless eyes point at the blue sky.

Rosa and I go downstairs to the kitchen and make some preparations and change into our day clothes. Doing "last rites" as she calls them, in pajamas, didn't seem appropriate.

On the terrace again, we wash his body and begin to cover it with a mixture of honey and oils that Rosa had prepared. A tall man, grey haired, thin but not gaunt. Clean toes and fingernails. I'd closed his eyes and his mouth seemed to be at peace. After last night's talk, with all the pain of loss and worry for Rosa, his mouth had somehow now slackened into a less contorted shape. And although he was in the open air, no-one in the city could see the body from any angle unless a low-flying plane, or a drone took notice. Or you actually stood by the slate slab.

I think again, will crows pick his bones? Gone in two days seems unlikely. Bodies take time to decay. I feel that things are going to be messy for a long time. And smelly.

"Won't he be attacked by …?" I start to say.

"Mama was gone within two days. Disappeared. I don't know how it works."

"Did you wash her body like this too?"

"Yes, with my father. It is our way."

"How old were you then?"

"Six."

I don't know what to say. Tough ask for a kid who's six, cleansing a dead body, let alone a 10-year-old. But bodies don't disappear from slabs! I had a sinking feeling that perhaps after Rosa's mother was placed on the slab, her father had come back and disposed of her body while Rosa slept. I feel very uneasy, especially as the weirdest looking bird has just landed on the roof lintel. It has grey, shaggy feathers, a bald black head and red eyes, with a horrible knobble on its hooked black beak. The creature looks like some feathery dinosaur.

"Go away," I say, "shooo!" waving my hand at the horrible looking bird. It cocks its head and ruffles its scruffy feathers.

"Don't," says Rosa sharply. "The friarbird lives here in the garden and keeps her eye on things."

The bird goes *squarck!* which I understand as: "That's right." I can only nod an apology to the friarbird.

Rosa continues putting her unguent on her father's body, gently dabbing.

"Are there any words we should say? People who need to say goodbye?" I add. I'd been to funerals. My mother's, those of friends – too many friends blinked out by circumstance – accidents and overdoses. But Rosa just shrugs.

"Not that I know."

Then she pauses, thinking back to her mother's death. "And Papa said: *Death is the parting of the molecules and the ways. You rise with the dust and settle with the dust. There are no words that can possibly overwhelm death, so, why say anything?*"

The friarbird listens attentively and said *oich!*

"Papa also said: *Instead, use the fist of your mind to grasp and hold onto your best memories of your mama, and let the sadness wash over you again and again for a while, like the ocean waves, until all the sadness is washed away, and when you open your hand, the memories will be beautiful smooth stones that will last forever.* But you don't say that to the body, you say that to yourself," she finishes.

Rosa stands back with a smile and a tear in her eye. "I love you, Father," she finally says in a small voice.

I think, this kid is very unusual. If this happened to me, to someone I adored the way she adores her dad, I'd be a soggy, devastated mess, like I was when Mum died.

Rosa and I wipe our hands on an old towel which I put in a zinc bucket with the empty bottles of oil and honey jars.

*

"Come on," she says and we walk down the third side of the Hall of Justice, which is less overgrown. Just an azalea border against the wall and some old wisteria creepers throwing branches and purple flowers onto the roof. She reaches up to a thick wisteria vine and scales up onto the roof tiles, landing on all fours like a zippy cat. "Come on," she says.

I'm urbex. No problemo. I reach up and haul myself over the guttering in a flash. We walk nonchalantly to the roof ridge and stand on the capping – her balance is easy, relaxed, and I'm completely unworried for her safety. There's quite a breeze, and her black hair, released from the plaits for the ceremony, floofs about a bit, but she's fine on the roof ridge. I am too. We tightrope walk along it to the end and look down on her father's body. He's plumb in the center of the slate slab, in the sun, pasty-pink.

"Papa's at rest now," she says. I see the gloomy friarbird perched in a tree nearby.

Over the wall, across the road down at street level, there's a small local park with high railings round the outside, so I presume only residents can get access using a key. Further down the hill, Rosa's street hits the main road, and it's full of people walking hither and thither, going to work, or the shops. A tram flashes past, followed by a convoy of cars and motorbikes. Far off, beyond the houses and the docks is a streak of green-blue – the ocean, and clouds way over on the horizon. A couple of jets cut the sky, leaving a trail of cloudy vapor.

"I used to come here after Mum ... left ... to talk to her."

"I often go to high places too," I say. "It's peaceful here above the city. You can think more clearly when you can see a horizon."

She asks, "Can you do flips?" then stands and flips gracefully three times along the high line of ridge-caps, like a folding wave, into a handstand on the top of the attic. I smile at this astonishing display of acrobatic skill as she dismounts, slowly, carefully, feet finding the point of the roof.

The roof is steep, slippery slate, precarious. I slowly bend backward, curving my spine right back and feeling for the metal, and then I copy her graceful handstand. She peers at me through her eerie eyes and seems to nod. Someone who knows balance and strength. Maybe she wants a playmate, or some sort of protector when the chips are down. I banish these musings because I must land cleanly. Again I feel my way down to the ridge cap, feet touching the narrow surface. A little bit dangerous, adrenaline surging. I feel that she's testing me, but in serious little kid mode she just nods and says: "Good one."

Then we sit in silence for a while. I sense she wants to think things through, while sitting with someone for the comfort of being with an-other. I can almost hear the cogs in her mind ticking over, trying to reset her situation, readjust to the fateful circumstance. Maybe to remember the sequence of events last night.

*

I'm correct.

She finally asks me to describe what the Caiman had done, but I start at the beginning, where I break into the attic up until she moves the chess piece. The rook. The last thing she remembers.

Sitting on that roof ridge, I find that I can't leave one item out, in fact, things I'd forgotten pop into my head at the retelling: such as, how my eyebrows were slightly singed when Tau al-Gorz combusted, the heat being so fierce; the Caiman's glance at me, the swampy smell of its breath, and how understanding seeped into my mind; the tail stretching out to Rosa's body, the agonizing wait while life seeped back into her veins. It's like I'm compelled to bear witness.

"And father hit Tau al-Gorz?"

I confirm with a nod. "Struck him on the face."

"And a combustion happened?"

"Yes. Do you remember anything after you were stabbed?" I ask.

"Well, no. I was dead, wasn't I?"

"Yes. Caiman knew you were dead, and somehow I understood her thoughts. When the Caiman sighed and looked at me, I knew."

Rosa pondered for a bit, then speaks.

"I remember the knife flash in my face, but it didn't hurt. Just went dark in a milli-second. Not scary dark, just blank. But I wasn't asleep … after I felt the short burst of burning heat, then blank again, and after a forever time I woke up but couldn't move or talk because my mouth was soooo dry. That's all Mr Benjamin."

We sit in silence again, in the sunshine, on that roof, until she says, "Come on" and we slide down the tiles onto the terrace below.

Back in the big attic room she walks over to the chess game – gold king prone on the board – and says, "Hmmm".

"Hmmm," she says again.

I point at the rook she'd moved.

"I remember this," Rosa says. "I came in and immediately was in the game. Tau al-Gorz was losing. I tried to help with the rook, but he couldn't see the path to checkmate. He thought it was a childish error. Wasn't! I was being nice, helping the loser. Would have been checkmate in two moves."

"He thought it was a childish error 'cos you're a child."

"The childish error was mine because when the course of justice flows on its own, I should never interfere. That was the error. He was going to lose and I was trying to be clever, but I am a child. I have learned a big lesson. And it is probably good that Tau al-Gorz combusted."

Then, one by one, Rosa puts the pieces – that I was unable to lift – into place for the next game.

"This is my job – to set up the board," she says. "What I always did for Papa. We played all the time."

I pick up a pawn and it is as heavy as I'd expect for a silver chess piece. I toss it up a few centimeters where it flashes in the sunlight and catch it in my palm. Still light.

"I couldn't move these pieces last night."

"The weight of justice is now lifted," she explains to me. "The game is over. The judgment has been meted out."

"What judgment?"

"On Tau al-Gorz, on my father," she says in a little voice, "and on me."

THE ELBOW PARK

Rosa and I enter what she calls the "junk room". A tall, narrow, gloomy room adjacent to the kitchen. There's a sliding wooden hatch-window against a counter that opens to a dining room on the other side. The junk room is filled with shelves loaded with boxes that are loaded with stuff. The shelves head for the ceiling like steps. On a hat rack at the end hang hats of all sorts and sizes. There is a strange bronze statue of a cowboy throwing a lasso on a bench.

"This was once a butler's pantry, in the old days," Rosa says grandly as she shuffles through the boxes, "where he would buttle for my grandfathers and grandmothers. Prepare plates and trays on the bench and then pass them through the hatch. The drawer is somewhere here," she says, crouching under the counter. "Yes. This one."

A drawer full of spectacles and sunglasses. We sift through the tangled spectacle arms and find a small pair of round tortoiseshell sunglasses.

"Mum wore these," she said simply.

She put them on to obscure her weird eyes. I show her in a little red mirror on the butler's counter, and she nods in approval.

We are going out.

Her father lies in state, or at least in a state of nature, high on the roof terrace, and Rosa is satisfied her "last rites" have been successfully carried out under the friarbird's watchful eye. Now it is time to go to the elbow park and find my crew.

I'd asked Rosa, gently, if she was up to coming with me, because I need to tell my friends I'm peeling away for a bit, and I owe them an explanation. She'd nodded and said: "Fine. It will take my mind off things."

I want to introduce them to Rosa and tell them I now have obligations, and for a while, I'll be elsewhere.

A big word for me: "obligations".

I never imagined I would have to care for anyone except myself, and in a collective way, my crew. We look out for each other, make sure no-one starves, or gets sad and suicidal, but really, it's not a caring role. We watch one other's backs, but mind our own business at the same time. Except for Yusif and Sukki who care for each other. They are an item. But for the rest? I'm in love with Elodie the alpinist, but she is always cautious with me in return, says she doesn't want to get attached, so my love is a one-way street.

I lock the front door and, in the sunshine, we descend the eight steps to street level, where I spot an iron gate and steps to a little flat below the level of the pavement.

"Who lives down there," I ask Rosa.

"Mrs Cimbalom. Our cleaner," she says.

A cleaner. I didn't know.

"Mrs C comes on Tuesdays and Thursdays, and she used to babysit me."

"Does she know your dad was The Judge?"

"Oh yes," says Rosa.

"Won't she notice he's gone?" I ask.

"She already knows," says Rosa.

We catch a tram, one of the old ones. Wood-paneled, turn of the century. The conductor clips our tickets and looks at Rosa strangely. Maybe he glimpses her eyes behind the glasses, but he moves on up the tram clipping tickets. He has a job to do.

We get to midtown and walk up one of the narrower, tree-lined streets, past the older town houses, much like hers, then down another hill to where the elbow park is. The trees look refreshed and green with the overnight rain and the city air is quite clear.

The time is past 4 p.m. now. It has been a busy day and I feel very tired. Rosa is full of bounce, but looks nervous because I have explained that I must part from my crew for a while. She is worried, and on the tram she had told me why. They may be angry with my decision and, as a consequence, hate Rosa.

But right now the crew can't live in the house with us, because it's Rosa's house, and she'll be grieving, and her father's corpse on the roof. I'm also uncertain about my responsibilities, and I've had a growing suspicion that when I picked the oldy-timey lock so easily, up on the roof terrace, the house let me in on purpose. I feel bad. I was looking for a new hang for the whole crew, and I ended up finding a mansion just for me. Maybe they can all move in later, but not just now.

The elbow park is shaped like a folded elbow. Named after some dead general whose big bronze statue gets pooped on by birds, but we (the crew) have our own nickname because of the shape. The park is wide at one end, narrow at the other where there's a Y-junction. Paths lead through it under beautiful oak, ash and elm trees.

Down one end, there's a concrete skate bowl where Chaz and I used to come a few years earlier, when we weren't much older than Rosa, and hang out and waste time doing halfpipes and ollies. This is where we met Sukki

, who is also a skater. This is where things took off for the crew, like a high kick-flip. We can't stay away because it's like we own the park.

My crew are all there at our usual table, having coffee and ice-creams at the kiosk and they wave as I approach. There's a playground across the central pathway from the kiosk, so that mums and dads can sit at the cafe and chat and watch their kids, and further along a bunch of older guys, who look like walnuts in suits, play bocce on a sand rink under some trees. They're always there around this time of day. Plenty of late-afternoon promenading is going on, and people heading home from work, kids from school, one or two joggers. A friendly park.

Yusif, the handsome Greek Adonis with his black beard, Elodie the alpinist from France, blonde and tall. Sukki, the Tokyo ninja, and Chaz. He and I were born and bred in the city, and its alleyways and electricity wires course through our veins. We've lived here all our lives while the other three are trapped in the city by circumstance. But we are a family, because I believe when you look out for people, they are family, and I look out for my crew.

And right now, I'm feeling bad, and Rosa is super-nervous.

I buy Rosa and myself an ice-cream cone, then sit with the crew. I introduce my new friend who sits in a wire chair beside me. The crew are curious and friendly to Rosa. Who wouldn't be friendly to a small well-mannered girl in cute tortoiseshell sunglasses licking an ice-cream?

Now I have to find the guts to tell my four best friends the bad news. Slowly, I explain that last night her father went away, and he'd asked me to "stay with her" for a while.

Won't say "look after her" because I get a feeling that Rosa is capable of looking after herself. She sits, licking her ice-cream in a rather hypnotic, lizardy manner, examining my friends closely.

"Where's your dad gone?" Elodie asks in a curious and slightly stressed voice as the whole arrangement around some random kid has happened so fast. Elodie has a friendly face and can relate to a strong girl, but Elodie likes me to hang out with Elodie!

"Away. He will be gone for some time." So, Rosa can lie. I'd asked her not to explain what happened last night and she's kept her part of the bargain.

"I'm living at that house with the rooftop garden where Yusif and Sukki jumped," I tell the crew. "I won't be exploring for a bit." I find those words so hard to say out loud.

"No, no. We can explore," says Rosa, slightly horrified. "I don't want father's sentence to cramp your style, Benjamin. I'll just have to come along."

Yusif and Chaz are disbelieving and angry. Yusif looks at me and mouths the word: "Sentence?" Clearly Rosa hasn't guessed what the urbex crew do.

After my announcement sinks in, Chaz's look becomes more thunderous, like I've betrayed everything. But he doesn't question my decision.

"You better come back soon," he grunts. "We're family."

Elodie's reaction is even worse, which both upsets and heartens me.

"So when will we see you, Benjee?" Elodie asks, still with a disbelieving eye on Rosa, who is nibbling at the edge of her cone. Elodie, my on-again, off-again girlfriend looks really upset at my "peeling off". I try to smile.

Angry Chaz changes tack. "How old are you, kid?" he asks. He's wearing sunglasses too. And his climbing shoes, ready for action. And a green tank-top and shorts. Muscles burst like tree roots from his arms and legs.

"Ten. But I have balance and can climb."

"She has," I confirm.

I'm glad we're onto another subject, even if it's a grilling of Rosa.

"Climb that tree," he suggests, pointing to a towering ash near the kiosk that is at least 30 meters high, a mass of summer greenery which fountains into the sky. An impossible tree. He's now being an arse. The first lateral branch is about five meters up a huge trunk.

"Really?" I ask Chaz, and he smirks.

But Rosa hands me her half-eaten ice-cream and is gone. We look around and Sukki turns a shriek into a muffled squeak and points up. Rosa's already on the roof of the kiosk. How did she get up so quickly? No-one notices, though there are plenty of people around. She reaches up. A thin, hanging branch laden with leaves seems too high for her arm, but somehow she springs and grasps it and flips herself up to a standing position. How did she do that? I glance around and no-one else sees this feat, except my hypnotized urbex crew.

"She's a little squirrel girl," says Elodie, astounded, a hand framing her brow as she stares upward.

Now walking along the branch (its leaves shake slightly at each footfall) Rosa leaps up to catch hold of a semi-vertical branch that she scales with ease until she disappears into the foliage, unseen. Then, almost at the top of the crown, where the branches must be perilously thin, she appears between a bunch of leaves and hanging on, gives a cheery wave.

"Huh?" says Yusif.

Elodie and I wave back. With a precarious running jump along a lateral branch, and a flick, she leaps onto a high branch of the next tree and disappears for a while into that crown. I start to worry. But then, like a trapeze artist – or is it a squirrel? – Rosa uses thinner branches to bend, catch, bend, and descend in a twinkle, until she jumps onto the back of the kiosk roof with the slightest of bumps and disappears. A few seconds later Rosa appears around the corner as if she's just visited the toilet block. She's hastily replacing her sunglasses which had been stuck in her pants belt for the climb and descent. I hand her the ice-cream – it has hardly melted. She gives me a secret little smile, while trying to look cool.

"Ok?" she asks the group.

Stunned into admiration, no-one knows what to say. Except Chaz.

Chaz laughs. "You'll do," he says. He likes adrenaline and Rosa just delivered him some, vicariously. Even Chaz can't sprint along branches.

Chaz is my best mate. He started as a juvie criminal, in and out of foster homes and jail from the age of 10. A strong little boy, both physically and mentally, son of African refugees who couldn't hold it together. At 14 he was sent to by a dumb judge to bootcamp to "knock some sense into him" and he did two weeks in the mountains at an outward bound where he learned ropework – climbing, rappelling, hitting those ledges like a chamois goat. That changed him from a lippy standover kid in one of the drug gangs in the city's east, into a proficient cat burglar. So much for "sense being knocked into him". The only sense he acquired was a sense of space and body strength, and he'd been taught how to plan meticulously. For a couple of years he stole and survived, but finally he was caught on a hidden camera and sent back to jail. He promised the parole board that if the authorities found him a job at a gym learning to be a personal trainer, they'd never see him again. The authorities agreed and Chaz powered up in the weights room and rock-climbing galleries. He quit after his parole period ended and became an excellent, uncatchable cat burglar, which is how we met. He's still a personal trainer, but only to his friends.

His manners are smooth, his tactics excellent, but inside, after his rough start, Chaz is hard as nails. Still, he is my loyal friend and always up for some fun.

"So when will we see you," grunts Chaz on behalf of the crew. He's still not happy with me, even if Rosa has delighted him.

"Next week, I think. There're things we have to sort out. Tutors and stuff." I make it sound humdrum. I don't want the crew hiking along the roof and finding the dead judge on the roof. They can come over when the birds have picked his bones.

"I'll pass by the hang and get my pack now," I say and start to leave with Rosa. The crew quarters are not far away from the elbow park where I'll collect my clothes, sleeping bag, a couple of books, my phone charger, all the possessions of an urban nomad.

"Okey dokey," says Chaz. "We don't have anything planned until the Embassy. You will turn up for that, won't you?" he adds.

"Yep."

There's a long pause as he darts a pissed-off look at me.

"Chaz, I'm okay, man. I'm on for that," I reassure him, maybe too much.

"Me, too," says Rosa cheerfully, but Chaz doesn't smile this time. The interloper is wrecking his crew.

Rosa sucks the last of the ice-cream out the bottom of the cone, and munches the rest, as I kiss my unhappy friends goodbye and hug a pissed-off Elodie.

As we walk off, I can almost feel their eye-daggers in my back.

"Chaz was angry," Rosa says.

"I have a responsibility to you now. They're still my friends. Things will smooth over," I tell her in a bright voice. My tone is fake to reassure Rosa. Inside I'm very upset, but as I hit the boulevard I remember her dad's direction: *You will protect her from the folly of the human world.*

Easy to say, not easy to do.

THE JUDGES HOUSE

Rosa is super tired, recovering from the death of her father and the trauma of her own resurrection. I'm sure these events still have not sunk in. After I read her *The Bone that Rapped* again, tuck her in, and almost close her bedroom door, I resolve to explore the house – after all, I'm still urbex!

It's still early but we ate a big dinner of honey chicken wings and chips that we made together and a dessert of ice-cream mondae (a concoction of ice-cream, mango, and honeycomb choc). After that, Rosa was ready for bed.

So far in this rambling house, I'd been at the tip of the top – the roof, witnessed a murder in the Hall of Justice and cooked in the kitchen. I'd also explored the third floor with the comfortable bedrooms and bathroom. But the rest is a mystery. The Somberly home is large, heavily furnished and beautifully decorated, and it seems Rosa's family has lived here for a very long time, judging by the old-timey oil portraits.

I don't start at the roof because The Judge, as far as I know, still lies there in state. We'd already been up before dinner to make sure he wasn't being predated on. He lay on the slab with the guard friarbird standing on his left foot. The crinkle-headed bird gave us a friendly *clank!* and sideways nod. Not a carrion fly in sight, even after a day of lying in the sun.

The exploration begins on the fourth storey, down from the short flight of attic stairs where the red lightshade hangs, and one level up from the bedrooms. There were two doors at the lift, either side of the landing. One room I enter is some sort of laboratory, an big L-shaped room. I assume this was where Rosa's mum, the chemist, worked. There are beakers, and racks of chemicals in jars; big microscopes, and advanced-looking electronic equipment covered in plastic dust protectors; a barometer on the wall which points at "fair". A chemical smell pervades the air, metallic and sharp.

At one end is a huge bookcase full of notebooks and folders. A big, solid safe in the corner – goodness knows what is in there. I pulled a notebook from the shelf and saw it contains complicated chemical formulas written in a neat, clipped hand. Each book was dated alongside the signature, *C Somberly*, on the inside cover and I sit for a while, trying to make sense of the notes. On a blackboard is a scribble: *"Chemicals were always there. Humans just caught up with the play and named them"*, and underneath that, *"Don't forget the milk"*. As if Rosa's mum had just gone to bed too, with a reminder on the board. Had her father left everything as it was after his wife died? Possibly.

C Somberly was clearly a scientist. I open some drawers and see partitions in which sit chunks of colored wax with stuff embedded in them. I pick one up to sniff, but it doesn't smell of much. I put everything back in place.

The laboratory is unvisited and dusty. I assume Mrs Cimbalom doesn't clean here much. I turn the light off and enter the smaller room at the end of the landing.

A bedroom, with an old wooden four-poster bed and some delicate etchings on the wall. The tall, sash window looks onto the street, four-stories down. Orange light from a streetlamp pokes up through the top of the plane tree below, like marmalade squeezing through mesh, and cars are parked, bonnet to boot all the way along. A man in the park across the road and down to the right kicks a football with a boy who looks about the same age as Rosa. The dad is no doubt trying to tire his son before the boy's bedtime. Kick, kick, kick, they go without pause. There is plenty of lighting in the neighborhood, so the football players are pretty accurate.

I take a closer look at the many delicate etchings. They are portraits, but with lines etched so finely, they are almost spiderwebs. If it wasn't for the grade of ink and the coarseness of the print paper, they'd be invisible. The faces are all lifelike. I think I recognize a younger Judge Somberly in one, and a woman who looks like an older version of Rosa in another. The scratchy line at the bottom says *Ciara*. Maybe Rosa's mother, whose name starts with C. I move to look at a portrait of a dog with fur swept like fine filaments with the name *Old Fuzz*. Another shows a rather faded Alsatian dog with the name *Vieux Flic*. The dresser and wardrobe in the room are empty. Perhaps Rosa's mum slept here when she worked late in the laboratory? Was she a restless night owl? The radiator is turned off and the room is cold, but it could be cozy.

That's floor four.

On floor three are the bedrooms. Judge Somberly's bedroom, where I'd helped myself to pajamas and dressing gowns, is a room without many flourishes. A bright oil painting of fruit and leaves, a very good one. I look at the signature and it says *G Courbet*. Crew business means I know a bit about art, and I know if this is an original it's worth a lot. Some books on The Judge's bedside table: a mix of biographies and travelogues.

Rosa's room is opposite her father's, and my room – the guest room – is beside hers. At the back of the landing is a spacious bathroom with big white tiles, brass taps, a bath with impressive eagle-claw feet (Rosa showed me them with glee), a long sink where my newly purchased toothbrush sits in a mug with Rosa's little red one. The room is bright and modern. A separate toilet next door, and then a elevator door. The stairs, with the iron balustrade, appear to become a little wider as I descend to the second floor, where a vast room runs along the front of the house with a view across the street – Judge Somberly's study. Both parents have imposing workplaces, and this one is packed with books, his big desk, on which sits a human-skull candle holder (a little bit over the top, I think, because the skull is real), lots of papers, a rack for pens, a comfy chair, a chaise lounge on which to recline.

The dead Judge kinda told me the answers to our future challenges were in his books, and here they are. The bookshelves reach to the ceiling and seem to keep going until I realize it's a painted ceiling to give the impression of an endless library all the way to the heavens. A chandelier sits plumb in the middle. The skull candle holder is for show, as there's also a sensible reading lamp on his desk next to wooden trays filled with papers. Another reading lamp with a shade depicting goldfish swimming round and round is placed behind the chaise.

I'm drawn to a large old-fashioned globe on a stand. Twice as big as a basketball, it's made of wood and, looking closely, I discern areas showing the world's deserts, oceans, forests and mountains, the North Pole with white on blue, and Antarctica. This is not a political globe with pink and yellow countries and defined boundaries, but a topographical one, or even a bio-geographical globe, with terrain. I look more carefully and can see swirls of cloud. I look even more carefully still and I'm startled. They appear to be moving, as clouds do, above the land and ocean. I find a large, thick magnifying glass on the desk and concentrate on one swirl of thick cloud and am amazed to see a flicker, lightning perhaps, on the surface. I gingerly move the globe round and stare at the Amazon basin, which I know is Caiman's home, and see wisps of smoke along the edges of one river and then, for a while, I am hypnotized by the whorls of weather around the North Pole.

Uneasy, I put the magnifying glass down and sink into The Judge's desk chair, a very comfortable leather affair with a footrest and padded arms. Yes, there are law books and briefs piled on the huge desk, along with letters addressed to Judge Somberly, or Mr Roland Somberly, his full name. From this angle, the heaped papers in the in-trays look formidable, but I vow not to go through the paperwork until Rosa is with me. And at my elbow is a half-finished glass of wine. Judge Somberly must have been sitting here when Tau al-Gorz started roaring "sabotage", and he'd sprinted upstairs to his death.

"I'm sorry I didn't stop Rosa being … hurt," I say to no-one in particular, and the walls seem to bend in, infinitesimally, acknowledging my apology. Not that I could have done much to save the black-eyed Rosa from the ogre, Tau al-Gorz. For a huge disheveled lump, his knife hand was fast and deadly.

For a while I sit in the comfortable chair and think about this weird situation and realize I know nothing, absolutely nothing, about what I've promised to do. Zilch! Nix! Nothing!

What the strange house means? Rosa's role is as "Judge"? Or a basic question: what sort of judging do the Somberlys actually do? Clearly, they are not part of the country's criminal justice system. It's weird as!

This lightning bolt of realization shocks me out of the semi-comfortable feeling I've had over the last day. I sigh and resolve to answer some of the questions so I can help Rosa a little better. What floats in my mind's eye is the vivid scene of Somberly's corpse saying, "Protect her, keep her safe. The house is yours, my boy. Yours and Rosa's."

Another shock goes through me ... the dead Somberly seemed to know I was homeless, rootless, looking for a haven. Now this busy, busy house was emptied of its adults, its owners, and left to a little girl and me, a vagrant youth.

After sitting in the big chair, and swirled with mixed feelings, I finally move to further discovery.

Next to the staircase, the lift, and at the other end of this second floor landing, another large room across the back of the house. I enter, turn on the light, and stare in amazement.

A treasure gallery or a museum? Many paintings on the wall of all shapes, sizes and hues. Big old display cabinets rest on the floor, and up at the end are ancient Greek pots, a tree of mummified owls, classical sculptures of naked men and women, formed from both marble and bronze. I walk around the museum room and it seems much larger and wider than could fit the back half of the house, but maybe it's an optical illusion. The ceiling is painted too – golden cornices, and birds in a tangle of vines and plants, and there are several mirrors confusing my sense of space. What a beautiful, curious room. I look at some of the paintings: they are all well-lit, and I do recognize one signature. *Picasso*. I know about Picasso from a job the crew did last year, and this one could be from his famous "blue" period.

Wow!

After looking at the treasures for some time, I look at my phone and am surprised to find that it is way after midnight. Time has whizzed past. So I turn out the light, close the door, and descend to the first floor, which I know quite well. The kitchen where Rosa and I have had a few heart-to-heart's and toasted sandwiches, then the butler's pantry which leads to the dining room, again fronting the house, with a long table that could seat 16 or 18 people, sideboards, a full sized suit of armor on a plinth that I tap with a teaspoon and hear the ring of metal. It is real.

The room has high, fancy curtains and a lower view of the street, at a midway point of the plane tree. I look out between the drapes and there's no-one in the small park. The soccer playing man and boy have long gone to bed. And the pavements are clear of people.

Down to the ground floor via a grander staircase, with beautiful, polished railings held by a cast-iron balustrade of interlaced leaves and flowers. Again, from the art jobs we sometimes do, I know the ironwork style is art nouveau. This is the entry staircase, flaring out to impress the visitor as they come through the front door. The steps sweep down to the very large vestibule, with its ornate floor tiles and the big front door flanked by window sections. The windows contain some sort of stained glass decorations, which I hadn't noticed before, but can't make out. I'll look in the light of the morning. To the right of the front door is a comfortable, intimate living room, a big table at a bay window, and cozy upholstered chairs, and a large brick fireplace with a mantelpiece covered in small bronze and marble busts, plus a vase full of fresh flowers. I walk up to the fireplace and run my finger on the grate. Soot. Still used, clearly, although fires are frowned upon in a modern city. A nice comfortable room. A family place.

Then I'm surprised.

In none of the other rooms is there a television, or a computer, or even a digital clock (all the clocks are mechanical), but along a sideboard is a high-end music stereo system with a turntable and a CD player. I open the bureau underneath and it is stacked with classical records going way back to the time of thick shellac discs and all the way forward to LPs. I nod approvingly at the collection. Still *olde worlde,* but an electronic form of entertainment. Someone in the house loved music.

The room to the left of the vestibule is long and thin. Smaller than the lounge and more formal, also with a fireplace. A low table and chairs and a beautiful long painting, almost a mural, four panels of the four seasons – Spring, Summer, Autumn and Winter - depicted as young women. The girl that depicts Autumn, with reddish hair and sweeping gown, looks faintly like Rosa (though Rosa's hair is black), or maybe the woman, Ciara, in the etching I saw on the fourth level. This painting is in-your-face style – it ripples with color and line. I look at the signature and it says, *Alphonse Mucha*. Never heard of him, but he's good.

A room to receive people. Clients of the Judge perhaps?

There is also a baby grand piano at a bay window, and a couple of music stands stacked in the corner. A music room also? This is where Rosa has her lessons.

Behind the sweeping stairs are smaller rooms, two each side of a corridor and a bathroom at the back. Empty and abandoned. Servants' quarters, perhaps? Or for kids? One or two rooms have single beds with bare mattresses. There's a small bathroom, but the fittings are a bit rusty, the sink stained. No-one has used this area for years, it seems, but there's a back door leading to the small garden. It's locked with an old-timey lock, but I can't be bothered picking it. The garden can wait.

I'm much more interested in my favorite thing about houses in Old Town. I open the door set in the side of the staircase and inhale the scent of the cellars. A dark smell. We urbex love the cellars, the tunnels, the routes below the pavements. I have a bright torch this time, but there's a switch that lights the cellar stairs so I turn on the wall lights, and I make my way down.

Well, of course – there's wine. Lots of dark bottles, necks sticking out the racks like condemned heads stuck through the guillotine. I don't know if the wines are any good – a beer drinker myself – but they are kept cool and I understand this is important. They are stacked between the brick foundation columns.

Ancient paving stones – very large slabs – line the floor. I move past the wine along a wide passage which is used for storage. Garden tools and a mower, some empty animal cages. And I round the corner, startled to find a bigger space. The walls and columns are decorated stone carvings which look like moonscapes, and in the middle of the room is a dark-colored slab, same size, I think, as the one on the roof. It's dim here, so I flick my torch on and examine the surface and it has fossil imprints. Fern shapes, mostly. Black on the dull-green stone, but rather beautiful. Although I could smell the cool of the earth, or the stone, it wasn't at all moldy or musty. The space smelled fresh.

I wish one of those moments of osmosis would happen – like when I had a clear understanding from nowhere about the Caiman, or The Judge. I wish some explanation would pop into my head, but I was in the strange cellar and none too cluey. I couldn't work anything out, especially the meaning of the giant slabs.

I am now very tired. There is more to the underground part of the house, but I decide to call it a night. Rosa could help me explore next and tell me what she knew. I wonder if there were exits into the maze of the city's tunnels – old medieval passageways, or war bunkers, or even sewers and other utility tunnels. I knew they were many and varied.

There are at least two heavy iron doors with green padlocked latches set into the far wall, and there's another passage. But I'll have to leave the cellar for another time.

I'm tired, so take the lift upstairs, puzzled, discombobulated, but in no way frightened, even after witnessing some quite traumatic events. There is a dead man on the roof. A child who has part-morphed into a crocodile.

And yet ... in my bones I feel safe, as if the house is a sanctuary, guarding its inhabitants.

Until that stabbing, even the Ogre and the Caiman hadn't been frightening, although unsettling, for sure.

Yes, there was a level of contentment and peace in the atmosphere. Surrounded by beautiful objects and such wonderful decorations.

What a strange house.

I fell onto the bed, closed my eyes and had sweet dreams, all night.

THE CASE OF THE ANGRY CATS

At the front steps are many, many cats. Thirty or 40 cats, waiting in the sun, one or two pacing, others grooming or asleep. Tabbies, greys, Siamese, street cats and pampered white and black fluffers. Human passers-by look worried by the feline agglomeration, but Rosa doesn't.

It's been two days since I moved into Rosa's house and we've been shopping. I carry two bags full of milk, biscuits, chicken legs and vegetables. She carries the light one with the ice-cream.

Rosa scowls at the cats and looks at me through her large sunglasses.

"What are they hanging at the house for?" I ask.

"Probably a legal dispute," she mutters, small face lost in the rain-jacket's hood. "They want father."

I can't believe it. As we ascend the stairs, the cats flow apart like water, as if we were the prow of a boat pushing upriver. Up to the door, I unlock it with the key, and we enter with the cats gushing in around our legs.

Rosa thinks for a moment, and then pushes open the door to the comfortable sitting room on the left and says: "In here."

Normally a quiet room where you bring breakfast to read the paper in the morning sunlight which crosses the park and shines through the bay window.

The cats, numbering at least 100, swarm in and inhabit the room as only cats can. They claim ownership of every cushion, perch, patch of rug, and armchair arm. They sit between the busts on the mantelpiece, along the top of a tall bookshelf, everywhere. Tails – ginger, grey, black, speckled – flick and curve, eyes peer at us with the common insouciance that cats own. Even though cats are clean, the room is permeated with a strong animal smell.

The windows out to the street are high and I can see the trunk and first branches of the plane tree outside. The neighboring apartments, a relatively modern set, are opposite, but the tree obscures our strange assembly from view.

Rosa removes the sunglasses and scans her audience.

The cats gasp. Have you ever heard a cat gasp? Some tails wave wildly, almost angrily, from fright. There are also purrs. A mixed verdict. Her crocodile eyes look like a cat's eyes.

"So it's true," says one cat near me, and another nods. I can now understand cat language, in this strange house.

"My father is dead," Rosa tells the assembled cats.

"That means you are The Judge," says one of the larger cats, close to Rosa. I am shocked that I understand its yowling tone.

"I'm an apprentice judge. A judge in learning."

"You are not allowed to be. There must always be a Judge," says another fat tabby with a scarred nose. "By the way, nice eyes you got," it adds, and there is general consensus among the cats, though a white fluffer near me says, "This may prejudice her decision. She's been touched by the wild!"

A Siamese beside it says in a quiet gossipy voice: "Interesssting point. You're right. This may taint her judgment."

"My understanding is that Bastqut, Elemental of the cats, is responsible for your law," says Rosa showing more than a little knowledge.

"I am," says a voice at the back. I can hardly see the shape that is talking, but it is certainly a large cat shape. "This dispute should not come to your jurisdiction. It is squarely in mine," Bastqut says. "And you are just a child."

Rosa looks slightly panicked by the last remark. The larger cat shape at the back of the room starts to take more form, smoky black, yellow eyes much like Rosa's. At recognition by Judge Rosa, its form has become more solid. Bastqut holds what looks like a rod with a fluffy dangle on the end.

"Why are you all here?" I ask. At this point my head is spinning.

"Who's that?" spits a cat, noticing me for the first time.

"My ... Associate, Mr Benjamin," says Rosa.

Ahhh. That'd be me.

Strangely, I don't feel uneasy or under threat. There's no tension in this room despite the presence of a cat god plus 100 cats, many of whom appear anxious. Rosa later tells me that The Judge's house is strictly neutral territory.

Rosa explains to me, in front of the cats: "I believe there is an unresolved dispute between parties."

There were growls and mews of agreement.

"They may want to appeal a decision by Bastqut here, who is their Elemental."

More noises of agreement.

"Cats must eat," says a rather scraggy tomcat up on top of a bookcase. Then it proceeds to lick its paw.

"And why cannot Bastqut preside over this dispute?" Rosa asks the crowd.

"There is a view among WE, of the city street cats and wildcats, that Bastqut is prejudiced against our kind," says the scraggy cat

"Okaaay," says Rosa slowly. "And why is that?"

"He oversaw and encouraged the domestication of the cat in Egypt – our original home – to make life easier for cats ... some cats ... and therefore he finds in the favor of domesticated cats, always."

"Always, Bastqut?" Rosa was holding her own. I was impressed.

The smoky cat form at the back seems to grow in size: "We cats are independent animals with the utmost dignity," he says. "I seldom have to mediate. Cats know what to do. They are of great intelligence, wild or domestic."

I can see Bastqut's silvery whiskers now, great spikes emerging from his cheeks, and smoke is swirling around his eyes.

"Who will make the appeal for the street cats?" calls Rosa, but a small cat on a table interrupts.

"Why are we not on the roof? In the Hall of Justice?" it shouts.

"For now the roof is a place of mourning. The great slab holds my father's body. It would not be appropriate."

"Ahhh," say some of the cats. One licks its lips which unnerves me.

"And this is just a preliminary hearing," she adds, slightly panicked. "Justice won't be served today. I ask again, who is the appellant for the street cats?"

A huge ginger tom waddles forward.

"I am the appellant," says the growly tom.

"Your name?"

"Mason."

"Your case?"

Mason clears his throat and begins: "Because of the terrible climate, the heat, and the water shortage, there are less and less birds, and less and less mice in the cities, in the parks and wastelands, and along river and canal banks." Mason is an orator. Eyes flashing, he was just getting going.

"While house cats are fed by their human slaves on a daily basis, we street cats have to survive in the wild. However, it had always been the case that there was plenty of hunting for all. Now, we are finding slim pickings. The birds aren't breeding so well, the rats and mice are being caught, and there are fewer lizards. We are going hungry. We need to eat! Our plea to Bastqut was that the house cats eat their canned food and dry kibble, and stop hunting our food. But this was denied."

There's a general purring from the assembled street cats, while the house cats swished their tails.

I nod and pass a note to Rosa:

As a street human, I've noticed not so many birds in the city as before, possibly. Might have to check this.

She looks at my note and gives a curt nod.

"Have we a representative of the house cats?" Rosa asks. The Siamese cat who had made rude comments about Rosa's eyes stepped forward.

"Me! Missy Wiggins. I present an objection to The Judge's fitness to hear this appeal. Should you not disqualify yourself from this case?" says the arrogant little Siamese. "Recuse yourself! Your eyes are like ours. I am concerned that you have been touched by the wild."

The cat even steps forward, flicks her tail, and sniffs Rosa's leg. "You smell swampy. This may be prejudicial to the case of the domesticated house cats."

"As you all know, I am the only judge that can hear such an appeal. I assure all cats that I will make a fair judgment," says Rosa in a calm voice. "I may have been touched by the wild, but I am also tame. I hold both worlds in my heart and this will assist me in finding the balanced decision." She glances at me for reassurance and I nod.

"Tau al-Gorz could hear our appeal," says the snippy Siamese. "He is all-powerful."

I look at Rosa in shock. *Tau al-Gorz?*

She doesn't flinch.

"Firstly, he is indisposed at present, and secondly, he has no standing in our system of justice. So I'm afraid not," says Rosa in a level voice as she talks about her killer. "Proceed with your petition on behalf of the house cats."

Missy Wiggins puffs herself up. "As Bastqut says, birds, mice and lizards are fair game for all cats. Some owners imprison us with a foul fetid poop-tray in our houses and flats, and these felines are the victims of human cruelty. Miserable cats. But most of us can get out and about to hunt. This is important for our mental health and a varied diet. It is medically recognized that a diet consisting of only dry kibble can cause kidney damage. We must also eat flesh and blood and organs and gristle and brains."

"That's your claim?"

"Yiss," says Missy Wiggins.

"Thank you for your petition," Rosa says in a polite voice.

"And Bastqut, you have previous ruled on this dispute between the street cats and the house cats and denied the petition of the wildcats? What were your reasons?" she asks the smoky black form at the back of the room.

"Some years ago, I heard these complaints," the cat Elemental says, his voice low and slightly menacing, "but as always in the precedents of feline law it is 'every cat for themselves'. We are hunters. Cats must hunt for mental stability, house cats and wildcats alike. Just as domestic dogs, for their mental health, must go for a silly walk round the park once a day on the end of a rope to pee."

When Bastqut disses the dogs there is general snickering from all cats.

"This case was heard already in the Court of Cats, and I ruled that every cat, no matter their station, could hunt. That's the end of it. That is the way of the cat!"

"And when was that ruling?"

"Only 32 cat years ago," hisses Bastqut.

Rosa makes a note: *four years back.*

"Not long ago," she murmurs. Then Rosa addresses the crowd.

"I will study Bastqut's previous ruling. And street cats, I will ask my Associate, Mr Benjamin, to do some research into your claims about the lack of birds and mice while I talk to house cats about their diets. This Court of Last Resort will reconvene here in one week's time."

"Can we make the hearing at midnight," yowls the cat called Mason. "Much more convenient for cats. We should be napping now."

There's a general purr of approval in the room.

"So be it!"

The cats clear the parlour, and flow out down the stairs into the street in a great furry wave, and then Bastqut seems to be gone too.

"How come I understood what the cats said?" I ask in wonderment.

Rosa looks gloomy and says, "Parts of the human mind have been clogged up for a long time," as if she was reciting a lesson. "The house helps to unlock those blockages and you now understand more about other forces in the world. Language is everywhere. People have forgotten to listen," but she is distracted, and looks down at her notepad.

Rosa sighs and then puts her hands on her face in despair. "I am sooo out of my depth. Sooo difficult. A cat ambush! I'm not ready to be Judge."

"You sounded very sensible. The cats treated you seriously."

"That's because in their eyes I am The Judge," she says earnestly. "But what sort of judge will I be? I don't know anything ..."

"You seem to know a fair bit," I say reassuringly.

"One thing I do know ... I feel sorry for the sparrows," she says.

*

Yusif is older than us and went to college. Although he's well read, he hated his humdrum existence as a philosophy tutor and threw his lot in with the urbex crew. His new motto was: *To think life, you must live life.* Chaz had toughened him up and, of course, he found Sukki, who is the absolute love of his life.

Yusif sits alone in his favorite Greek cafe at the small table at the back, reading a book and sipping an expresso coffee, looking thoughtful as usual. I sidle up to him.

"Hey," he says, pleased to see the missing crew guy. Yusif is very mature about people and the decisions they make, so he holds no grudge that I've left the crew. Also, Yusif is as funny and happy as a rebel philosopher can be. A few years back he got me into reading from the sack of books he lugged from hangout to hangout. I've read all the greats, Plato, Jack Kerouac and Agatha Christie.

During my old life, in between training together and thieving work, we talked about philosophy stuff and he helped me to think more clearly about how the world works. He was like a personal tutor. And I taught him some home-truths too, like *living a good life is about trusting your judgement,* and *never burn a friendship that's worth having,* which still makes me feel queasy about Chaz's current attitude with me. Apparently he's started referring to me as a *snake in the grass.*

I order an expresso likewise, and sit and say, "You know a lot of stuff, so can you advise how someone can work out how much wildlife there is in a neighborhood?"

Yusif thought the question was funny and laughs.

"Why?" he asks.

"Oh, we got a mouse plague at Rosa's and I've noticed less birds in the trees. Just interested."

"Get a cat," he advises.

I think about the river of cats and smile.

"Yeah, no. Can you measure how much wildlife there is?"

"Forget the cat. Get an ecologist...they'll know...they measure these things." He looks a bit professor-like with his handsome beard and thick black reading glasses. He points me to an ecologist he'd once known at the university. Then we chat about other stuff. Yusif says Chaz will come back – we've been brothers in arms for too long. "Life goes on. The others will get over it, bro. After all, we're still the same crew," he says, making me feel a little better.

After a couple of hours of hilarious chat, I pay for his sticky black coffees, thank him, and phone Professor Ebeneezer Fleezlemeyer.

*

Next morning I go down to the stoop to let in Mrs Gamelan, the piano teacher. Lying on the doormat were three dead blackbirds, and several rat and mice corpses. I apologize to Mrs Gamelan as I usher her in, and while Rosa plays her practice pieces on the baby grand, still wearing sunglasses, I bury the rats and birds in the small backyard plot.

The practice pieces float from the music room, strange chords form tunes that remind me of bells blown in the wind.

After the lesson Rosa looks down at the rat and bird grave and says the cats were now trying to bribe her with gifts, but she didn't know whether it was the house cats or street cats who were responsible.

"They're disgusting," she whispers.

By seven o'clock that evening there's another sizable mound of mangled mice with their little guts hanging out, chewed up sparrows and headless lizards at the front door.

"I thought cats slept during the day?" I say as we stood looking at the doormat.

"I think *both* sides are trying to bribe me," she says.

"Can't we stop them?" I ask. "It's a massacre."

We take a shopping bag of dead things and a large kerosene lamp through the back door and out into the garden and I dig another hole. I notice shadows moving stealthily along a back wall, and there's a rustle in a tree that overhangs the laneway behind. Rosa also senses the surveillance. We're outside and it is clear the trees have eyes and ears.

"Cats," she announces, rolling her eyes, "while I appreciate your gifts, they won't sway my decision. My ruling will be on law, reason and precedent. I won't be bought," she adds more loudly, into the dark. "The decision will be mine alone." She almost shouts. "If you are indeed hungry, take these creatures and eat them." And instead of putting them in the hole, she lay them in a line along the top of the garden wall.

Still, her performance does not stop the bribery. The next day, on the doormat, was not only quite a sizable pile of sparrows and blackbirds, but a squirrel, eyes glazed and dead.

"Only Wednesday. Four more days of this senseless slaughter," she mutters.

By then, without telling Rosa, I'd placed a small motion-sensitive night camera on the stoop, pointed across the doormat. So I connected the camera to my device and turned it on. Was it house cats or street cats trying to bribe The Judge?

I lay in bed watching the feed from the camera on my phone. One by one, cats of all shapes and sizes scuttle up the stairs and leave a gift. As I lay there, I watched in horror as a huge walleyed tomcat dropped a small Chihuahua in the pile. The dog was still twitching, and looked quite badly wounded. Mice were bad enough, but a Chihuahua?

I spring out of bed, tiptoe down the staircase, and open the front door. A half-moon is slung in the sky like a hammock, and the tiny dog is trying to stand up, but kept falling over onto a pile of dead rats, mice, birds and lizards. The Chihuahua has a bloody bite on its neck and under its tiny front leg. As I bend over to help, I smell a hot stinky breath behind me. Suddenly the steps and the half-moon disappear in a haze of black smoke, then something grips me around my chest.

"Hey," I yell. I'm suddenly held in a huge stinky mouth, a wet raspy tongue under my stomach. I'm grasped gently, but between the points of evil, sharp teeth. The monster that holds me in its slobbery grip springs from the porch, high off the ground so the night world whirls past in a blur until things slow for a moment as we descend onto a thick branch. I focus on some cars parked along the street below my head. I feel the creature tense, and spring again. Leaves and twigs smack my face as we bounce through a tree crown. The world whirls by in another blur and I fly higher, still helplessly trapped. Suddenly, in front of me gripping a wall, I see two shiny, black cat paws with sharp white claws that are the size of basketball hoops. Beside the wall, and between curtains in an adjacent window, a man in a room, smoking a pipe and reading a book. I want to be him!

"Let me go," I shout, and hear an evil snicker from the back of the cavernous throat.

Then up we go in another blur of brick, me and my captor. We fly across the space in a couple of bounds, onto the rooves of the row of townhouses which snake up Rosa's street. I see chimneys, stars and slate tiles wheeling in my vision.

"Put me down," I shout. The giant cat snickers and, holding me tightly enough to not let me fall, but gently enough so its teeth don't bite through my body, the cat leans its head out over the edge of the building and dangles me. I'm genuinely freaked out now as I'm face down in a soggy mouth looking at the footpath and the tiny toylike cars below glowing in the streetlamps. Worse, my stinky captor starts to open its jaws, its slobber making my pajamas damp. Slowly, deliberately, the jaws part a little and I grab at a slippery, wet incisor tooth to try and hold on. There's nothing between me and the ground, but air and the smell of old fish. With an electric rush of terror, I fear for my life. Don't want to end as a pavement splat.

"Not over the edge. Drop me on the roof!" I shout. The creature tightens its toothy grip on me, flicks its head to the side, and spits me out so I cannon off an old chimney block onto a flat area of lead roof-lining. There's a sharp crack and pain in my bum as I land. I see we're on a roof five or six houses down from The Judge's because in the faint moonlight, I can see Rosa's extra story and the higher garden wall with the shadow of a treetop peeping above.

In front of me, crouched with a cruel smile on his lips, is Bastqut. He's shrunk back to less than human height, but to lift me up four-stories onto the roof, he must have grown, somehow, to the size of truck. Now he's merely the size of a sleek black jaguar.

"I saw your camera, spy!" he says. "You human creep!" One claw pops out of his smoky paw and he pokes my pajama leg, ripping the cloth and scratching my leg.

I'm flat on my back, so I pull my leg back and sit up with a groan.

Bastqut is half visible, yellow gleaming eyes looking cruel. Poised for a pounce. I can just see a black tail whisking back and forth in the night.

"Don't interfere in our business," he hisses. "Too many humans interfere in our business."

"Can I ask, wasn't it you that encouraged cats to interfere in the business of humans 4000 years ago?"

"Hmm," says Bastqut with a hint of amusement, "of this I am accused, you clever man. But it was for cat preservation and comfort that we manipulated our Egyptian people."

"A very clever move," I say.

"Thank you." Bastqut looks pleased. "But still, cat business is my business. Not yours." This time he pokes me playfully with his paw. "Stay out of cat business, and I promise not to eat you."

"Well, don't try to bribe The Judge," I say.

"Why would I try and bribe The Judge?" he says. "I'm not an appellant. I am merely making sure that the judgment is fair."

"The Judge is annoyed by the pile of dead things on her doormat."

"So you decide to find out who is doing this? And tittle-tattle to The Judge."

"It's research!" I say. "Wheelbarrows of creatures are being slaughtered and left uneaten because cats can't agree." Bastqut's eyes flame slightly.

"How do you know it's cats?" says Bastqut sounding surly.

"Who else drops dead offerings to the people they admire? Also, you need to eat some raw chicken wings, Bastqut. Your breath smells."

Bastqut narrows his eyes in sudden fury and his cat shape swells.

"I might eat you, and use your puny ribs to clean my teeth, Mr Associate," he threatens, and stretches out a paw, which becomes quite large. Another single claw popped out like a machete, ripped my left pajama pant leg and scratched my shin, deeper this time. Blood wells up through the wound.

"Ow, that hurt!" I exclaim.

"You are no friend of cats," he hisses, "I can tell. This is a warning. Stay out of the business of nature."

Then in a puff of black fluff, he evaporates into the half-dark night. I stand, my pajamas wet with cat saliva, feeling bruised and shaky. I look up. The friarbird from the roof garden is perched behind me.

Kwook? it asks. *Are you okay?*

"Yes. Bit bruised and lacerated. Never been hunted before – and toyed with."

Kwook! says the friarbird.

"Would you have told Rosa if I'd been flung off the roof? Is that what she means when she says you keep your eye on things?"

Kah-clonk! nods the friarbird in acknowledgment.

I think, perhaps, the vigilant friarbird saved me. Bastqut was hardly going to murder me if he was being watched by The Judge's bird.

"Thanks for bearing witness. I think you may have saved my life."

Clank! says the friarbird quite intently. *My privilege.* The bird was agreeing and accepting my thanks at the same time.

I add: "I am not liking those cats."

Clonk!

"Yeah? Not your friends either?"

The friarbird didn't answer, but I knew birds were no friends of cats. I find my balance and walk to the garden wall while the friarbird hopped ahead of me. I use a pipe to shimmy up from the townhouse roof and onto the terrace, while she simply flew over.

I'm on the outside end of the Hall of Justice garden where Rosa's father had lain in state for the past three days on the mortuary slab. Now he's gone, his pale naked body mysteriously absent from the blank slate. Rosa said it would happen, but I'm still thunderstruck.

"Gone," I say, pointing.

Carckle, says the friarbird, matter of factly.

"Taken?"

The friarbird doesn't answer, but points its beak at the moon. I don't understand that gesture.

"The moon?"

But by then the strange bird has hopped into a small maple tree at the corner, ruffled its feathers and started preening.

"Thanks again, bird," I say. My night isn't yet finished. I'm wounded and sore so I take the lift down to the vestibule. The front door is still ajar, but the Chihuahua has gone from the bloodied doormat. Perhaps it had staggered home, but I don't think so. Too injured.

I hear noises upstairs so I lock the door and go up to the kitchen and there's a tall, dark woman wearing a beautiful pink and green silk dressing gown and a pink towelling turban. She holds the Chihuahua on the table and wields a cotton bud.

"Who are you?" I ask.

She must be around 60, judging by the fine wrinkles around her eyes adorned with magnificent eyelashes, but the rest of her face is smooth and glowing, her hair jet black, and her lips are curved in amusement.

"I'm Mrs Cimbalom from the downstairs flat," she announces. "I hear this little fellow whimpering out front so came up to help him." Her accent is soft, but confident. A massive first aid kit is open on the kitchen table, but it bears a purple cross, rather than a red one.

"I'm Benjamin. Staying with Rosa," I explain. "The Chihuahua's badly injured," I add.

"Nonsense – this doggy is a Prague ratter, or Prazsky krysarik!" She pronounces it like she was tearing paper. "It is nothing like a Chihuahua," chides Mrs Cimbalom. "This breed has a proud lineage!"

I stare at the small, brown creature. Not much bigger than a rat, with a brown and tan snout, oval ears, and spindly legs, the dog's eyes are rolling around in their sockets from the pain, blood soaked in its fur.

"Nothing that we can't fix," she says. "Hold this." Her fingers are long and thin . A syringe.

"Now make up the preparation." She handed me a bottle with a stopper that said: *Panic retardant. Administer with 2 parts water by mouth.* I fill the measurements.

"Now squirt into the mouth."

So while Mrs Cimbalom holds the little dog, I administer the calming syringe stuff, then she rubs *suture juice* (some sort of antiseptic?) on the wounds, and they immediately stop seeping blood. It may have broken bones or internal injuries, I don't know, but I hope that it survives. She washes the dog gently with a wet rag (it didn't take long) and patted the wet areas with a towel.

"He'll live," says Mrs Cimbalom, who tucks a towel in a plastic washing up bowl and pops the sedated dog into the makeshift bed. "He can come stay with me until this cat business is over. Then we will look for his owners. Cup of tea?"

I smile. "I'll put the kettle on."

She looks down at my torn pajama legs soaked in cat saliva and blood and says, "You've been in the wars too. Here. Some suture juice for you also." She dabs the scratches Bastqut had inflicted. The scratch is instantly soothed by the dark brown juice.

"I'm not a fan of cats, either," she adds, as if she knew what had happened.

"Have you lived downstairs for long?" I finally ask.

"Since forever," she says, rolling her eyes. "You wouldn't believe the tasks The Judge and his dear wife have requested from a simple cleaning lady like me. So many tasks. And Rosa – I am glad you are looking out for her. She is soooo young."

"You seem to know a lot."

"I am the cleaning lady. This is my job."

Her eyes are black and soft as Rosa's had been, her nose quite aquiline. Her lips stay playful as she speaks.

"I'm sure we will become good friends, Mr Benjamin. And don't forget, the bell is over there if you need anything. Rosa is always happy to ring it too," she says pointing at a white handle on the wall. "I have a key to the house."

Mrs Cimbalom finished her mug of tea, packed up the first aid kit and put it in a cupboard, then picked up the plastic basin with the sleeping dog. The panic retardant had knocked it out. Its breathing was wispy, but at least it breathed.

"Goodnight," she says.

"Goodnight, Mrs Cimbalom." I walk her to the front door and she wafts down the eight front steps and turns into a little gate on the street, down into her flat. I can just see a window below street level, where light pokes out from between curtains.

"Must ask if there's a Mr Cimbalom," I mutter.

*

The cats preferred the Hall of Justice for the verdict, because they could reach the room from the rooves and trees without congregating in the street. I'd thrown the French doors open along the top garden and they slinked and slunked out of the dark and into the room, cat after cat, in the hours prior to midnight.

The days of summer rain had cleared but it was warm and humid. A pleasing jasmine waft perfumed the air.

At one end, Rosa sits studying papers behind a small, but chunky desk. She looks so serious. Her father has died and she has inherited a family job with a huge burden of responsibility: The Court of Last Resort. I found it unfair that any child of ten should be so serious.

The room is lit by three standing lamps. The same lamp near the landing door which had cast the shadows of Tau al-Gorz and the Caiman, a second over Rosa's shoulder so she can read, a third near the back entrance. The room is well lit, but not bright. The cats are comfortable.

On the dot of midnight, a shadow or was it a mist, arches into the space, and there is my foe, Bastqut, lounging at the back on his stomach.

Rosa peers over the desk – we'd found a hard, bolster-style pillow to elevate her above the desk, to see the cats on the rugs in front. Mason is there. The snippy Siamese, Missy Wiggins is there. Rosa's golden eyes are spooky and unblinking as she surveys what must be around 200 cats. Plus their Elemental at the back.

"The court is in session," she says. "Here is my verdict."

The room hushed.

"The street cats submitted to the court that the edible wildlife in the city is being reduced in numbers by drought. This means less food for them. The domestic cats are taking too many mice and birds and the street cats say they are hungry and demand the house cats stop hunting their food and stick to their kibble, supplied by their humans. This is the argument.

"But from the start, large quantities of dead, uneaten creatures have been left on The Judge's doorstep. We counted 380 sparrows, 48 blackbirds, 270 mice and 400 rats, plus a squirrel, and unfortunately a small dog ..." There are sniggers. "And I thank you for your gifts." Rosa is most polite.

"My Judge's Associate, Mr Benjamin, has studied these numbers. He also screened and identified some of the felines that presented these gifts and there was indeed a mix of domestic and wildcats at my doorstep leaving these mouse and rat corpses. I understand that domestic cats present gifts, such as mice, to their human carers as a token of love and respect, or possibly to tempt their lazy humans to start hunting for themselves."

More snickers.

"And I am sure the wildcats were trying to match the kindness of the house cats in leaving these delicious bloody gobbets on my doormat." So diplomatic!

"In zoology studies there is a special formula that allows interested parties to track the numbers of wild animal populations to see if they are in abundance, or whether an animal is endangered. My assistant spoke with an ecologist who looks at such things and they did the calculations together.

"And I can assure you, the catch rate per cat presented on my doormat for this neighborhood over a week, and beyond, proves there is still plenty of street food for all cats, both house and feral."

Rosa is treading a fine line. She doesn't want to offend the appellants – the street cats. And she doesn't want the house cats to think that she was on their side either.

"Facts matter. We can count things on our doormats. There are many birds and mice in the city. You have all helpfully provided me with the evidence for this judgment."

"My judgment is this." (There's an intake of breaths). "I uphold Bastqut's original determination in the Court of Cats. All cats can hunt."

She could have said "And the street cats appeal is dismissed!" but she's decided not to, because it sounds rude – the sort of rude thing which would be said in a human court.

I was expecting complaints, an uproar, angry tail flicking from Mason and his street mob, but they took the whole thing well, reassured as they were by the court that there was still food. I hoped myself and Professor Ebeneezer Fleezlemeyer, the ecologist, had calculated the dead things properly, and therefore the live populations, but he'd seemed the expert.

Bastqut appears to expand in size at the back of the room, casting his furry blackness.

"Very well," Bastqut says, which was as pleased as he was going to sound. And he then slowly winked at me with a fiery orange eye, which was unsettling.

"Two more determinations of the court before I end this session," Rosa commands in a very judgey voice. "On exit, leave the friarbird in the garden alone. I will not abide her being harassed. And do not leave me any thank you gifts on my doormat. There is no need. If you are indeed as hungry as you claim, eat them. The case is now closed." She bangs her gavel.

And in what looks like a moving wave of fur, tails, and little pink bottoms, the room empties of cats within a minute, leaving myself and Rosa alone.

"First appeal, Mr Benji," she says.

"Well done."

"These cats. They talk about food, but there were a lot of wasted mice and birds on the mat."

"Mostly put there by the well-fed cats, if the truth be told, but it was a nightly sample of the number of creatures available around this neighborhood."

"Thanks, Mr Benjamin," says Rosa with a yawn. "Will you read me some more bedtime story now?" She pulls *The Bone that Rapped* out from under her judge's notes.

"Sure thing," I say, so we sit in the chess player's easy chairs for 10 minutes while she listens and yawns, and she then goes to bed while I wish the friarbird a goodnight, and lock the doors of the Hall of Justice to prevent people, like me, from breaking in.

THE EMBASSY JOB

We Urbex prefer roofs unless we're traversing a dark tunnel or exploring the innards of a broken old factory. In fact, I have a tattoo on my back – started when I was 14 – that maps our underground city, and every time I explore a new tunnel Sukki inks the new route to the map. The tattoo is now very intricate. It looks like the winding roots of a giant tree.

My on-again off-again girlfriend, Elodie, and I could have sipped our coffee in the quiet parlor room above, looking through the big bay window, but we prefer outside, among the plane trees. We sit on the top front step – spacious stoop, an elevated view up and down this lovely street which angles gently down to the main road, lined with those big trees.

The sun scatters down and Elodie sits with her hip against my happy hip, watching the people who make the city hum.

We've just finished a tough three-hour training session – without Chaz. Elodie says he's still angry with me and is sort of ignoring me. He mutters under his breath, she tells me, that I'm a traitor to the crew, which makes my stomach lurch. I've known Chaz since we were kids and we've supported each other through the bad patches and partied during the good ones. I'm sad and uncomfortable about the sitch.

So Elodie and I sweated hard together on a muscle-numbing workout – a long run, climbing, parkour through a housing estate that has high walls and steps, and finally, strength lifts at the park's primitive gym equipment. Now we're sore but chill as we drink coffee from big mugs and I try not to think of Chaz's fury.

Elodie is dressed as usual – very simply – in three-quarter length climbing pants, a cropped midriff shirt with a deep V-line neck, which lets the sun warm her skin, and white canvas sneakers. Her blonde hair is already escaping a pink ponytail scrunchie. Her briar rose tattoo runs up her left hand and arm with three red roses flowering on her bicep. Elodie is lovely, with green almond-shaped eyes and freckles, though unfortunately, she is smoking a small cigarette and creating fume stink.

Elodie is a self-declared "difficult person". She's not happy with me either. Last couple of days she's asked me: "Why do you want to hang with weird little squirrel girl and not me?"

I kind of enjoy the jealous anger in her eye, but she has nothing to be jealous about. I love Elodie. I explain (again) that I've moved in with Rosa because I promised her father I'd look after her for a while.

And she'd say: "We have a good thing going between us."

I'd say: "When you're talking to me, it's fantastic."

And Elodie would say: "I talk to you always, Benji."

And I'd say: "Sometimes, sometimes not."

And she'd say: "Well if I don't sometimes, it's because I'm a difficult person."

"Why?"

"Because ... I've seen a lot of things."

That was her response. I'd sometimes say: "What things?" and she'd look gloomy and clam up. That was often how convos between us went, leaving me frustrated by her silence. Last two days we've had this weird fight. I've said, "Move in with me and Rosa – there's plenty of room," and she's said: "Don't want the commitment, and Chaz would get even madder," and then she'd add: "See – two good reasons."

But today Elodie is great, though she did, yet again, complain about my living with the "weird little squirrel girl". I shrugged and said again, "You can move in too, there's plenty of room," and she went, "No, no," as if it were a shocking suggestion, and then moved on to urbex gossip about various crews around the city, rolling her cigarettes and blowing smoke from the side of her mouth.

"It's charming here, but it's not Paris," she sighs, stubbing the horrible cig on the stone step.

No, it is Not Paris. It's Not San Francisco, it's Not Tokyo, it's Not Budapest, it's Not London, it's Not Mexico City, it's Not Shanghai, nor Sydney. It feels like somewhere else. Especially in the house. I kiss her softly on the lips. Elodie and I often kiss when we are discomfited or, indeed, happy. In other words, a lot. A wisp of her loose blonde hair tickles my forehead. She's 22, three years older than me, but we like each other. The kiss is a tonic and my stomach goes fizzy. We hold each other tightly and kiss again, with passion.

At this moment, Mrs Cimbalom emerges from the downstairs flat and looks up.

"Mr Benjamin," she calls. Elodie and I disentangle.

"Oh. Hi, Mrs Cimbalom. This is Elodie, my friend."

"I can see that," she says smiling. "Hello, Elodie."

Elodie is smiling too, at the intrusion as well as the unusual view of Mrs Cimbalom in a red felt hat, a swathe of colorful silk scarves, a tartan shopping jeep, and the now recovered Prague ratter doggy.

"Miloš and I are going to the grocery store, Mr Benjamin. Do you need anything?"

"Milk, please," I say. "And Mrs Cimbalom, could you mind Rosa tonight?"

"Sure, sure," she says.

"Elodie and I are going out on a date." I can tell Mrs Cimbalom knows it's a lie before I finish telling it. Inside the house it's impossible to tell lies, but we are out on the street, where lies emerge lamely.

"Sure, sure."

Miloš trots after her on a skinny lead as if he owns the street. Mrs Cimbalom is still scouring the neighborhood, trying to find its owners.

"She's odd," said Elodie.

"The cleaning lady, and everything else," I say.

"Why can't she be Rosa's carer? You could come home."

"Not sure. But I gave my word to Rosa's father."

"He's actually dead, isn't he?" Elodie asks. Elodie is a very perceptive "old soul". She's watched me and Rosa dance around the subject of Rosa's dad.

"Rosa looks too sad," she adds.

Rosa is upstairs in the visitor's parlor attending her mathematics lesson with Mr Zither, a small portly man in a neat grey suit and goatee beard.

"Yes," I finally admit. "Her dad died in front of me. In fact, he asked me to look after her from beyond the grave. So weird. He had a scratchy voice, but his mouth didn't move ... at all. But his eyeball moved and stared at me. I made him a promise. I cannot break my word on this one."

"Oh, Benjee," says Elodie, "you made a promise to a dead man. That is one serious promise." I'm amazed she believes me, but she does. She's had her fair share of tragedy in her 22 years and shivers at the idea of promises made to corpses. She clearly feels for Rosa too.

"You could move in here, though. Plenty of room!" I offer again.

"Oh Benjee." She says my name again in her French accent. "It wouldn't be right," I don't know why it's a question of "right".

Elodie and I aren't officially dating. She's very independent, but I'd love her to be living with me.

"Well, the offer is there," I say simply.

"Thank you, *cheri*." We engage in a slow succulent kiss. "I must go, Benji. Ten tonight. At the meeting place."

"See you there," I say, and feel a bit breathless as I watch her walk off down the sun-dappled street.

*

Money is no object in this house. There is a petty cash drawer in the study which always seems to be full of notes, fivers and 100 notes and everything in between. Maybe Mrs Cimbalom replenishes it when she's dusting and cleaning. I pay Mr Zither with a 50 on his way out.

We are standing in the vestibule, and I'm struck again by the translucence and beauty of the leadlight windows on each side of the front door. Greens, aquamarines, oranges and reds, twining vines and hummingbirds, lilies and all-colored light thrown and glimmering on the white marble floor tiles.

"Miss Rosa is doing very well with her advanced algebra. I think she is what you call a *savant*," says Mr Zither. I nod.

"She's very smart."

Rosa stands with us with her little smile, sunglasses on.

"She told me what happened to her father. Very sad. My condolences again, Miss Rosa."

"Thank you, Professor Zither," she says. Suddenly the mild smile is gone and she looks like she's about to cry. I show Professor Zither out and take a mournful Rosa upstairs for morning tea. She sits on a kitchen stool in a huge gloom.

"It's normal to be sad and mournful," I say. "When my mum died, I went to bed for a week."

"How old were you when you went to bed for a week?" she asks.

"Ten. And then two years later my stepfather threw me out on the streets because he found another woman. A stepmother who hated me. He said, 'you're getting between me and Melissa', and I said: 'but I'm your son, and he filled a sports bag with my clothes and otdered me to go and live with my Aunt."

Rosa shook her head at the unfairness.

"I'll be sad forever," she said with a glum face. "I miss Mum more than Dad, but I know I'll miss him more as time goes on."

"That's true," I said. "Missing people so much shows you still love them, which is a good thing. Love lasts. Love lasts whole lives."

In consoling Rosa, I'm making it up as I go along, but I also know what I say is true. We sit in silence for a while as she sips tea. I'm already full of coffee so I just sit and talk.

"Mrs Cimbalom is going to look after you tonight. I'm going out with Elodie."

"I saw you two out the window kissing," she said in a gossipy voice. "Is this the Embassy thing?"

The kid was smart alright. She'd remembered the discussion in the elbow park a week back.

"Yes," I said.

"Is the Embassy thing a good thing?"

"Not really," I said. "It's a job. And you are The Judge, so you don't want to know what sort of job."

"What sort of job?" she asks, of course.

I couldn't lie to Judge Rosa in this house. The truth just blurts out. "We have been asked to steal an ancient artefact for a rich collector. I won't be the main thief, but I'll be helping."

"An accessory!" Rosa yelps. "Aiding and abetting a crime. You shouldn't steal!" chiding me in her judgey voice.

"I know. It's a very rare artefact. An ancient bronze piece in a new exhibition in the Embassy gallery."

Rosa shakes her head slowly but says nothing.

"I'll be home by morning."

"Whatever." Again her gloom descends and I worry that my confession has clouded her sad mood even further. I don't want her to end up with depression.

*

We've decided this morning to go into her father's study and go through the papers on his desk. There are letters, legal briefs, scribbled notes, receipts, even a couple of maps, neatly assembled in piles.

We start with the letters.

Begging letters are politely replied to, stating the former Judge has died. We pay bills through my phone with a credit card that Rosa has found. Then there are letters with detailed requests for a judgment. From all sorts. Opposing farmers in the hills who are in dispute over water in a lake; a fishing town that is at war with its council; an impatient president in a faraway country; two fruit sellers who are almost at war because they want the same roadside stall site. We put them in the in-tray.

There is a letter from two sisters, who are fighting over the same man who has led them both on. Worse, they are both pregnant. A terribly sad letter, but funny all the same as the sisters wrote it together.

We can't make him choose between us, they write. *When we ask him to choose he keeps bursting into tears. This is very frustrating for us both.*

Rosa is very interested in this last one, but I counsel that this is not a matter for a judge, this is a matter for their own hearts and for them to work out together, the two sisters and the man.

"But he's a bad man."

"How do you know, Judge Rosa? Maybe he just loves both women and doesn't want to decide on one and hurt the other's feelings. Or just can't. And they find that hard because they both love him."

How come I became so wise so suddenly? Are these the "follies of the human world" that Rosa needs to learn about?

We end up writing to the sisters. It ends: ... *your problem is not a matter of law because it is not so much a dispute, as a muddle. A matter for three hearts that should get together in the same room and resolve arrangements both personal and geographical, remembering that now, there are children involved who require the proximity of parents.* Rosa signs it: *R Somberly, Judge.*

By the time we've written letters, filed documents, paid bills and cleared up the desk, it is 4 p.m. – ice-cream time.

*

At dusk, Mrs Cimbalom whisks past me on the steps as I leave the house. I'm excited as I haven't hung out with the crew for a couple of weeks. Even if they are cranky with me they are my friends. We've shared a lot of adventures over many years. I walk briskly on the pavement through the twilight feeling the thrill of the chase to the tram stop at the bottom of the street. There I stall for an hour in a little cafe and drink another coffee to keep me sharp and I ponder how to handle Chaz, and decide to be friendly and firm about my new situation. The cafe has wood paneling, a long bar, and is a pleasant place to linger. The brisk waitress has a tattoo of a bull's head, with a snout like a drill-bit on her arm and the words El Toro.

That's a chunky-looking ink, I think.

"Why did you get that design?" I asked her.

"Dunno. Saw it in a magazine and just liked it," said the waitress as she walks off.

Then I catch a tram to a corner near the Embassy and walk a short way to a vacant lot between a cobbler's shop and a stone church. I'm third to arrive. Yusif and Sukki are already in the church shadows.

"Hello, stranger," says Yusif, and I feel guilty for leaving the crew.

We kiss cheeks, I ask after them.

"We've moved out too, for a bit," Sukki says with a hint of excitement.

I'm shocked. My action has caused a reaction. The crew is breaking up.

"We busted into an empty flat in the seventh district," Yusif adds. "Sweet little place with a comfy bed. Owner likes being cushy but is overseas."

"We're having some 'us' time," Sukki says with a happy face.

"That's great," I say, congratulating them. Then Chaz arrives from the north, and Elodie from the south.

Chaz is in full operational swing, pumped. His eyes are shining, but he still has a sour-note go at me: "Nice to see you've turned up, Benji-man." A little sneer accompanies it. I just nod.

"Gallery is on the ground floor of the apartment block next to the Embassy. You know all that. Big show floor on the ground and a mezzanine floor. The target is in a display case on the mezzanine. The bull exhibit. The funerary offering. That's what the client is after.

"Embassy has its own guards who are persistently good, but the gallery is next door, so they do random irregular checks there. The guards are more interested in looking after the ambassador's house than an exhibition. A private security company does drive-bys at midnight and 2 a.m. Sukki is eyes out back, Yusif is eyes out front. Ping us on text if we've been made, two pings if someone's really coming for us. The front door has serious alarms and cameras so we go through the roof, down the tenement stairwell, in through the gallery firedoor where Ell will kill the cameras. Me, Benji-man, and Ell on the roof. Benji, you're inside lookout. We should take 20 minutes max, in and out."

We all nod.

"No cameras in the apartment stairwell, but the gallery has lots, so hoods on."

We hood up.

"Benji, stay on lookout in the stairwell in case a resident enters or exits. We'll text you if we need help in the room. Phones on vibrate only!"

We slide into the shadows and wait for the midnight drive-by to pass. Elodie the alpinist, climbs a four-story house, using a corner drainpipe and masonry and brick as hand and footholds. A steady climb in her fingerless gloves. She is careful, takes her time, doesn't flail. So strong, she shimmies up the drain and reaches the roof gutters – I see her legs slide over, and she drops a fixed line which unfurls toward us like a thin white snake. Chaz and I swarm upward, hard work, and I'm puffing a little at the top. It's dark in this street as trees obscure streetlights, but the houses are not dissimilar to Rosa's. The street is just a little wider and fancier.

A car drones past, headlights throwing globs of light on the road, but we are in the skies and I'm already rolling up the line over my shoulder. Leave nothing behind. Chaz has cased these roofs and knows which tiles he unhooked earlier and placed back for easy removal. One, two, three … he passes them to Elodie and then me and I stack them against an old chimneypot wall. So useful. Elodie and I exchange a relieved smile, cos Chaz is now calm and on the job as he disappears down the roof hole. We drop through into a narrow attic, then through the attic hatch onto the top landing of the tenement stairwell. We land almost silently. We don't want to rouse the residents.

An old-style set of apartments, with stern wooden front doors on each landing, curved metal balustrade, and stone steps, which we silently descend with pin torches lighting our feet so there's no tripping. Sensor-activated stairlights, but the lights are feeble and turn off on passing. The adrenaline is starting to surge now. At the vestibule at the bottom of the stairs, a pair of glass doors to one side lead to the gallery. I entered that door weeks ago, when the exhibition had just opened, to scope the crime scene-to-be. Instead of the main gallery doors, we take a back door, behind the vestibule passage, into a narrow hallway – the fire exit. The alarm was disarmed by Elodie some time back, and no-one in the building has noticed.

In the dark, we aim our pin torches at the lock, while Chaz cracks it with a special pick and he and Elodie enter. She finds a security camera and puts a clamp behind one of the camera lines and nods to Chaz. Did I tell you she studied electronics? Camera system down.

I move back, just behind the hallway door, deep in the shadow of the stairwell, so I can watch the front door and the stairs.

Some ambient street light comes through the glass frontage, and then I see her, standing in the vestibule, like a small acrobat in tights and a black top, small black runners. No sunglasses here. She's looking at me with her golden eyes which seem to glow in the dark.

Rosa.

Ah, the kid has followed me into one of Chaz's operations. Not good. Chaz succeeds because of control freakery and detailed planning. There is never room for deviations, however minor. He goes nuts if someone improvises and I don't want him even more ballistic with me. Then I remember she'd put her hand up to come on the Embassy job, back in the elbow park. Maybe she took Chaz's "you'll do" literally.

I wave her over and she sidles up.

"You'd best go, Rosa ... we're pulling a robbery," I hissed.

"No, I can't."

"You must!" I hiss again. "This is no place for The Judge, or a kid, and you're both!"

"Mr Benji, you have a problem here."

"What?"

"I've come to help." She looks quite upset from my sharp tone.

"We have a plan. We have to stick to it." My hissed voice quietly shrill.

"Mr Benji," she says, her golden eyes sharp, "Mrs Cimbalom did a cast. I don't think you could foreshadow what is about to happen."

"A cast?" I know the crew is now into the gallery and sorting out the theft.

"With her greegrees. Bones and sticks and things. I can explain later but we must hurry."

Greegrees (whatever they are) sound ominous. I look at Rosa's urgent face and I'm suddenly filled with dread, and can only think Elodie is now in danger. We head down the narrow corridor and into the gallery, stealthily. I still don't want Chaz to see that Rosa's here. I can see their thin torch beams up high at the back of the mezzanine, where they are fussing about over display cabinets. There's a sharp cry – from Chaz. And a weird light sparks on. Then a thin guttural voice starts to whisper through the dark gallery, becoming clearer, speaking words I don't understand. The words now echo from each high corner of the room.

A strange glow-shape starts to bulge out of the stone wall, a purplish colour. The bulge balloons further and brightens to a shade of grape. And the distant voice of a woman starts floating from the ceiling above the bulge – her voice sounds pleading and sad. I see Elodie crouched against the exhibition cabinet looking stricken while Chaz's face is illuminated by the vague purple light from the wall bulge. He's holding an object, but he's frozen with fright, and now a hand, connected to a thin bare arm, emerges from the purple bulge.

So freaky.

The hand starts to slowly extend toward him and the glinting object he's holding. Chaz, staring wildly, is still rooted to the spot. Meanwhile, Elodie is crawling on the floor, trying to skirt around the purple bulge to get to the stairs.

"Oh dear," says Rosa, "Mrs Cimbalom, you were right!" She scampers up the metal mezzanine step at top speed, and grabs the object from Chaz's hand. Chaz jumps back as Rosa then vaults the mezzanine balcony down beside me, a leap of about eight meters. She lands without a sound.

Rosa shows me the small bronze bull we'd been tasked by a private buyer to steal. Sharp little horns, a strong bronze neck, with some decorative rippling in the metal, to represent hair. The strange voice is unrelenting. I cannot recognize any language.

"A tau," she says. The bright purple bulge of light has slid quickly along the wall and down, following the tiny bull like a magnet and the arm starts to extend out, now from the floor, toward Rosa and me and the ancient bull. I see the hand is small and shapely, a female arm and hand, beautiful fingernails. It looks solid, fleshly, muscular. In my torch light, perhaps it has dark, olive skin. A gold bracelet on the wrist. Chaz and Elodie, I see, are hanging over the railing, looking peak freaked. They start to descend the stairs cautiously. Some electricity now sizzles in the air between the hand and the little metal bull, little blue sparks, but Rosa stands firm with a quizzical look on her face.

"I've never done this before," she says, suddenly grinning at me.

"Well I hope you know what you're …"

"… me too."

She pulls a pink plastic spray bottle from her belt and sends a squirt of liquid straight into the outstretched hand. Then another puff of spray. And another. The scent of rosewater permeates the room. The hand stops stretching, and shudders for a moment. The low distant voice stops speaking. Then starts again in a tone of sorrow, a more apologetic tone. The hand slowly retreats into the purple bubble which then deflates into the floor, turning to grey polished concrete and throwing the room back into darkness. For a moment, there's silence. Rosa wraps the tau in a handkerchief and tosses the bundle to Chaz, then tucks the bottle into her belt.

"Let's get out of spookville," says Chaz, looking stunned, and the four of us exit the dark gallery as fast as possible, treading lightly up the tenement stairs past apartment doors.

"You're cool," Elodie says to Rosa who is running up the stairs beside her.

Rosa says, "Actually I'm quite hot," so I explain that Elodie means Rosa is worth knowing better.

"That's what I mean," says Elodie when we get to the top landing. "The squirty bottle thing. You saved us from I know not what!" She shudders.

At least, I thought, "You're cool" was a step up from "That weird little squirrel-girl."

We heave ourselves out through the attic ceiling onto the roof where we slide the slate tiles in rapid fashion. The night air is cold and I take a couple of deep breaths to calm myself. Elodie is sitting on the roof ridge, looking equally as frazzled by the events we just saw. The strange voice is still ringing in my ears. Low, long vowels and guttural stops that made it rhythmic, almost songlike. The arm stretching out of a purple electric cloud.

We sit and listen but there's no song now, no sound of police sirens, or cries from below.

"Come on," says Chaz. "We'll be wanting an explanation about all that chaos, Rosa, but right now, let's decamp!" One of his favorite phrases.

Then it's a matter of a quick shimmy over the other side of the houses, down a double drainpipe, and two thin ledges, into a tree to jump down to the street. One, two, three, four, Rosa again making not a sound as she lands while both Chaz and I land with dull thumps.

Chaz check-texts Sukki and Yusif and we split and head for the meeting place, Rosa with me.

"What was that thing?" I ask, as we walk briskly toward the tram stop.

"Mrs Cimbalom says old, old undercurrents of energy surround those taus. Things not even my dad and mum understood."

"And why did you follow me?"

"Mrs Cimbalom said you might need some rosewater. She said there might be a brouhaha. Soon as you left she threw the bones and the pattern foretold – you were stealing a tau."

"She's a fortune teller?"

"No, no. She's Fortune. Cimbalom Fortune. That is her name."

I'm even more confused. I'm not sure what a brouhaha is and how Mrs Cimbalom would know that a brouhaha was brewing. Now things feel more weekday normal. I sit silent beside Rosa in the tram surrounded by young people heading home from clubs and slightly drunk workers who've visited bars on the way home, stayed too long and look a bit screwy. Rosa in her dark glasses watches the crowd with interest. Some of the adults look at Rosa wondering why a kid's on a tram at midnight. Then I press the tram stop bell, a reassuring ding, and we hit the bustling street with the all night diner, *Cafe Nova*.

*

Everyone is there already, at the booth. *Cafe Nova* is busy with hungry night owls, the nocturnal clientele of the city. White tiles, the smell of old hot fat. The elderly Turkish chef is especially stained this evening, in his cap and beard, cheerfully flipping food for clients and shuffling fish, veggies and chicken around on the grill. His wife, the cashier, looks tired after a long night's haul. But she cheers up when she sees us.

"Evening, crew. Who's the kid?"

"My niece," I lie because I'm not in the house and lies come easily.

"Bit past bedtime?" says the caring woman.

"Aww, let her be, Gonca," says the old man. "Obviously having an adventure with this lot. How're you, Yusif?"

"I'm good, Manny!"

Coffee is good, but I need something stronger, so it is beer for the adults and lemonade for Rosa. She doesn't hide her eyes from them this time, as it's now apparent that strange things happen when Rosa is involved.

"Your eyes?" gasps Sukki.

"I take after my godmother," Rosa says proudly.

Silence. No-one knows what to say after that pronouncement, so Chaz changes the subject.

"What did we thieve?" he whispers to Rosa and the booth. "You obviously knew something'd happen. Armed with that squirt bottle and all."

"You stole a tau. A funeral offering from the early Bronze Age ... maybe earlier," Rosa whispers back. "The recipient wanted it back, from their grave. A very old grave, I think. A grave protected by the Great Goddess."

"Tau as in bull – Taurus?" asks Yusif. All eyes were on Rosa.

"Actually, before Taurus."

I start wondering about Tau al-Gorz and Rosa looks at me sharply as if to say, *keep quiet about that.*

"Maybe from ancient Minoa," she adds, as Manny put plates of burgers, and cheese and bacon toasties in front of the crew. Rosa turns her eyes away from Manny as he bends over the booth with the plates.

"Who are you?" asks Chaz.

"You know me. I'm Rosa! My dad was a judge and my mum was a chemist. And Benji is looking out for me now. I don't get out very much.

Your burglary was very interesting. Stealing is a serious crime, but I enjoyed the outing."

"It was sooo spooky," says Elodie to Sukki and Yusif. "This purple bulging of the wall and a hand that came from nowhere. Did you hurt that hand, Rosa, with the spray? It seemed to flinch away and react."

"I am not allowed to hurt anything. I don't *want* to hurt anything. All I did was spray rosewater," she says, "which reminded the hand's owner that she shouldn't be here, in this world."

"What world did the hand belong in?" asks Sukki.

"The world of the dead," Rosa says.

"So spoooky," said Elodie again.

"Will it come back again to claim the tau?" asks Chaz. Obviously Rosa was now the expert.

"Maybe. The fact you woke the powers of the tau with your bioelectric energy somehow alerted its owner. If you keep the object covered in cloth and don't place live skin against the tau, then it will remain an object and not some conductor of elemental forces. But humans are walking talking batteries, full of zap and zing. Luckily, in most museums, people now wear gloves when they touch objects, so I suppose the very few objects that are connected like that to the past are protected. But if you touch with your naked hand, a current is set up."

"You're right. I did that," says Chaz. "I took my glove off to feel the metal. I thought it might be gold."

"It's bronze, from the Bronze Age. The Minoans were pretty clever with goldsmithing too, though."

"So we saw a real Minoan hand?"

There is an exasperated explosion from the other side of the booth.

"Pah! This story is entirely unbelievable!" snorts Yusif, who of course was outside the gallery at the time. "There's no such thing as disembodied

Minoan hands coming out of walls. It's poppycock." His dark brown eyes glare under his black eyebrows. Yusif is the skeptic and the scholar.

Sukki looks at him. "Still sounds scary, Yusif."

"It's not rational. Its bull … shit!" he announces, shaking his head. "We are here, on this planet without ghosties, ghoulies or the undead!"

Chaz looks at him with a fixed grin and a gleam in his eye and fishes out the small bull wrapped in cloth.

"Want to bet?"

"No," I say, suddenly worried at the eye-gleam.

"Yes!" says Yusif. "One hundred from my share is yours if you can summon up a spooky disembodied hand! It's not possible!" Yusif is looking very cocky now.

Little Rosa sitting beside me is startled by the male shoutiness. Manny is flaming some chicken on the grill, and a flare shines off the huge commercial rangehood, casting a fiery gleam on the bronze of the artefact which Chaz holds up in its cloth, careful not to touch the metal.

"One hundred says it's true," Chaz says.

"You're on, brother!" says a delighted, confident Yusif, and they shake.

"What are they doing?" Rosa asks me.

"Gambling," I growl.

"You betcha," says Chaz, "I'm taking 100 from that sucker!"

"Don't, Chaz," I snap, but it's too late. His inner daredevil is awakened.

Shuffling the cloth, Chaz holds the bull with his naked fingers and lifts it high in the air.

"No!" says Rosa. "No. No! Before, the hand was moderated by earth. The earth in the walls. Here there's … FIRE!"

With a whoosh, the flame grill blows into a huge flare that bends up and under the rangehood toward our booth, singeing cafe roof. Manny is thrown backward and his wife dives under the counter. People queuing to order scramble outside, boosting the flame with a gust of front door oxygen.

The same low voice starts to wheedle and plead from the continuous arched flame, and the hand and then the arm start to emerge. Bigger, more lifesize, but still slim and feminine in shape. Chaz swears and drops the bull, but the flaming arms and hand, almost blue with heat, keep coming, and this time a shoulder appears and the side of a desperate woman's face: young, dark eyes with long lashes, her hair in neat black ringlets falling through the flames, red lipsticked lips, intent on the bull. We can see her singing, pleading now, the voice right beside us as if she is in the booth, which she almost is, but suspended above in a flame.

My crew drop beneath the table or over the back into the next booth. The arm and half body of the Minoan, stretch across the passage between the counter and the booth in the bending flame. Yusif looks particularly terrified as the voice keens. Rosa jumps on the tabletop and starts to squirt her bottle but of course the mist gets nowhere, because the spray turns into steam well before it reaches its target.

"Woah! Water! Quick!" I shout.

I stand on the seat grabbed my beer and a water jug and threw it at the hand, while Elodie finds another couple of jugs in the fridge. Rosa unscrews the top of the rosewater bottle.

"More water," she shouts, while Elodie, and Chaz, who appeared with a bucket, and I, chuck several bottles worth. The cooling effect is minimal, but Rosa pours rosewater straight onto the hand, which flinches, the young Minoan woman quiets and looks infinitely sad, staring straight into my eyes where, for a moment, I connect with someone from 4000 years ago with a wave of sorrow down to my toes. She shakes her head once and retreats, clearly remembering she is dead, and that the funerary offering is not within her grasp.

The flames disappear. I gather my wits.

"Chaz!"

"Ouch, sorry." He has lost an eyebrow in the flare-up. He's still standing with the bucket. I had to think quick, find some explanation for the flames.

"Nasty fat fire," I shout to Manny who'd been flat on the floor and missed the disembodied woman. Manny pulls himself above the counter, looks through the salad display.

"What on earth have you got in that chip oil, Manny? Petrol?" I ask.

Manny looks embarrassed. I start to feel sorry for him, but my empathy was interrupted by the sound of sirens and the red and blue flashing in the street outside. From her phone under the counter, Manny's wife had called the fire brigade.

"Regroup at Rosa's. We need to talk about this!" I say calmly.

Chaz had already wrapped the bull and is out the door. Yusif and Sukki are off out the back. I point to Rosa motioning her to put her glasses on. Elodie is nowhere to be seen.

*

We come together upstairs, in the Hall of Justice, though after the tumultuous night, everyone arrives at the front door, rather than the rooftops.

Elodie disappeared early because she'd been in the cafe office removing the CCTV feed on the way out. The vision of spooky hands is likely to make it onto the internet, along with us and Rosa. Our thieving urbex crew usually try to stay low-key as. Elodie has a small hard drive in her hand and looks pleased with herself.

"Nice penthouse room, kid!" she says to Rosa, curled up in one of the armchairs, looking around at the decor.

We'd made cups of Mrs Cimbalom's bitey tea. On the way through from the kitchen up to the roof, Chaz and Sukki are particularly interested in the art on the walls, but I give them both a look as if to say, *don't even think about it*. Sukki, especially, knows her art stuff – she has been to college and makes jewelry, and I'm sure she'd have clocked a couple of million worth of art just on the landings. Luckily, all the other doors are fast shut as if the house knew it was being invaded by thieves.

Now in comfy chairs and a sofa, Chaz is still agitated, and Yusif looked perplexed and haunted all in one.

"You shouldn't steal," Rosa chides. "Although you say this was a special circumstance. Who is this client that wants this tau, Mr Chaz?"

Chaz begins to mince with the truth, and suddenly realizes he can't. Rosa had asked a judge question in the Hall of Justice. I'm amused by his contortions as he tries to lie. But he has no choice but to answer The Judge truthfully.

"A man ... an old guy and his wife ... no ... not really, no ..." Then the truth comes out in a rush: "It was ordered by a multi-multi-millionaire called Dawson Kennedy who lives in the first district. Big house with the red roof on the hill. His assistant contacted us."

"What is his assistant's name?"

"Mrs Simply. His private secretary."

"And Mr Kennedy collects stolen taus?" asks Rosa.

"He collects antiquities of all kinds and most are legit. Bought at auctions. We've purloined him some small Assyrian pieces in the past. And a very early Cycladic figurine from the Greek islands. He is interested in very early stuff ... Hey, this is need-to-know biz! Why am I blurting it out?"

Rosa ignores his question.

"These objects are very powerful things." She holds up the tiny bronze bull using a napkin to shield her fingers. "They are a sacrificial link directly to the beginnings of human settlements and all that followed. Comes from a time after humans generally stopped being foragers and hunters, and learnt how to herd cattle like the little bull, and cultivate crops which led to colonization in villages and towns and farms. This tau is a living link between hunter-gatherer people and their creator goddess and your world. The tau belongs to an archaic, but powerful force of change. You cannot deliver this to Mr Dawson Kennedy unless he is aware of its risks."

Chaz nods dumbly.

"Until then it must stay in this house."

Chaz nods again. He can't speak. He's been sentenced by The Judge and he doesn't even know it. He is now locked into an Elemental's community service order.

"And take Mr Benjamin as a witness. You will need him," Rosa further orders.

*

A feeble first attempt of dawn light is poking up behind the black skyline, but the light quickly gets stronger revealing a cloudless sky. Rosa and I are outside on the roof garden. The others are gone.

Rosa insisted on keeping the tau until such time as Chaz was satisfied with Mr Dawson Kennedy's tau health and safety check. And Chaz was slightly relieved too. Rosa seemed to know what she was doing. I didn't know how much Chaz had brokered for payment with this Mr Dawson Kennedy, but we always got a good windfall after a burglary job.

We sit in the garden looking at the tiny object sitting on the napkin on the table.

"Such a pretty thing. Rosa, what would have happened if the Minoan woman had picked up the little bull?" I ask.

"I don't know. It could have disappeared back to wherever her grave lies. Or she would only have fondled it. Maybe we should let her have it?" Rosa looks at me with intensity. "I'm sorry, Benji. I have no idea what my father would have done."

She is still a small judge. A child.

"I understand," I say in a soothing voice. "And thanks for turning up and saving us."

"Stealing is a crime," she adds, yet again. "Someone stole the tau from this woman's grave a long time back. It's been from owner to owner, I'd guess, in collections. But she is dead. It's a reverse loop, the tau bringing her back to life rather than it being her ghost wandering the planet, looking for her property. She is dust and bone and has been for 4 or 5000 years as I had to remind her with the rosewater. But I'm very interested in that bet. Why did Yusif and Chaz bet on the spooky hand?"

I shrug. "Well, Rosa, Elodie would say in her angry voice: *Men are mad!* It's what guys do."

I know I'm mad, and Chaz was an even madder risk-taker than me.

"Will Chaz keep Yusif's 100?"

"Probably not. It was a bit of fun between them."

"I don't understand how taunting the dead is fun."

"They didn't understand what they were doing," I explain. "I still don't understand what happened."

We sit in silence for a while, feel the cool blast of dawn air carried on a southerly wind.

"Dad said everything has their elemental structure, atoms, molecules, bioelectric pulses. They bind and separate and rejoin for different reasons, under the laws of physics and life. Elementals are how these powers and forces communicate. There's a lot more to physics and chemistry than is understood by humans yet, but we're slowly getting there. Somehow, Elementals have understood these things forever. Mama was teaching me, father was teaching me. Unfortunately, our branch of the family is not immortal, while other Elementals are. With us, knowledge and powers are passed on, but I didn't learn everything. And now I feel lost."

Rosa is sad and tired as her gaze wanders along the garden's branches and tendrils, and at the slab where we'd laid her father.

"This is too big for me," says Rosa.

"I'm here to help you."

"I know," she says.

Another silence as Rosa started to tear up in the corner of an eye. Did I tell you she was small for her age? I feel helpless.

"Benji," she finally says, "I am going to sleep. I am missing my mum and dad. I need to think. I need to be sad. And, if you don't mind, I have decided to stay in bed for a week."

How can I object?

I once did that too.

ODDS & SODS

Rosa is still in bed. Three whole days mourning so far. I'm embroiled in a deep conversation with Mrs Cimbalom in the kitchen.

"No, Mr Benji," she says, "I am just the old cleaner who dusts and polishes."

"Ye...es, Mrs Cimbalom, but Rosa also said you were Fortune. What does she mean by that?"

"Even an old lady cleaner can be Fortune. That's what that means."

"Like a small orphan girl can be justice?"

"Exactly! Or a big strapping man like yourself can be loyalty."

Ah, she was being tricksy-dicksy. I gathered, somehow that Mrs Cimbalom is an Elemental too, but she parries my questions with her sneaky responses. Yes, I am very loyal. I am a promise keeper, and caring, too, but I'm also filled with unquenchable curiosity about Rosa's world. I wanted to observe this strange girl as well as help her.

The little smile played across Mrs Cimbalom's lips as if she was reading my thoughts. Hers was an endearing smile. I liked Mrs Cimbalom a lot, and I knew she cared for Rosa as well. Her smile forced me to grin back.

"Cheers to loyalty, then," I said lifting my glass of wine and Mrs Cimbalom clinked it against hers and sipped. I usually drink beer, but wine from The Judge's cellar was rich and warming. Electric soup, I'd read somewhere.

"You tell fortunes though, don't you?"

"Indeed I do – divination, tea leaves, I Ching, tarot, runes, greegrees, the innards of sacrificed fowls ..."

I wasn't sure whether she was joking about the last one.

"Meet my greegrees." She pulled a velvet bag from the top of her skirts, opened the drawstring, and placed a series of objects one by one on the tabletop, naming them as she did so. "Two finger bones, two four-faced pyramidic dice with pictograms on them, a hazel twig, a mummified mouse head, and a couple of uncut gems – an angular emerald and a rounded black onyx."

The collection looked awfully witchy.

"I can throw these, and give you answers, but to ask the wrong question is a beeeeg risk."

"Why so?"

"Because you can't avoid the future. And when people know what is coming they can desperately try to alter and deviate their true course and this can lead to further disaster. A painful journey."

"Do you know your future?"

"Oh, yes," said Mrs Cimbalom. "But I knew mine before I was born!"

"Big claim," I responded.

"Ah, Mr Benji, fate is always set for one like me."

I sipped and considered. I looked up through the skylights angled above the kitchen wall and saw leaves wheeling through the sky in a gust of wind. A gust under rain clouds. Autumn was coming.

What is in the wind? I think. The smell of rain? Diverted birds being blown my way? The hard truth heading toward us on a cold front, flushed with lightning and drenching reality. In the bruised sky? Do I want to know my fate?

I could ask: *Will Elodie and I get married*? I could ask: *How will I die*? I could ask: *Is it my pledge to look after Rosa forever? Am I trapped in this house?*

Mrs Cimbalom cocks her sculpted, and possibly tattooed, eyebrow at me, rattling her handful of dry, ominous greegrees as if to say, are you ready for it?

If I'd drunk another glass of this magic wine, I think I'd have said "'yea", and asked Fortune those questions, but I wasn't yet reckless drunk. Just happy.

I shake my head in the negative and she sighs and nods.

"Wise boy. Foreknowledge never did no-one any good. You toughen up from dealing with the unknown. That's life." She pats my arm in approval.

Since Rosa's mourning period began, Mrs Cimbalom and I have looked after her, going upstairs regularly, taking a breakfast tray, then morning toasties, a lunch snack and a big roast dinner. Then, about nine, a bowl of ice-cream is delivered to her bedroom. Not that Rosa's eaten very much, but we try. She's been there three days, lying surrounded by books, or watching age-appropriate movies on my smartphone, which she'd begged from me. Or just lying looking upward at the roof. Tissues, damp with tears, surround the bed and Mrs Cimbalom and I scoop up handfuls and bring her more boxes.

Sometimes it's me that takes up the tray, sometimes the cleaning lady, but we're in a groove and I appreciate her help.

Mrs Cimbalom has been teaching me about different wines, and we finish the evening with a glass (now a little ritual after ice-cream time), and then Mrs Cimbalom softly calls to Miloš, the unclaimed Prague ratter, who faithfully trots out after her. While animals can clearly be understood within the house, Miloš has remained mute since being mauled by the cat. I even try a little Russian on him, but he just scratches his ear. Maybe he's embarrassed at being bested by a tomcat and doesn't want to talk about it.

I think about tomorrow, when Chaz and I must carry out his part of the sentence for stealing the tau and visit Mr Dawson Kennedy, and I must make sure this millionaire collector knows the risks.

*

Chaz and I walk to the top of Nobbs Hill in the ultra-wealthy first district, with big, stack homes bristling with security cameras and razor wire along the tops of garden walls. Our pace is strong, and we float almost effortlessly up the undulating boulevard of affluence: show gardens, mansions, carports with hotrods and fancy EVs.

In my pocket, double-wrapped in thick cloth, the tau.

As Chaz's associate, I'd prepared a speech to first assess whether Mr Dawson Kennedy was aware of the perils of such powerful artefacts, and if not, to advise him on proper handling.

Chaz is much more interested in the business of the crew. He's still grim about me leaving and busting up our crew so he's in a sour mood. When we met at the corner down the hill he snapped, "When are you coming back, man?" and I shrug.

"Gah," he says in deep frustration. "Suki and Yusif are gone now – having a break they say," he said. "They won't be back."

"They're in love."

"Yeah – so man? Aren't you in love with Elodie?"

"Well, yes." I surprise myself, don't even hesitate to answer.

"Well?" He leaves the question hang. He's in a cloudy mood and I understand.

For Chaz, the crew were a tight-knit bunch from when we were 13 or 14, learning the streets. To Chaz, I'd abandoned my brother in crime and urbex. Except, not really. I'd just moved out.

"Bet Ell moves in with you, and I'll be stuck by myself. Brothers don't abandon brothers!" His anger – it's a fair call. My departure was sudden and Chaz doesn't want to be lonely, and everything around him is fraying: our routines, our habits. I grab his shoulder and stop him before he totally explodes. Look into his eyes.

"You can live with us at Rosa's."

"That's just it. It's Rosa's," he grunts. "Not even yours! You're an interloper!" Chaz doesn't want charity. He's proud to be independent and make his own way. Proud and angry. I can deal with angry, but not an angry Chaz. I hate the tone of his voice battering against me.

In my mind, I can see the eye of the dead Judge watching me, Rosa lying in bed grieving, Mrs Cimbalom's curious smile, and even Bastqut's angry fangs.

"You'll just have to trust me on this, Chaz," I say calmly. "Things'll get better. We're still working but looking after the kid is something I gotta do."

"Ok. I understand. I think. But the kid's weird. Those eyes," he mutters.

I watch his foxy face under the neat black beard as he walks with intent, looking at the road. He changes the subject, and starts on about how, now we've "busted up", we gotta schedule our fitness regimes properly. Our core business of urbex and burglary is still front of mind. He can't let go.

"On Saturday, let's do those old-style water towers on the south-side – time trials up and down them for strength and practice. Bottom to top in four minutes and top to bottom in 20 seconds, rappelling from the lid of the tank down. You'd be in that, wouldn't you, Benji-man?"

I nod, grunt "of course", and move on from the hint of bitterness in Chaz's voice to focus on the ritzy houses.

"These places are harder to bust into with concrete walls round the yards, and razor wire."

"Yep," said Chaz glancing at the sharpened metal along the wall-tops, "but there are ways and means with razor wire. It's the cameras that are the bummer."

"Too many?"

"Too many to fill with Ell's electronic jam." Curt and grumpy.

We reached the crest of the hill and meandered up a gravel driveway to a gate with a console on the wall. Clearly, Mr Dawson Kennedy had acreage here in the city. We could see a park-like garden with old chestnut and cypress trees.

Chaz buzzes the console and said: "Hi, Mrs Simply, Chaz here, we have a consignment for Mr Kennedy."

"It's not a good time," says a quavery voice.

I looked up the driveway. There were a couple of sleek cars parked in the drive, red and black.

"Can we just drop it in?"

"I'm afraid there's been a strange and terrible accident. I don't think we can receive the consignment," said the quavery, disembodied voice.

My heart sinks. Into my boots.

"Mrs Simply," I say, "I'm Chaz's consultant on these collectible objects." Chaz gave me a sharp look. "Can I come in and discuss something with you. It may help explain the accident."

There was a long pause. Then a buzz and the gate swung open.

I don't know what she was expecting. A tweedy academic? All she saw when she opened the door were two dressed-down urbex dudes. Conversely, I was expecting an old secretarial type in a pastel pink suit with greying hair and spectacles on a string, but Mrs Simply was maybe 30 years old, a woman who looked Ethiopian, with a coffee complexion and long limbs, tumbling braids in a green head scarf, and a short summer dress. I was confused. Chaz hadn't warned me about how beautiful Mrs Simply was. I couldn't see her eyes. They were behind dark glasses, and I could sense she'd been crying.

And she was a snob.

She looked us up and down disapprovingly, as she spoke. "I am Heloise Simply." She extended an elegant hand for me to shake, limply.

I try to channel The Judge's voice. "Mrs Simply. I'm Benjamin, Chaz's associate. Can I ask you, does Mr Kennedy have any more objects that look like this one we have acquired for him?" and I opened the palm of my hand. On a leather cloth was the tau.

"He collected those, yes. His little funeral offerings. That's what got stolen."

"Stolen?"

"And then an accident occurred during the theft." Her voice starts to quaver again.

"What happened?" My fake judge's strong voice holds. She pauses for only a moment before nodding.

"Well ... if it helps to explain, please come through to the scene of the terrible crime."

Mrs Simply leads us through a spacious ground floor lobby area into a large, sunlit gallery at the back of the house, lined with white French windows and doors opening onto the greenest lawn I've ever seen rolling down to a tangle of woods.

The gallery is amazing. Among the Mayan statues and Assyrian friezes along walls, and artefacts from everywhere, a glass showcase is smashed and empty. Scattered shards of glass lie on the floor, and numbered police tags are plonked around the room.

"All the little votive bulls were taken from the vitrine." A fancy word for showcase, I guess, and Mrs Simply is certainly fancy.

I look around the room. Black scorch marks cover the cream wall and the roof, which is intricately plastered. She gestures elegantly.

"The police say it's a robbery and aggravated assault leading to death. That's all they can tell me. They are hunting down his killer."

"When did it happen?"

"The day before yesterday. In the evening. I heard the kerfuffle. Then glass shattering, and cries, and so I came down. Dawson was .... on the floor. Slightly ... charred."

"How many of these did Mr Dawson Kennedy have." I show her the tau again.

"Five little bulls. They have all been stolen."

"Hmm," I say. "Possibly another collector."

"That's what the police said."

"You never saw his collection, did you, Chaz?" I ask my friend.

Mrs Simply shakes her head. "Of course he didn't. No-one was privy to Mr Kennedy's private museum, except family and close friends."

"Did the police say where the ... combustion came from?"

"They are looking into it."

"Looks extensive. Looks almost ... supernatural," I venture, pointing at the scorched and slightly burned wood of the cabinet.

Mrs Simply shook her head and muttered "Nonsense", but I could see she had the same thought.

"Are you okay?" I ask in a less official tone.

"Not really, but I have to deal with the situation. Mr Kennedy's family are coming here for a meeting today. I'm organizing that. And then there are the company rearrangements. I am the company secretary, after all."

What a puzzle. "Hmm," I say as if I was pondering the scene like a true detective.

For the first time that morning, Chaz looks amused. He almost bursts into a laugh, but thankfully contains himself.

I finally ask, "Did you hear any strange noises? Chanting or anything ..."

"Chanting, of course not." She stares at me as if I was mad.

"Did you see anyone at all? Any human figures?"

"Well, it was dark, and there was a flaring little fire in the gallery from burning bits of cabinet wood, which illumined the garden, and I told the policeman I thought I saw a small child fleeing down the lawn."

She goes on. "The police looked, but found no footprints. Could have been a figment of my imagination. By then I was terrified. I rang emergency."

"How old do you think this possible kid was?"

"Six years old, maybe younger. Very small, but wearing a hat. I saw that. A little hat and raincoat in the firelight. Maybe it was a midget?"

Not a midget, but I'd glimpsed mini-people before – on Tau al-Gorz's chest.

"I believe you, Mrs Simply. Certainly you saw a small person. And only these items were stolen?"

"Yes. Nothing else. His little bulls, as I've told you. They were in this case. Looked exactly the same as the one you have."

"Was there any security camera footage?"

"The police have it, I'm sorry. Anyway, I'd rather this accident, or perhaps murder, be left in their hands."

I almost blurt out that the murder is way beyond the knowledge of any police officer, but then thought better of it.

"So cops think it was kids?" Chaz says. "Looks a bit targeted for kids."

Mrs Simply arches her glamorous eyebrow a moment. "I know other people who hire kids to do their dirty work."

I laugh. "We're well and truly classified as adults under the criminal laws."

She almost smiles. She's only a few years older than us, anyway. More than just Mr Kennedy's private secretary, I guess. She's deeply sad, in mourning like Rosa.

"Thanks, Mrs Simply," I say. "We'll let you get on with your business."

"I'm sorry," says Chaz. "I liked Mr Dawson Kennedy."

"I'm sorry, too," I say.

"And I'm sorry that I can't buy the .... ah, consignment."

We both nod. I'm a little relieved, as well, as it's best kept in Rosa's house.

We shake hands. Did I mention she is very elegant, the sort of person I don't often meet.

"One moment," she says, and disappears into a side office. I look around the gallery, especially at the scorching. There's no fireplace to summon Minoan ghosts. But fire had burst out around the room somehow. I've seen that before, too, in the Hall of Justice when The Judge struck Tau al-Gorz.

Mrs Simply emerges and hands us 1000 in 50 notes.

"For your trouble and understanding," she says.

"Thanks, Mrs Simply," said Chaz, who pockets the money. "We can look after this object."

"Thank you, Charles, and just one other thing. I'm sure the police are surveilling the area, so if you are asked, just say that, as friends of Mr Dawson Kennedy, you've been offering me your condolences."

Chaz is unsettled, but I nod.

"Done, Mrs Simply."

"Call me Heloise," she says in a lighter voice. "I'm glad you understand."

Chaz and I head back down the drive and out of the gates. I see the cop car in the corner of my eye, but ignore it and pretend to chat about any old shit to Chaz. He's seen it too, and doesn't like it, as he's got an even longer juvie record than me. I only have misdemeanors, but Chaz has done time.

At the bottom of the hill, he's swearing under his breath.

"It's all okay, Chaz. Mrs Simply … Heloise … will cover for us," I say. "She won't want to hint that she's part of some crime."

"Possibly, but we should expect to be stopped and even searched," says Chaz. "Story is we were friends of Mrs Simply and paying her a condolence visit."

"*As friends of Mr Kennedy*," I add, reminding him of Heloise's line. Chaz is indeed rattled.

"Easy," he says, with a doubtful tone.

"Easy," I repeat and then I add: "She'll vouch for us in her uppity accent. Wowee, she's a beautiful woman. You should have warned me!"

"You noticed," says Chaz slyly. "She's 150 per cent."

"More."

Then I remember the tau wrapped in my pocket.

"I need to get it back to The Judge's house," I say.

"So is that what happens if the Minoan lady touches the tau when you're holding it? You combust spontaneously like Dawson Kennedy?" Chaz eventually asks.

"I don't know," I say.

"Is that what happened to Mr Dawson Kennedy?"

"Possibly. I'll tell Rosa. She might know." I'm even more worried about the bulge in my pocket.

We walk the rest of the way in silence, thinking of what might have happened the other night if the spooky hand had grasped the little bull. Would we have all been electrocuted or blown up in the cafe?

Soon we're in the guts of the city business district, wandering with a large crowd. Chaz slips me 200 in cash.

I don't need any cash thanks to the money-drawer in the study, and the cash was way less than we pulled for a normal job, but it's the principle.

"Thanks, man."

"Dawson's death was bad luck for him and us too. We were promised 5000." Chaz muttered. "Here's 100 for the kid. She's weird, but she aced it with the spray bottle. And text if the cops check on ya. I'll do the same."

"No problemo. Catch you in the park."

We separate in the middle of a crowd, and I head for home through a historic arcade, and while no cops followed (I doubled back to check) I'm certainly followed by a dark cloud of foreboding.

*

As soon as I walk through the door, I go straight up to Rosa's bedroom to tell of the events at the mansion.

"Siddley? She saw Siddley?"

"Siddley?"

"You know - Tau al-Gorz's nasty tattoo? His bad conscience?"

"How do you know it was Siddley?"

"You said it was a small figure that didn't leave footprints. A small troll who throws fireballs at people? He's violent, malicious and horrible."

"Fireballs?"

"Yes – he's Tau al-Gorz's worst impulses. Why is he loose by himself?" Rosa is perplexed. "Stealing taus. Killing old men who collect stuff."

"The lady said Mr Kennedy had five funeral taus."

"Is she sure? Could have been later Greek offerings to Zeus. They've found tons of them at Olympia."

"Naw, was specific. Mrs Simply knew what she was talking about."

Rosa decides to get out of bed.

"My mourning period is postponed," she announces.

Rosa makes me fetch the tau from the study while she showers and dresses and we head to her mum's laboratory where she finds an exercise book with what looks like a recipe.

"Mum's own. I helped her with experiments like this. We are neutralizing the ancient energies."

We eat chocolate-coated licorice bullets from a bowl as I help her with the task. We follow the recipe meticulously which includes beeswax, bismuth powder, and a number of other elements, from a row of chemical bottles. We dole out exact quantities with measuring spoons, which she adds to a beaker over a bunsen burner.

We both wear goggles and thick gloves to make the goop, and to handle the object, and finally Rosa pushes the tau gently into the warm mineral wax. While it dries and cools we remove our gloves and finish the bowl of chocolates.

"What are they?" I asked, waving at all the waxed objects in the drawer, filed in rows.

"Not sure. My mum called it her odds and sods drawer. Other objects with power, I suppose."

"Hmm," I say for the second time that day. "If Siddley, or whoever, is stealing these things and killing people, these need to be under lock and key."

"I agree," says Rosa. "We'll lock the lab."

Once the goop cools and hardens, she wraps the blob in tissue paper and places it in the odds and sods drawer and adds a record of the item to an index book that is placed in the thick, solid safe in the corner.

Then we leave the windowless room and she uses a big green padlock to secure the door.

How did these Elemental creatures come and go? I wonder. Arriving unannounced, causing havoc. Disappearing off, down a lawn, leaving no footprints. While I stir cheese sauce into some macaroni and spinach and put it in the oven, Rosa does her maths homework on the kitchen bench, perched on a stool, so focused and applied. She looks like a normal kid, a nice one, sensible and friendly.

Almost a real person.

*

Old clockface with glowing green radium hours peers at me. An art deco delight, I'd borrowed it from the chemist's bedroom on the fourth floor, though I wasn't too sure about the green radium. The big hand moves toward the hour of 2 a.m., with five minutes to go. It's the early hours of the morning. My eyes open to a sound and I lie in bed staring into the landing where a glow of red on the back wall follows the steps down. I hear voices. Rosa's and another.

It's cool and I grab a thick silk dressing gown printed with pink hibiscus petals, and walk up the stairs and the attic steps, under the red light to the Hall of Justice. Rosa is in discussion with Caiman. The reptile Elemental, as old as the earth, lay there on the floor in full croc form, no robes this time, just bumpy and ominous on all fours, greeny-brown, with the same unblinking golden eyes as Rosa's.

Rosa's curled up in one of the armchairs in her pajamas, unfussed. Neither looked at me when I enter as they are in mid-conversation.

"Godmother, you know I can't do that," says Rosa.

"So what do you mean can't, Egg? Tau al-Gorz is imminent! Finish the job!"

"Not my job to 'finish him'. I am The Judge."

Hrumpph, snorts Caiman, and she lowers her snout for a moment. I can see the wicked teeth, the landing light casting a red sheen on her brutal enamel.

"I can feel his baleful influence, coming from the north. Your father failed to finish him."

"My father lost his judgment in what is the house of balance – The Judge's house. That's why the banishment is so short," Rosa says, "and papa paid with his life, godmother. For his mistake, his outburst of bias. As Judge, you must not hurt anything or anyone and he was stricken with what he'd done. Losing his temper like that." Rosa began to cry.

"Rosa," I start …

Caiman lifts then smacks her tail once on the ground behind her, and a pot jumps off a shelf and shatters.

"This conversation is private, familiar."

"He's not my familiar," says Rosa, fighting through the sniffles. "Mr Benjamin is my Associate. He looks after me."

Hrumpph, said Caiman, sounding unimpressed.

"I thought Tau al-Gorz was dead," I say. "I saw him …. combust in a fire tornado."

Caiman turned her murderous knobbly head toward me and I'm enveloped in her swampy breath.

"Tau al-Gorz is a tough opponent. He was disintegrated and banished to the Tundra momentarily, but he and his Giddley and Siddley are reforming, pushing their way back into my rivers, killing my trees, whose roots hold the earth in their moist embrace. He sucks the Jurassic era from the ground and burns it in the Holocene. All my beautiful old fossilized ferns.

Come back to haunt. Causing chaos. And this Egg is powerless to stop him!"

"I am not," says Rosa sounding cross, "but you must present me with the crimes. I must summons him."

"As if he'd come."

"I am The Judge."

"You are, Egg. But you are also an egg."

By now I'm sitting comfortably in the other armchair, hypnotized by Caiman's twitching tail and teeth.

"I dealt with those cats," says Rosa.

"By telling the cats they could be cats? Hurrr...umphh."

Caiman appears to be laughing. As if crocodiles had a sense of humor.

"It was the correct judgment."

"It was, Egg, though the birds tell me they are not pleased."

"Well, then, feel free to eat a cat on your way out, godmother," says Rosa.

"Hurrr...umphh." Caiman appeared to laugh again.

"Perhaps you are not so egg-like, Egg. I will send petitioners – victims of his crimes. They will give you proof that Tau al-Gorz is a backslider and has not learned a twig from his puny banishment that your late father meted out."

"Do that, godmother," says Rosa, lightly. "And I," and she waves at me, "and my Associate will attend to the judgment."

Caiman seems to nod, then, without a farewell, she slithers through the door onto the garden terrace and round the corner. I follow, but by the time I'd reached the other side of the house, there was no giant croc to be seen.

"Sorry," says Rosa at my side. "Godmother is angry, but what father did to Tau Al-Gorz wasn't going to change anything. The ogre requires a judgement, not revenge."

"... and Caiman wants revenge."

"She wants justice for her domain."

"And the chess game solved nothing? Even though the gold king was checkmated?"

"I made things worse. There was no resolution. They had been playing for a timeless eon and it was a waste. In the Elemental world, time is not measured in heartbeats."

THE CASE OF THE RELUCTANT FOREST

Most days find me in the study, reading.

Me! Man of action! Reading books!

Light streams in from the high sash windows, but the room is deep and dark, lined with walnut bookcases filled with old volumes. The air smells papery and serious, but not musty.

I lie on the couch, or sit reclined back in the office chair, with a light switched on, wearing a dressing gown of muted yellow bananas and pineapples, which I've come to like very much. The house contains a plethora of dressing gowns that I constantly wear. And I sport a pair of brown carpet slippers which I bought the other week. Slippers that seem to suit the house.

I read to understand. About gods and archetypes from long ago. I can't quite work out what this house and its inhabitants are about and feel the answers may lie in past myths, or in history. It's a mysterious plot that is coming together with all the telltale signs, and red herrings, and hints. As if the solution is on the tip of my tongue, but beyond understanding at the same time. Like, I feel I should know, but don't.

From big wooden filing cabinets I pull out the Judge's notes to read, going back decades, maybe even centuries. I randomly plunder these files to see if Tau al-Gorz, the ogre, Rosa's killer, features in past cases, but there are so many files which appear to go much further back into the cabinet than is possible for the deep wooden cavity. There's no mention of the ogre.

Today finds me leaning back looking up at the ceiling to the ever-continuing cliff of bookshelves that head for some celestial vanishing point painted as a fresco above the actual shelves. Knowledge starts, but never ends. Up there, I think, in the painted stacks, there's a painted shelf of books that no-one has read yet, about ideas that have not yet arrived in the minds of writers not yet born.

The files reveal some case notes so ridiculous that the words make me laugh, but the written judgment is always in a clear hand that finds a fair conclusion to the dispute. Some disputes are hair-raising. Some seem ordinary, but reading between the lines I think the decisions of the court could well be concluded between the ogres and angels, adults, bears, children, even fish. They are all blurred together.

I read about family fights, territorial disputes between beasts and men, the edges of responsibility for hedgehogs or kings. Nothing is quite sane, but the judgment always seems to stand. Anything sentient with a beef, that cannot be resolved, ends up in front of this Judge in this Court of Last Resort. Especially the outliers. Even humans, who have their own courts until they find no justice is delivered, come to this Judge. And some judgments seem very old.

Very perplexing. I looked up at the ceiling again with the sky and the bookshelves disappearing into a long, painted perspective, blues and browns and golds.

I think: *How can I help Rosa move into this difficult space? What does she need to know?*

Then I catch a slight movement on the ceiling. What looks like a bird, or a big brown fruitbat, swooping through the painted stacks, what I think is an optical illusion.

I rubbed my eyes thinking it might be dust and look up again. Down and down something falls, becoming more distinct, until I see a brown-covered book. As if it has fallen from a painted shelf. I realize the book is heading straight for me. I reel back in the chair as it lands with a thud, right in front of me, closed, on the big wooden desk. A beautiful artefact. The polish in the desktop catches the browns and golds of the spine and binding.

I bend forward in the chair. The fallen book is solid. It opens to rough, old paper leaves and black printed words in classical fonts.

The old, leatherbound book is titled, *Beyond the Rule of Claw*, in gold embossed words. Truly, it is a beautiful book that has fallen down in front of me and one that may well answer my question.

Beyond the Rule of Claw was written by Miss Edith Shecklestone, barrister-at-law. Only 100 years old, this tome, around the time when women were first allowed to practice in a court. Still, it's a strange book, because her introduction claims: *the purpose of this book is to take violence from the streets or battlefields, and tame it with words, rules and reason.* Turning disputes that might lead to bloodshed into cast-iron agreements that both parties sign.

I glance at the ceiling again, scared that a bigger, heavier book might land on my head and brain me, but there are no more offerings tumbling from distant shelves.

Don't know whether this suggested reading by the house is for me or Rosa, but Miss Edith Shecklestone became a Kings' Counsel, and a judge, in England many years ago. I find a *Who's Who in Law* on the reference shelf behind my head and look her up. Libraries are useful. Stuffed with almost-forgotten facts that can't be found on the internet.

I then get halfway through the first chapter of *Beyond the Rule of Claw*, when the raw clang of the doorbell interrupts me. That particular clang is the house indicating a stranger is on the front step. The door chime is more forgiving for Rosa's teachers and friends, including my friends, sounding a pleasant chime when they press the button. And when Mrs Cimbalom presses the button (only once, when she'd left her keys inside) it sounds like the songs of butterflies.

This clang is sharp and high – a warning.

I descend the staircase and open the door and am confronted by two men in overalls and a man in a suit.

"Is The Judge at home?" asks the man in the suit. His hair is long and grey and he wears very thick glasses through which his eyes bulge like eggs.

"Judge Somberly has passed," I say. "His daughter is The Judge now. Do you want to speak to her."

"Of course," says the man. Though in a suit, he has a working man's accent.

"I'm Mr Benjamin, her Associate. And you are?"

"Apologies. I am Leopold Hack. These are my brothers Germane and Gus, from Hack Brothers, Timbergetters."

Leopold is a small skinny fellow, but his brothers are huge – burly shoulders, long beards, bushy eyebrows and hands as thick as posts.

I summon them in and sit them in the visitor's parlor where they gape at the four seasons frieze by Mr Mucha. Germane Hack, in particular, looks at the beautiful woman who represents spring, but then I realize he is more transfixed by the trees behind her.

Hmmm, I wonder.

The men don't blink when Rosa appears. She's dressed in a matching tracksuit with Nike written across the front. Nike, goddess of victory, daughter of the river Styx, the river that leads to the underworld. I know that now. But Rosa is not victory. I know that also. And anyway, it's a brand name stuck on clothes that kids like, not a goddess.

I gesture to the table and we sit around it, the three Hack brothers on one side, Rosa and myself on the other.

"We have a problem with a forest, which we own. It is making trouble. The forest does not understand that it belongs to us and its time has come," said Leopold Hack, getting to the point.

"What do you mean 'its time has come'?" Rosa asks.

"We are timbergetters."

"Ohhh, so you want to fell the forest?"

"Well, make a start on it," says Gus Hack, scratching his bushy beard. "Tree here, tree there. Let the sunshine through to make baby trees."

"It's the forest's time," says Germane Hack in a rumbly low voice. Sad but firm.

"So how is this forest resisting?" asks Rosa, very interested.

"Like they all do. Sending wild boars against my men. Dropping fat branches on machinery. And it has somehow summonsed greenies. There's a camp of greenies on our property, and I've had the police remove them five times, but they just persist and come back and chain themselves to marked trees."

"Bah! Greenies!" barks Gus in disgust.

"Surely that's a civil matter? For local authorities to arrest trespassers?" Rosa says.

The three lumberjacks nod, and Leopold says, "But the boars and branches aren't. So they are part of the overall ..."

Leopold opens his bag and pulls out a folded map and an ancient piece of parchment that was almost a meter by a meter, with a large circular red seal at the bottom. The seal is made of wax and is dark with age. The writing is spidery, from a pen, and almost indecipherable, written in an earlier version of the language.

Rosa draws the ancient legal document toward her and places her hand squarely on the seal and closes her eyes.

"The seal of an ancient emperor. He was old when the wax was melted and the seal impressed. An old greybeard of much power ..." She shudders. "Your ancestors had done his bidding in the north with their yeomen, and these lands, your land, were their reward, a much bigger expanse than you now own. This title deed is over 800 years old. The parchment was drawn up by the Emperor's chancellor with your ancestor, and written by a scribe, Friar Ned, who was terrified of making a mistake, or leaving a blot on the parchment. Scared for his life. He was also very hungry at the time."

Rosa shakes her head sadly, then continues: "Your ancestor was given all the lands in the valley. Many more farms, the town, and one further to the north, a valley to be farmed and tithed. The deal, though, was the valley must be protected too, by your family, from barbarian forces of the north. The valley was a trade route and an invasion route, a river of people, traveling both ways. An easy entry into the country. Your ancestor was quick to agree and take the land. He was a fearsome man who ..." Rosa shuddered again like an electric shock had gone through her, "had fought on behalf of the Emperor, and killed many people - knights, soldiers, villagers and children alike."

She takes her hand off the seal, as if scalded by hot wax.

"And so your ancestor was rewarded for his services by the old Emperor," she finishes in a level voice.

She looks at the three astounded lumbermen and then unfolds the map, of much later vintage, on the tabletop. It's a beautiful map made from linen and paper fibers, with deep clear inks of black, green and blue demarcating land and topography, and freehold and leasehold, near a town 200 kilometers north of the city, halfway to the mountains. Here was their swathe of land. A couple of big farms adjacent to a river and even a small village embedded in part of their property. The forest sloped up behind both farms.

The Hacks are much more than timbergetters, I think. They are still big landholders. On second glance, Leopold's suit looks much swisher and in his old-fashioned waistcoat is a gold fob watch on a chain poking out of the fob pocket. He points with a skinny finger.

"Here's the Forest of Nairn. Our forest. Been in our family since the Middle Ages. Harvested in the distant past, the old way, bit by bit, allowed to grow, left to get tangled and murky for periods, sometimes left untouched, although my grandfather took out nine small coupes over his years of ownership and now those coupes have regrown and are ready for harvest. We want to clearfell other parts, too."

"Have you other forests?"

"We have two tree plantations here and here." He points at the map where another old forest is marked. "But they are underdone," says Leopold Hack. "Used to be an original forest, but my grandfather clearfelled it and planted pines."

"A few more years of growth to be had in those pines," says Gus Hack.

"We will have to inspect these areas, especially the Forest of Nairn," says Rosa, eyes shining at the thought of a visit. She wrote down some notes. "After that, I'll attempt a hearing of the parties." The three men nodded. I wondered, how can a forest be a party to a legal dispute?

"We will visit tomorrow," she adds. "You clearly want a ruling."

"We are in the right! This is our title," Leopold Hack says grumpily. "I want this resolved."

"Resolved!" said Gus.

"You will make the forest understand it is time," Leopold says more forcefully.

"Make the forest understand?" asks Rosa puzzled.

"You know what I mean. You legal eagles are best placed to persuade!" His tone becomes loud, shrill and angry. He is a tall man, and Rosa appears frightened.

I cleared my throat. "The Judge is not a legal advocate on your behalf. The Judge will hear from the parties and make a judgment on this dispute."

"Well, we are in the right," says Leopold. "Here is the original ... 800 years, you say ... title, so I await your judgment on behalf of us."

"The forest may have a counter claim," says Rosa.

"How so? It's a forest," snaps Leopold Hack, making Rosa grimace.

I put my hand up. "The Judge is obliged to hear both sides of the argument. The forest appears resistant to your machinery. We must understand why."

"We have title to it," exclaims Germane Hack.

"Are you a greenie?" asks Gus Hack to me. "I hate greenies."

"No, I am the Judge's Associate. I don't even like leaving the city," I add. "But you've come here for a judgment, so Judge Rosa Somberly will make one. For the best."

"Better be!" says Gus, standing up and leaning over me, his beard brushing my forehead. I stand up and push him out of my space gently.

"The right decision will be made." I pat his shoulder and Gus sits down nodding.

Little Rosa smiles nervously at Gus and me, and then turns to the other two brothers and says, "I will listen to your arguments and my decision will be fair, but it will also be final, and the matter will be closed. Do you understand?"

The three men nod. They have made their plea, and have no choice other than to agree, in The Judge's house.

"Fair enough," says Leopold. "We'll see you tomorrow."

And I show them out.

*

Rosa leads me along a winding path through a field. We'd walked up toward a green hill, carpeted in trees and leaves, and then through a little gate. As we enter the forest proper, it becomes darker, so Rosa takes off her sunglasses and sticks them in the elastic of her walking pants. I'm discombobulated – it's all new to me – but she seems to know exactly what she's doing, just walking under the muscular boughs and leaf-laden branches.

I've never been in a forest before and find it pleasant. I know city trees, planted evenly in rows along kerbs, or scattered through parks, pruned regularly, picturesque … additions to an architectural streetscape of stone, glass and brick.

In a forest, the trees rule. They are spread randomly, thickly, in amongst bracken, rocks, and little twisting pathways. The air is much cooler than in the city. Sometimes something squelches underfoot and with each squelch the socks in my runners start to feel wet.

We keep climbing the hill, first along a little trickling stream, a beautiful sound as the water wriggles and splashes against the stones, then we move to the left, following a rough path away from the stream. Every so often a bird bursts and whirrs out of bracken, or ferns, or from behind a pleasant lichen-greened rock, and heads into the canopy. They are all plump brown birds, the size of tennis balls.

"Quail," says Rosa, knowledgably.

At a ridge, which is lined with pretty conifers, we stop and have a glug of water. We sit on a pair of boulders.

"Thanks for explaining to the Hack brothers what I do. I'm not used to people and their emotional outbursts. They may have a kernel of justice behind the emotion, but I have to find it. People are odd."

She seems grateful. I'm surprised at this admission, but then, she is a kid and the Hacks come from a long line of aggressive men.

"That's okay. People have their own ways. Like me. I have always lived in the city. This is all ..." I wave my hand around, "... very strange to me."

Rosa puts her finger to her lips and says *shhhh*. We sit in silence. The leaves move with the tiny breeze, and after a while I hear light footsteps scraping leaves, higher up the hill.

We stand and walk toward the sound.

An old man shuffles forward between two large and twisted boles, raising his hand in greeting. He is nut brown, with long twiggish fingers and a bulbous red nose as if he's been drinking a lot. He wears brown boots, a tan shirt, baggy pants covered by a filthy apron stained with resin and dirt.

"Here I am. You came to see me, Judge."

He knows who Rosa is!

"Hello, Old Man of the Forest. This is my Judge's Associate, Benjamin. He assists with my deliberations."

"Welcome, Mr Benji-man," the old man says.

He approaches stiffly, like he finds walking difficult. Rosa isn't wearing her sunglasses and the old man looks surprised and squints at her face.

"My friend, Caiman, told me you'd been touched by the wild," he says. "Your eyes remind me of my little frogs."

"Godmother revived me with her powers after I was killed," says Rosa.

"Caiman told me so. Ugly business. I believe Tau al-Gorz is involved in this horrible problem I have."

I'd been expecting a hearing with the forest – a discussion with a tree or something. Or a disembodied voice among the bracken. The fact we are talking to an old man amazes me.

"Why are you human?" I blurt. Because he is. He smells of sweat, and his face is patched with leathery wrinkles and moles.

"I'm not human, lad, neither am I a tree." He has such a creaky voice. "I am this whole forest. Our roots intertwine in the dark underfoot, and our leaves tickle each other in the breeze, and when autumn comes, we sigh together and the leaves fall, and we buckle down for winter. See, our leaves are starting to turn now." He points down, and there is a scattering of wet brown leaves on the grass and moss.

"Problem is, humans can't see beyond their noses, so that's why I too, must have a nose. To look like them. How remarkably vain of humans that they can't communicate with entities other than in their own image. So many Elementals have to look human to impress their followers. If humans could only see us as we are and communicate. But no. Humans are too self-regarding. It's such a shame."

"So you're a projection of this forest in human form?"

"We are the forest. This is just what you see. The forest can't see this. Those birds up there probably can't see me … or maybe they can. I don't know. I'm a forest, not a psychologist."

"Tell me what's happened?" Rosa asks.

"Well, Judge, this is our story. We knew things were turning bad when a couple of workmen turned up and started painting an X on some of the younger trees. Then the greenie kids turned up with their camp, which is always a harbinger of doom. Those protestors turn up when there's no hope, but to their credit the camp held fast for a while. The humans chained themselves to some of our trunks, and to the Hack brothers' machines, but they were removed by other men, and Hacks' people started to saw through bigger trees. We kept dropping branches on them, but they kept coming. I got a couple of boars to charge and bite their legs, but they were turned into sausages. These humans are remarkably persistent. Years ago, my agreement with Mr Cyrus Hack gave the forest safety to grow freely in perpetuity, he said, but now the Hacks are back with chainsaws."

"You had an agreement with their granddad? What sort of agreement?" asked Rosa, her interest sparked.

"He agreed that this forest, the one you see around you, would be spared, from the length of the mountain heights to the valley floor. I showed Mr Cyrus the way of the trees. That's why he put pine plantations further up the valley, all those years ago, standing in the silly rows the way humans like, with less to-ing and fro-ing of life. The plantations aren't so bad, but they are very limited."

"In your discussion with Cyrus Hack, did you write something to the effect that he'd leave you alone?"

"Write? It was an agreement between the woods and the human who was under an illusion that he owned the woods. Here, I'll take you where we came to terms."

So this uncanny old man leads us up a hill over rock slabs and through bracken, down through a gully with a small trickling stream and up again. He shuffles along in front of us, occasionally grunting, and we walk for some time up to where the very old trees thinned out and younger, though mature, trees grew. Rosa's face is shining. She hardly ever leaves her house and this is like a holiday for her.

The Old Man of the Forest stretches out his knobbly arm and hand in a circle indicating where all the younger trees grow.

"Mr Cyrus Hack wounded the forest here quite a while ago. We have grown again. Back then, when we made our deal, fine old chestnuts and oaks lived on this slope, but here's where I held up my hand and said to him, enough. He was frightened at first, but to his credit, he listened."

The Old Man of the Forest's face drops and resinous tears appear in his eyes. "He and we stood here among the carnage of my trees. Most had been hauled down a track over there, to a mill in the village. Mr Hack's workers were burning cutoff pieces in bonfires. The roots of the trees were dying beneath my feet."

"And what did you agree?" Rosa asks.

"He promised never to harvest this forest again. Which was good. We are a very old forest. There's not many of us oldies left around the mountain ranges. And yet humans seldom ask, why are we forests here in the first place? We were here before people desired to build houses. Or make fires with our wood. We've been here for millions of years for reasons other than human comfort."

I sit beside the musty old man, on a tree trunk that had fallen naturally. It is covered in little white flowers and bugs going about their business. I press the wet moss gently and look at the bottom of the log where the wood rots into the damp soil. Again a squadron of little bugs work through the bark – ants, weevils, earwigs.

The old man also sits in his own stillness. All that moves is a stick in his hand, which he turns in a circle making a pattern in the ground. Rosa looks through what appears to be an infinity of trees stretching down the hill to a vanishing point, garnished with green light.

"Judge, there are not many forests like this any more," the old man says.

"I know," says Rosa gravely.

"When you make your decision, I implore you to think of the past as well as the future."

"I will," says Rosa.

The old man stands up.

"Here, please have this on me," and he produces a brown mushroom from the front pouch of his apron. Enormous, fresh, perfectly round, like a large frisbee, with beautiful gills around the underside. The topside is a most pleasing color brown with pretty mottles. An aroma is faint and yet beautiful.

"Just as you humans like them. As the moon has whirled round us, a million times, we've watched the people in the woods pick mushrooms, and at this time of year the spores grow rich and fecund. We understand that this is what brings the most delight and contemplation," he says.

The forest offers the mushroom to Rosa with his twiggy fingers and she thanks him. I help her to carefully place it in her backpack, holding the top open so it fits without being squashed.

When we stand, the old man is gone.

"Where did he go?"

"They do that," says Rosa with a smile.

*

We come out of the forest into the glare of the afternoon. Seems we spent more time in the woods than I'd imagined. Rosa dons her sunnies and marches smartly along a fence-line, down toward a village where a large farmhouse dominates the huddle of buildings at the bottom of the valley. I see a church spire at the other end of the village, and the river behind. I follow, breathing odors of poo and cut grass. A bit rich for a city boy like me. The fields are speckled with sheep and cows, and a blackbird flutters and hops down the fence, like a tiny beaked guide.

"Where are we going?" I ask.

"The Hacks," said Rosa.

There is smoke coming from one chimney on the large and beautiful stone farmhouse, an old brick grain silo nearby, on a rise on the village's edge. We trudge over the gravel drive adjacent to a big barn and an almost-empty hayshed waiting for the harvest offerings. A cat is perched on one of the few remaining bales – it spots us and angrily swishes a long tail, then jumps to the back of the shed, which was odd.

It is an L-shaped, two-story house with several chimneys, obviously the property of a well-off landholder. We walk round to the back door through a small kitchen garden. There is machinery in a back shed, including a red tractor and big portable band saws on trailers.

I bang my fist on the door and Gus Hack's massive beard appeared in the gap, followed by Gus. He glances at me, and looks down at Rosa.

"Oh, hello Judge," he says gruffly. "Come in."

Germane is sitting at a stocky wooden kitchen table reading *The Land* newspaper. He looks up and scowls.

"So here you are," he says.

"Where's Mr Leopold?" asked Rosa.

"In town. He'll be back soon." Gus is handling a pan that contains ham frying over a flame on the stove. "I'm just getting tea together. Would you like some?" he says suddenly, realizing he had guests and should be hospitable.

"That would be lovely," says Rosa. "Here, we brought this," and she fishes out the large mushroom from her bag. "An offering."

"To go with the ham," I add.

"Well, that's a handsome mushroom," says Gus, beaming. He spins it between his fingers examining the gills for dirt. There is none. He chops it quickly and adds it to the fry-up. The scent of the mushroom and ham is incredible. Germane stops reading and sniffs the air with a dreamy look in his small, close-set eyes.

"Won't wait for Leo. He'll be having a quick one at the Travelers Arms, I'm sure," and Gus divides the ham, mushrooms and some fried shallots between the four plates and loads each up with a thick slab of buttered bread. I have trouble containing the saliva in my mouth, the smell is so divine.

"Here's cheers," he says, and the two lumbermen tuck into the food as if they are starving dogs, while Rosa and I eat a little more neatly.

Then something happens.

Gus and Germane's face-stoking and shoveling slow down. They start to chew thoughtfully with a look of bliss. I suddenly realize why. The mushroom is the creamiest, sweetest, tastiest, savoriest thing I had ever experienced. My mouth glows with happiness. Each munch is a pleasure. Even serious little Rosa smiles broadly as she eats her plate of food.

"Oh, my," exclaims Gus.

*

The ceiling started to swim with the gold light of the late afternoon. Germane leaned back elegantly from his empty plate and burped, and his burp sounded like the clear pure chime of a church bell. We all sat in a reverie of bliss. I thought of the forest paths, and the dirt and the beetles, and the dripping rain turning into rivulets, then streams and then the river in the valley snaking between its green banks.

Between the silver rivulets trickling across the earth, the small bright green fernbuds pushing through and unfurling, and, yes, the mushrooms, bulging like globes and flattening into brown pancakes, or tiny red beads on the end of pin sized stalks, the smell of wet earth was sweet and over-whelming in my reverie. I seemed to be being led underground by the old man under the forest where I felt the comfort of soil, and thick and thin roots twining and holding the earth firm, and velvety pink worms, as the water crawled under, too, and wriggled between the roots into the deeper soil, or staying put for a while because the leaves kept the ground cool, and then seeping down, down for a while into the deep earth, emerging from the riverbank into the stream.

A chorus of birds sang like bells and flutes as they found grubs, or sipped honey in the trees, brought mushed worm to their little ones in woven nests lined with soft spiderweb high in the canopy. There the bees flew from their natural hives the forest, in hollow trees and caves and pollinated the fields in the valley ensuring crops, and flowers lifted themselves eagerly, for pollination, almost calling the bees over with their singing colours and I was a bee, and hopped from flower to flower with amazing intent, rubbing my legs and butt in the delicious yellow pollen which weighed down my heavy legs and I wobbled through the air unsteadily.

Bats that live in old dead tree holes and under rocks, fly through dusk to catch hungry insects that had their hearts set on the Hack's crops, thousands of bats, munching the millions of bugs and for a while *I was a wheeling bat chasing a bug and it was fun as.* I would make a sound, like a gong, and in front of me in the dark tunnel I seemed to fly through, *the bugs before me would light up like sparks when I called out ... bong ... a myriad of bug-sparks would set off in the dark,* along with larger, bright, swift lines, which were other bats in the dark, and I'd wheel and avoid my fellow bats at dizzying speed toward the nearest spark and munch it and then *bong, and there would be so many more sparks, like a fireworks display,* and I'd zoom downward, but dodge a flatter light like upside-down sheet lightning below me – the ground – which would fade slowly, *bong* ... sparks .... I'd zoom up and eat the next juicy bug-spark. It was dizzying, thrilling, vertiginous fun, until I emerged under a huge archway of branches and leaves and the sunlight speckled amongst the various greeneries above. I was again part of the forest. I could feel the water under the soil heaving below me, down, slowly but surely, sharing with the trees and the river.

*

Slowly I emerge from my reverie, while the Hack brothers are still leaning back in their seats in a daze. I look at Rosa and she puts her finger to her lips, shushing me, so we stay quiet and watch the sun dip down to the horizon. A car draws up in the driveway. The banging back door rouses the two men from their daydream.

"What was that?" asks Gus.

"What?" I ask.

"I had the oddest dream."

"Okay," I say.

Mr Leopold enters in a waft of whiskey, fussing with his coat and putting it on a peg at the door.

"Hi, lads," says Leopold. "Judge. Mr Associate."

"Mr Leopold," says Rosa, "we've been waiting for you. Mr Germane kindly made tea."

"No problems. I had a pie down at the pub. Shall we start?"

"We can't do it," says Gus, out of the blue.

"Do what?" Leopold says.

"We've got to wait until them pine plantations mature. Only a few more years."

"What?" says Leopold, taken aback.

"We need the bees," says Germane.

"And the bats. Bats are fun," says Gus.

Astonished, I realize they've had the same freewheeling dream as me. They'd been a dream-bat as well, swooping into clouds of sparking insects like a fighter plane, *bonging* (a slowed down squeak?), and hearing and seeing the sonar signal bounce just as a juicy bug was munched.

"What nonsense have you been putting in my brothers' heads?" Leopold asks Rosa. "What have you been saying to them?"

"Nothing. None. No discussion. We just had tea. We were waiting for you."

"I'm sorry, Leo. Weren't the Judge's doing. We can explain ... my vote is to leave the old forest up there, and concentrate on other things," Germane says.

"But we're talking at least half a million ... for the business," Leopold splutters.

"Sorry, Leo, my view too, " said Gus, who turns to us and says: "And I just want to point out, I'm no greenie. I'm a timberman!"

"Maybe there's no need for a judgment then," Rosa says.

"Don't think so. Sorry for troubling you, young lady," says Germane in a kindly voice. And we have another cup of tea, with Leopold glowering in the corner. Clearly, he was working up an argument for his brothers who'd just outvoted him. We leave and walk to the town up the valley to catch a train.

"What just happened?" I ask, as we wander down the Hacks' driveway to the road.

"We were all presented with the forest's deposition to the court in the form of an edible mushroom," Rosa says, "and I have to say, Mr Benjamin, it was one of the highest quality submissions to a court I've ever experienced in my short career as a judge. Mr Leopold doesn't stand a chance."

SIDDLEY & GIDDLEY

As we return to the city in the night-train, two large collie dogs, both with muzzles, are sprawled out on the floor of our compartment. One is brown, and one is black. Dogs by law have to wear tight muzzles on trains, but theirs hang off their snouts in an act of compassion by the owner, an older woman in a small black hat and a grey tracksuit. She sits at the window seat, with a big leather art portfolio folder beside her.

The collies both look up and shift uneasily when Rosa comes in (sunglasses on) and she pats their hairy necks and mutters something reassuring. Comforted, both lay their chins on the ground once more. As the dogs fill most of the floor space, we edge round them carefully to reach our seats as the train picks up speed. Rosa and I sit opposite the woman who is reading a book entitled *Love's Lost Song*.

After a while she looks up and smiles at Rosa.

"Is the book good?" asks Rosa.

"It's terrible. Completely unrealistic portrayal of love. Characters one-dimensional. But it passes the time," says the woman, who looks pained. Then she blurts out, "Would you mind watching my dogs. I have to go to the toilet."

The woman shuffles past her dogs, both of which suddenly look anxious, one sticking its snout out of the compartment door.

"She'll be back," says Rosa.

"Hope so," says the dog with its snout out the door. "She's a bit unreliable. Gets lost."

"All the time," says the other dog.

Rosa laughs. "It's hard to get lost on a train."

"What's the bet she comes out of the toilet and turns the wrong way, and then has to come all the way back," says the snout-out dog.

"What's your name?" I ask the dog, given that all understandings were heightened in the presence of The Judge.

"I'm Ringo. That's George," says the snout-out dog. "Hey, what was that?"

George stands and also sticks his head out of the compartment door. "Something's odd, but can't see nothing."

"Looked like a little kid," says Ringo, "but bald and horrible. I'm worried."

Rosa suddenly sits up and takes off her sunglasses.

"Could be Siddley," she says to me. The dogs alerted by her sharp tone, look round at her.

"Hey – you've interesting eyes," says Ringo, "but they unfortunately make you look like a cat."

The train clicks along, unrelenting.

"Marjorie's taking her time," says George, further craning his hairy neck into the brightly-lit passageway. "Toilets just at the end of this carriage. And there's a weird smell coming from that way ... and it's not a toilet smell."

Both dogs sniff the air in the companionway. Rosa and I look at each other.

"How dangerous is Siddley?" I ask.

"He likely killed Mr Dawson Kennedy. He can be lethal," says Rosa, "but probably not to me. Let's go and check."

Worried about their lady owner, the two dogs stand and pad after us as we head down the carriage. The train charges through the countryside in the night with very few lights visible outside, although some of the brighter stars can be seen if you stand still and stare. But no time for standing still! The carriage rocks gently as we move. I lead, cautiously, checking the adjoining compartments which are filled with evening passengers. Siddley is not sitting in any of them. The only thing lingering in either of the two toilets is the smell of pee. We cross into the next carriage, me in front, Rosa flanked by the two collies. We push the door and find ourselves meshed in white fluffy stuff, like ceiling insulation, but sticky – so we push through that and enter the bistro car.

Siddley sits on a stool at the bar in a small dark suit and tie. Maybe a Zegna suit? It looks neat and Italian, with pointy shoulders, and contrasts with Siddley's wildly swinging eyes, and tiny razor-sharp teeth. On his bald head, a black fedora hat.

Beside him, sitting on a stool, is Marjorie swaddled in the fluff-stuff, and behind the bar, the bistro attendant, who is swathed in fluff-stuff too, cocooned fast with only his head sticking out. His cocoon hangs off the ceiling on a webline, which sways as the train carriage sways. I can see a couple more white bundles further down the bar also hanging and also swaying, and at the back door to the carriage, more fluff or spider web blocks the doorway.

The attendant looks terrified, but can't move ... bound tight, or maybe he's been paralyzed like a spider victim.

"You okay, Marjorie?" says Ringo. The woman nods, not realizing she'd understood her dog.

"You're not hurt?" asks George, and she shakes her head. The concern of Marjorie's dogs is commendable.

Rosa slides in front of me.

"What's going on, Siddley? What have you done? Restraining these people against their will."

"Billeon is with me, to keep order," Siddley says with a wicked sharp smile. "Aren't you, Billeon? This is Billeon, my hench-spider."

Four or five large sharp legs crept over the end of one of the booths further down the bistro, followed by the eight eyes of a huge spider. The dogs start to bark and Rosa gestures for them to be quiet. The spider, with a fat thorax, sits above the booth and glares at us. Shiny-black and malevolent, the eyes glowed red.

"Let these people go, Siddley," says Rosa. She is very brave. Her voice, sharp and angry.

"I been following you."

"Let them go."

"No. They're my hostages. I just want to talk to you, hostage-taker to judge."

"I'm a judge. I don't talk to hostage-takers. The police do that."

"Well, take care, or you'll be dealing with my spidey. Won't they, Billeon?"

The spider snicks her fangs in a threatening manner, and slowly moves to the carriage wall and creeps sideways up the window, leaving a trail of silvery web behind her.

Siddley puffs himself up and declares: "We're very annoyed with you. Annoyed about the Hack brothers, now, too."

"The Hack brothers?"

"Stopping their forestry plans."

"The Hacks' made their decision, Mr Siddley. There was no case."

"Hmmm. There was a good profit to be made there. You tricked them so they'd back off harvesting that forest. What a wasted opportunity." Siddley had a whiney voice. But then corrected himself and returned to business.

"Anyway, that's not the point. The point is – when are you going to give us that other little bull? The stolen property!"

Siddley leaves the stool to sit on the bar. His suit is sharply tailored, and he is very animated. Can't sit still. He has a little walking stick and pushes himself along the bar, and slides closer to us.

"The bull?" Rosa says in surprise.

She looks concerned and I'm very edgy as Billeon, the hench-spider, has started to creep further up the window to hang upside-down on the carriage roof, then starts to creep closer to me and the dogs with malice aforethought and menacing intent. The hairs on the back of my neck stand up, and I notice the collie dogs neck hair is fluffed vertically too. Billeon has enormous fangs, and white filaments behind her, exuding from her spinnerets, strewing web across the booths and tables as she approaches. The huge spider is an unnerving sight in the dim carriage. And she smells weird, like electricity.

"I didn't know you wanted the little bull," Rosa says coolly, ignoring the spider.

"Course we want it."

I ask: "Why do you want it?"

Rosa didn't take her eyes off Siddley.

"Who asked you to speak?" sneers Siddley, pointing at me, his index finger sparking yellowy-blue. Yet another danger.

"This is Mr Benjamin, my Associate. Provides me with legal opinions. He's entitled to ask questions on behalf of the court."

"Oh," said Siddley, sneers, "an Associate? Can't do the biz by yourself, judgey-wudge?"

All the time Marjorie and the dogs look at each other. The dogs pant and yawn nervously staring at the woman, then the spider on the roof. At the same time, Marjorie watches her dogs and also, from the corner of her eyes, Siddley. I know she is more worried about her dogs than herself, and that was nice. We're all locked in a dangerous stand-off – Rosa, Siddley, Billeon, Marjorie, me, and George and Ringo, not to mention the innocent people swinging back and forth in webby cocoons.

"The bull belongs to the boss," says Siddley, finally answering the question.

Rosa goes on: "The tau is in safekeeping, Siddley. You can assure Tau al-Gorz ..."

Siddley slams his hand on the counter and screams: "We don't want assurances ... we want the bull!" The counter sizzled red with heat under his palm as the train went round a long curve *clickety clickety click*. The spider sways on the roof with the train, eyes glowing, snicking its fangs. The wrapped and dangling people sway and I can hear their muffled moans. My mouth is dry and my head spins at the precarious situation and I tell myself, calmness is the answer. I try to be calm and summon some saliva for my tongue and mouth.

"Why do you want the bull," I ask coolly, watching Siddley's fireball finger.

"For the connection of course. Dimwit!"

One of the dogs takes offense at the word "dimwit" and starts to growl, but Rosa again gestures gently, signaling it to stop. Siddley is a seriously angry Elemental with a lot of firepower in his finger and we don't want a fricasseed collie on our hands.

The connection. That was interesting. Back to the Bronze Age and the Minoan lady.

"Remember, I'm The Judge now, Siddley, so stop following me around and frightening people. You know the rules... you are NOT allowed to menace the Court of Last Resort. We are charged with remaining open for every litigant, so you can make an appointment to see me any time. You only have to ask."

"Not so much fun, phoning for an appointment."

Rosa ignores his sneer.

"Tell Tau al-Gorz he needs to visit me at the house and we'll talk," says Rosa, reasonably. "You shouldn't be a messenger boy. You are an important half of his conscience."

"Don't dare tell ME who I am," snarls Siddley. He hops off the bar (a long way down for the little fellow), lands silently and marches up to Rosa. He looks up at her. The dogs gave a warning growl, but Siddley ignores them. He met her eyes and said: "Expect us."

"And Siddley, let them go." She points to the cocoons. "Otherwise, I won't admit you to the house. As I said, no negotiation with hostage-takers or their bosses."

Siddley sneers again. The spider evaporates, the people wrapped in web fall to the ground, unwrapped.

"See, it's that easy," says Rosa to the little creature.

"The way I do things, Judge, nothing's ever easy, you can bet on that."

There's a strong (and smelly) gust of wind through the carriage, which turns into a swirling wind, and Siddley is sucked into it, disappearing from view. Marjorie's eyes bulge.

I vault the bar and try to help the barman up. He's fallen backward onto his bottom from where he'd been hanging, and he's terrified and crying.

"Come on, mate, let's get you sorted." I pull him up and brush him down and give him a tissue. Other people were dragging themselves to their bistro tables, or walking out the far door. I could see one other woman down the end, also weeping in terror, but the web had disappeared from the doorways.

"There," I say to the man. "Gone. Just a bad dream."

"Didn't feel like a dream," says the traumatized attendant.

"They never do," I answer. "Did you hear that dog talk?"

He nods.

"Well, it's clearly a dream."

"Suppose. Bad one though."

"Bad dreams always come from a bad conscience, even if it's not your own ," says Rosa. "Come on," and she leads Marjorie and her dogs back to the compartment, and I follow as the train begins to pass the outer suburbs of the city. Snakes of light from streetlamps and shop signs disappear in our high-speed wake. In my mind, the last image of the bistro is the shape of a small angry hand burned into the bartop. My heart rate starts to settle.

"Dream, you say?" says the woman.

"There are always spiders in bad dreams," I explain.

"That's true. Funny though, felt very real to me. What is the dream about?"

"A private matter, Marjorie," says Rosa.

The woman flinches. "How do you know my name?"

"Ringo told me. Your dogs are very brave. They were ready to protect you from the spider."

"They're good boys," says Marjorie, still under the impression she is asleep, and dreaming.

"We're coming into the station," says Rosa, in a neutral voice.

"Well, I suppose I'd better tie their muzzles on so the stationmaster doesn't fine us," the woman says.

"If you have to," says George.

"Rules are rules, George," says Ringo.

"Sorry, boys," she says.

Rosa kneels and strokes the dogs and helps the woman put on their muzzles.

I wink at Rosa who smiles.

*

I can't sleep – still too much spider-fueled adrenaline pumping through my lines, those capillaries and veins, turning my face and my pillow hot. I slide from bed in my purple silk pajamas and walk up the short flight to the attic and the garden to breathe cool air.

In the attic I find a mess. The gold and silver chess pieces glitter in the moonlight where they lie scattered over the floor and chairs and cushions. I'm suddenly alert and put the light on, but there's nothing else untoward in the room. A French door is slightly open though, so I push cautiously onto the terrace.

The air's cold, and nobody's on the terrace, so I stare out to the glimmer of the city and suburbs. I calm down, until something hits the back of my head. It's sharp and hard and I turn round to collect another sharp pebble on my nose.

"Ow!"

Sitting on top of the attic roof is a tiny person, throwing small pebbles at me.

"Hey, stop," I say, suddenly fearing Siddley and his fireballs.

"I'm not Siddley, stupid," says a scritchy voice reading my mind and throwing another pebble which whacks me on the head. "Get for me Rosa!" A sharp order.

"Who are you?"

But already I've worked it out – Giddley. She's in half shadow but appears to be wearing a shiny silver one-piece jumpsuit. Seems two-dimensional Siddley and Giddley ditch their grubby robes when they leave their boss's saggy chest and become well-dressed 3D trolls. She is sure dressed like a disco queen. A demented disco queen. I can see the glint of her yellow eyes, with black slits, just like Rosa's, but her eyebrows are thin and pointy – in fact, everything about her is pointy, including her sharp little teeth which are unnerving when she smiles.

"Rosa!" She throws another pebble.

"Just ask nicely and I'll wake her up," I say.

"Sorry sooky lala." Another pebble whizzes past me.

"Nicely." I hope I wasn't risking a fireball.

"No fire-pops from Giddley. Not nasty like Siddley. Get Rosa." Okay. Reading minds again. At least a pebble isn't involved this time so I take it as a polite request.

I duck downstairs and shake Rosa gently, hall light leaning into her dark room and across her bed. "Giddley's on the roof. She wants to talk to you. She keeps reading my mind." And Rosa is out of bed almost instantly and running upstairs. "Quick, quick, before she changes her mind and disappears," Rosa says over her shoulder as she vanishes upward.

Rosa scoots onto the roof before I even get to the garden. I haul myself up the wisteria and traverse the slates. The moon is a halfer, but bright, so there's some light – along with the city ambience welling up from below. Enough light to twinkle the sequins on Giddley's disco jumpsuit.

"Giddley followed us from the train after Siddley's performance," Rosa tells me as I reach the pair. Small Rosa and even smaller Giddley. "Giddley was watching Siddley who was projecting as a cat."

"I was spying on Siddley!" Giddley says proudly. "He was a spying cat, spying on you at that farm, nasty Siddley."

Giddley's little twin tattoo is about a quarter of Rosa's height.

"You've met my Associate, Mr Benji?"

"Hello, Associate Mr Benji." Giddley's voice crackles with a little laugh. "You a bit flimsy."

"Be nice, Giddley. He's not so weak. What's Siddley up to? What's Tau al-Gorz up to?"

"Can't betray master, but you know what he's like. My brother is..." She shrieked out a laugh, "unstoppable when he wants something. He'll be back, you know. He wants what you've got."

"The tau?"

"Yizzz."

"Why does he want the tau?" I ask, sitting on the roof ridge a little bit further away from Giddley in case of fireballs.

"He wants kill me. Hates me. With passion. He hurts me." She pulls up the sleeve of her glittering one-piece suit and there are bruises and bite marks on her arm. Suddenly, I feel deeply sorry for little Giddley.

"A nasty case of sibling rivalry?" I ask.

"He not my sibling. I am a conscience. Tau al-Gorz's good conscience. I always lose." Her head swivels around, and she scratches her neck with a clawed fingernail.

Rosa puts her arm around Giddley's tiny shoulder. "Thanks for coming and warning us."

"What Siddley done to those people was wrong. Billeon spider-thing is wrong, making people fear. The master should be better, but Siddley riles and razzes him all the time to be bad and greeeeedy." Giddley is crying now, making yowly noises and wiping glistening green snot from her nose.

We sit in the dark waiting for the little troll to recover.

"Giddley – the other month, just before Tau al-Gorz killed me in the attic, you and Siddley had a terrible fight. Were you fighting for me?"

Giddley nods. "Stupid chess! Stupid, stupid chess! I knew the master was angry and want to kill, and Siddley was stoking his anger. I try to stop the stoking – jump on him, but I was muzzled from speaking, like those hairy dogs on the train. Siddley won and Tau struck out, stabbed you."

"Thank you for trying." Rosa says gently.

"I am yours, Judge Rosa Somberly," says Giddley humbly, and softly. "Now must go. Master is looking for both of us. Wanting to know where Giddley and Siddley is."

Giddley looks up at the half-moon and without a sound, she seems to dissolve into a mist.

"Fak – what was all that?" I say, as the mist then melts into the nothingness of the night.

"Giddley's trying to help. She's not sure how. She's very scared."

"She's tough for what she puts up with, and Siddley's mad," I say.

"Only for effect. Siddley knows what he is doing. He's a bad conscience. Giddley is nicer. Seeing her just now made me remember. The last thing I saw during the chess game was Giddley trying to save me." Rosa looked very sad again, no doubt thinking of her father.

"Why did she say 'I am yours'?"

"I think she likes me for some reason. But I'm not sure if she believes in The Judge. She's part of Tau al-Gorz."

We have a mutual think, looking into the city lights that stretch to the horizon like a glittering net.

I look at Rosa's small face. It's now very late.

"Let's make a hot chocolate and try and get some sleep," I suggest.

"That would be nice, Mr Benji," she says.

THE CASE OF TEN PANGOLINS IN A BOOT

Through the skylight I see water shimmering below, moon-silver and shadow-ink. A 50-meter serious-swimmers' pool, the jewel in the crown of the city's old bathing complex with its ancient glassed ceiling. Elodie, Rosa and I crouch on the roof, with a view across Emperors Park, and our breaths form tiny moonlit clouds in the cold air. Winter has arrived and the moon's light casts snail trails across bare branches of stately old trees and throws vast shadows below on the grass. Being 1 a.m., no-one's about, not even revelers. Far too cold, unless you've drunk more than a skinful of spirits.

I slide a thin piece of metal under the skylight latch and snick it open lifting the window frame which squeaks on its ancient hinge. A chlorine stink and warm humidity wafts past me. The baths are always kept to a nice temperature for the public.

"Okay," I say, "let's drop in."

We are here at the request of Rosa. She's a swimmer, always a swimmer. But her crocodilian eyes make it impossible to swim when the public baths are crowded. The golden glint and black-slit pupils are too strange, and she's fearful someone would notice and scream in fright, so she's been bugging me for weeks for a secret swim. I asked Elodie to help me break into the swimming pool, so here we are, the three of us. At one in the morning on a roof. Our backpacks stuffed with towels, bathers and burglary tools.

Rosa has another slight problem. She is growing what looks like a tail from the bottom of her spine. There are five extra small vertebrae emerging from where her coccyx should be – at least, that's what Elodie told me. Although I was technically her carer, I knew it wasn't right for me to advise on a 10-year-old girl's body. I was neither family nor female. After Rosa told me of this growing tail-like structure, I had asked Elodie and Mrs Cimbalom to inspect the protuberance in the privacy of Rosa's bedroom, and they talked to her for an hour or so while I paced the landing outside, like a worried parent!

"It's a small tail, and I think manageable so long as it doesn't grow much longer," Mrs Cimbalom said afterward.

"What if it does?"

She'd shrugged and Elodie said, "Mrs Cimbalom will sew a tail hole in her swimmers so she can wear them." Elodie had looked deeply perplexed at what she'd seen, but remained practical.

"And I can tuck it in down my pants during the day. It's not too awkward," added Rosa. "I've been doing that for a few weeks." I saw right through her stoic act. Suffering in silence for a few weeks now. Poor kid.

"Is it covered in skin?" I'd asked, hesitantly.

Mrs Cimbalom shrugged again.

"Maybe. Maybe ... a little scaly," said Elodie.

"With a reptilian ridge?"

"A little one," said Elodie, grimacing slightly.

"It's okay," said Rosa. "Don't worry."

*

Now, in the middle of the night on the bathhouse roof, we rope up, slither through the skylight and rappel onto the cast-iron viewers' balcony above the pool, a short drop and easy slide. Elodie and I slip on our swimmers and goggles, because we might as well do a few laps too. The moonlight is serious, and where it shines, the room is bright.

"Didn't you pack your goggles, Rosa?" I ask.

"I don't need goggles. This skin thing under my eyelid goes over my eyes when I go underwater. It's excellent."

I'd heard about this crocodilian third eyelid.

"Can you see through it? The skin thing?"

"Yeah," she says as she ran down the stairs to the pool and dives into the water. Her small green tail protrudes from her one-piece swimmers, then she disappears into the ink, and surfaces halfway down the pool, swimming strongly. She'd told me she'd always loved swimming, at the beach, in mountain lakes and especially at the pool.

"That tail's a bit cute," I say to Elodie who stood beside me in her own one-piece.

"It is adorable, but I hope it doesn't grow any further when she reaches puberty."

"There is that."

Tomorrow is Rosa's birthday and the secret swim is an early birthday present. She'll be eleven years old. Elodie, Mrs Cimbalom and I have no idea what might eventuate with her Elemental powers as this strange girl turns into a teenager.

The dark water laps at the poolside and I see occasional splashes, caught in the moonlight which streams through the glass roof. The pool's edges are marble and sandstone, and statues and carvings sit in niches along the walls. They are carvings of classical figures – Neptune, Minerva, Thetis,

Peleus and more. I know them all now, as my search for an explanation of Rosa and her parents took me on a deep dive (so to speak) into Greek and Roman mythology. Shifting reflections lick the statues' faces, but nowhere did my searches give me clarity about The Judge, Mrs Cimbalom, the house, or the strange legal cases that keep coming through our front door.

After I splosh my way through a few warm laps, kicking off each end and sliding through the inky water, I emerge wet and sit on a seat with a towel around my shoulders, Elodie beside me, taking a warming swallow of brandy from a little silver flask I had found in the mysterious butler's pantry. I pass the flask to Elodie who lifts her wet, gleaming arm with its briar rose tattoo as she takes a swig. We watch Rosa lapping up and down with a strong and easy freestyle, a silvery moon-wake behind her.

"Is her adorable tail wiggling as well?" Elodie asks.

"I believe it is. Assisted propulsion."

We sit together for a while listening to Rosa's soft splashing in the huge room. I feel a sad pang - this is my last evening with Elodie for a while. I'm going to miss her and I feel so stressed for her, going off to care for her dying mother.

The French authorities agreed to allow her into the country over Christmas. Elodie was banished for a series of robberies she committed as a juvenile, one of which involved the death of a fellow robber. Her father came from this city, so the government cancelled her French citizenship and said she belonged here. So very unfair, as she was born and grew up in France, near Mont Blanc. It sucked. France had molded Elodie and that nation should have taken responsibility for her, but no – she was kicked out of the country without money or resources 24 hours after being released from jail.

Four years back, Chaz found the 18-year-old Elodie at the central railway station looking thunderous and abandoned at the same time and asked her what the prob was. When it was quickly established she was an alpinist and an outcast she came and stayed with the crew. Now, thanks to pleas from her dying mama's local politician, there was a short reprieve, and she was going home to see her mum in the care home.

"How long will you be in Paris?" I ask Elodie.

"I'm allowed two weeks, *cheri*, but I'll try it on and stay longer, depending on Mama."

"Fair enough," I say. I understand. Looking after Mama was humane, but Elodie was a canceled French citizen and they'd be glad to be rid of her again. Their loss, my gain, at some point.

"I'll miss you."

"So sweet. Me too," says Elodie, smiling. I could see her lips and eyelashes, also silvery in the strange light. Elodie is always elusive, so you never knew where or when she'd return after an absence. I know I'll miss her, but it's likely she will be back.

We kiss softly and I stroke her cheek, and suddenly she hugs me, damp and intense.

*

After 50 laps, Rosa finishes her swim. I kneel on the edge of the pool and she shows me her weird reptilian eye-film that slides up across her eye when she dips under water. I touch the edge with the end of my pinky finger and it feels like contact lens plastic.

"And it doesn't make things blurry?" I ask.

"A bit, but it's okay."

Finally, Rosa pulls herself from the pool and I throw her towel round her shoulders. Rosa quickly and methodically towels her hair and dries herself. I turn away to let her dress in tights and a thermal, a jumper, socks and her sneakers.

"Ready," she says.

The three of us return to the balcony and easily scale onto the roof, where I lock the skylight. We'd found a manageable route up, using walls and a portico above the entrance, so it's a snap to climb down. We scuttle down the pool complex's steps to the park and a quiet saunter out of the park gate to the metro entrance, and down the lit steps to the bright platform underground, discussing Elodie's departure plans.

Trains only come every half hour at 3 a.m., so we bide our time on the platform, inhaling the hot subway smell emanating from the tunnel. The dead of night doesn't worry any of us owls. We're used to operating at dark, and Rosa can sleep at the drop of an eyelid, and anyway, after the brisk swim we're all wide awake. Tomorrow is Sunday so Rosa can sleep in before her party.

This metro line was built in the 19th century. The platform is made from stone, and the walls are tiled in an old-fashioned hatch pattern, quite yellow. There's a drunk man prone on a bench further up, groaning, and a couple of people standing quietly, the woman leaning against a pillar. Elodie cuddles into me, and Rosa amuses herself by twirling her wet towel and flicking an advertisement on a rubbish bin with the end, with little snaps. Watching her is electric – the snaps are accurate and hit the same target, a photo of a goat on the side, multiple times at great speed. *Snap snap snap.*

We don't see the policemen approach until Rosa looks up and says, "Hello, officers."

The two cops are a bit raggle-taggle as if they've been on a long shift: caps and ties askew, shirt flap out in front of their gun-belts. One is a black guy, and the other a woman with very short grey hair. The man is a sergeant.

Elodie and I stare at them with deep distrust, Elodie because of her impending special trip to Paris, me because of past misdemeanors.

But Rosa's fine with the situation – being the Judge of the Court of Last Resort she relates to law enforcement.

"What can I do for you?" she asks.

"How old are you?" the sergeant asks her, looking utterly perplexed at the junior spokesperson.

"Ten," says Rosa. "I turn 11 tomorrow!"

"Is she with you?" the officer asks me.

"Yes."

The female police officer kneels down in front of Rosa and holds her hand.

"Sweetie, do you know this man?" she asks.

"He's my Associate," Rosa says. She suddenly realizes that the woman cop is tense, so there's something wrong.

"Associate?"

"Carer," I say.

At that moment the subway train blows into the station throwing that electric smell and lots of light over the platform. I see Elodie get on it and give me a little wave through the door window as it draws away. She wants no biz with cops just before departure on a special visa and I don't blame her.

"That's our train," I protest.

"Not so fast," said the sergeant. "You'll be coming with us. What's your name, kid?"

"Rosa Somberly. We were just going home, sir. We were only out for a swim."

The cop looks shocked. "But the pool is closed? How did you get into the bathing complex?" He looked at the wet towel around her neck. "You'll need to come down to the station with us. A kid up this late is neglect." He turns to me. "She should be tucked up in bed, buddy."

He then looks back at Rosa and his nose wrinkles slightly. Rosa wears her yellow tinted Bono glasses, but he can sense her weird eyes, I'm sure. Cops are trained to notice things. The woman cop in particular seems amazed that a small girl is at large at 3 a.m. in the morning with a big guy in a shabby hoodie and stovepipe jeans, with two days of bristle on his face. Only Rosa's bright-eyed, quizzical attitude is saving us from a big problem.

"Hey, where's the woman who was with you?" the female cop says looking round.

"Blew us off, I think. Caught the train. Had to get back to her sick mum," I say, too glibly. The cop gives me a dirty look and huffs.

"Come on, sweetie," said the female cop in the voice of faux motherliness, "we'll get you down to the station for a cup of tea and a blanket and talk to this man. Not sure about your situation. Might be a case for social services."

"Hardly," I butt in. "Her father asked me to take care of her ..."

"By illegally breaking into the municipal pool after midnight?" says the sarge. "I don't think her father will approve once we've told him."

Rosa is about to say something, but I look at her and she stops. She stops talking from then on, and we are escorted up the stone subway steps, and along the cold street to the squad car, a black Mercedes with POLICE on the doors.

We rip through the streets in the Merc, when suddenly there's a commotion on the radio.

A busy tinny voice: "Car with two possible bodies inside, alleyway off La Grange Street, Old Town. Nearest available cars, please attend. The Slammer Bar reported it in. A Mikail Tommasen called, bar proprietor. Suspect car is in the alley next to the bar."

"Aw, fak. Two streets away. We'll get it," says the sarge. "This pair can sit and dry off in the back. This is car 22, we got it," he says into the radio, a hint of excitement in his voice. Some real policing.

"Ok, copy," the tinny busy-voice says.

Now the sirens sound, but not for long, as it takes a minute to hove into the city's emptied-out party precinct. Quiet, there are only a few drunken stragglers in the shadows. We come to a narrow street in Old Town where there's a lot of bars, mostly closed-up, but still with their yellow, red and blue neon lights aglow.

"Sit here tight, you two," says the sergeant to us. "Secure the car, Fran."

"Yes, sarge." Click! The car is locked. We're in the back seat and there's a shatterproof divider between us and the front. And the child lock is activated. I try the door, but Fran had done her job. Dang!

The cops head through the freezing air to the doorway of the bar, where the proprietor, Mikail Tommasen, is waiting. He looks little drunk and smokes a cigarette which glows pinpoint orange. He gestures unsteadily to an alley at the corner with finger and cigarette. The alley was real black, no street light ambience penetrating – I can see old-fashioned chrome bumpers poking out, but that's about it. We are trapped in the car and my sightlines are poor.

I look at Rosa and she looks at me. She blinks once and the car locks pop open.

"Dad taught me that," she says. "Don't know how it works."

I laugh. We sneak out the car door on the side opposite the cops. My hair's still damp and there's now a biting wind making the tips of my ears cold.

"Okay, let's head home," I say.

"No," she says, "I'm going to look at the car and maybe help the police. You can leave me here."

"You know I can't leave you. I hate the cops. Let's go!"

"Benji, they have our faces on their body cameras." Her voice mildly exasperated at my stupidity. "Your photo will already be in their files. We have to talk our way out of this … arrest."

"We haven't been arrested."

"No, but you will be, if we leave. You'll be charged with escaping custody, child neglect, breaking into a swimming pool and illegal disposal of a body when they find out father has died. Lots of crime."

The Judge is right. I am the irresponsible adult.

After listing my alleged crimes and misdemeanors, she then says: "Let's help the police and get a caution instead."

So we get out and skulk our way through the shadows while the cops are focused on the alley car and its inhabitants.

The car's an old banger, one side mushed into the alley wall like it had hurtled into the corner. The light from the cop's torches were dancing on what looked like people in the front seat. Little bit of hair sticking out of a clearly round head.

"Hmmm," says Rosa. "I'm not liking this. There are pangolins in the boot."

"What?"

"Can't you hear them?" So I listen and hear scuffling and a muffled discussion about where to find ants. Rosa's ability to comprehend any witness is transferred to me as well, being her Associate. I can now understand pangolin.

"They're hungry and thirsty," says Rosa.

"Stinks in here," I hear a whiny voice say.

"How do you know they're pangolins?"

"Ant addicts," she says. "They crave ants."

The cops have walked away from the car into the light of the narrow street and start calling in people on their phones. Forensics and homicide detectives. I look back and Rosa's gone. Must say, by now (3 a.m.) I'm quite tired, but she's all Action Jackson. I sidle through the shadow toward the front of the car in the alleyway, and there she is, talking to the two corpses.

"We tried our best, Judge," the dead driver was saying. He'd been shot in the chest and I could just see something in the dark … blood still gleaming wet in the reflection of lights. A slumped neck and a mouth. As per my conversation with Rosa's dead father, the corpse's lips don't move, and I can't see the eyes in the shadows.

"There's a farm in the hills," the faint voice says. "Breeding and fattening up rare wildlife for illegal trade. We belong … belonged … to the group WLA, The Wildlife Liberation Army. Dee and I broke into this farm … the place is a big operation … sheds and pens full of animals. They also legally breed mink for a cover story. So we busted in …"

"Quietly, though …" says the dead girl beside the dead man. A more distant voice, another shadow in the car. She was slumped on his shoulder – could just make out a mop of blonde hair poking above the seat into some light. The rest of her was dark. "But they musta had CCTV in the barn. Ernst and I managed to pack ten pangolins into the car, but we heard doors slamming up at the farmhouse, so we zipped."

The other scratchy voice took over: "They followed us. Motorcyclists. Two Kawasaki trail bikes, very fast. Chased us all the way from down Albrecht into the city … tucked close. I tried to evade them, but those kwaka's are powerful. I try this alley and they just … corral us …"

"And kill us," says the girl. "Very quick. Pop. Pop."

Sorrow overwhelms me as I look at the corpse and listen to her ghost. Tears well up on the edge of my eyelids, but Rosa doesn't stop, forging on with her questions.

"Do you remember any features?"

"Couldn't see faces, but the arm that held the gun had an old blue bull-horn tattoo with a zappy snout. I remember that," says the dead man.

"Yeah. Bull horns, Judge," says the woman.

"Went *pop pop*. Two flashes."

I wipe a tear from my cheek.

Judge Rosa asks: "So where's this farm?"

"Horrible cruel place, Judge. Up Back Mountain Road above the town. Hidden behind a whole bunch of fir plantations. They got ..." and the voice started to fade "... pangolins, honey bears, poisonous snakes, stuffed in together in battery conditions. Breeding them up ... for foreign buyers. Been watching them for a while, but heard from Barnabas the pangolins were going to be shipped out tomorrow ..."

"So we rescued the pangolins ... at least they're safe ..."

Rosa sounds very serious: "Who's Barnabas?"

"Our spy in the farm. He's a good man."

"You did well Ernst and Dee," says Rosa in a kindly voice. "Go on your journey now. We will find justice for you."

"Thank you, Judge," says a faint voice. "Remember ... Back Mountain Road ..."

"Hey," says the sergeant angrily. "What are you two doing here?"

We spin around.

"Officer ... the girl is still alive," I say, brain whirring, thinking quickly, trying to meet his angry tone with urgency. "She just told us the car boot contains ten pangolins which these two people rescued from an illegal breeding facility in the hills above Albrecht. Along Back Mountain Road."

The cop looked at me in amazement. "But she's been shot in the heart!"

"Did you check for life signs?" I ask.

"Well, no. I didn't have to."

"Pop the boot," says Rosa beside me, and she blinks once and the boot lid popped up and ten pangolins look out, beady little eyes set in scaly faces.

"See, pangolins!" Rosa's got the idea.

"Oh, my god! Just as the girl said! Call an ambulance," I exclaim.

"And the zoo people, too," says Rosa, pointing at the pangolins. "They'll need ants."

"Yes, we do," shouts one of the pangolins. "Whole nests!"

"We're starving hungry," says another.

"Aw shit," says the cop pushing past us and reaching in and putting his finger on the girl's neck to find a pulse. "Ahhh...she's gone now," he mutters.

I move with the cop out of the darkness, into the street, and tell him the story of the hit, the two motorcyclists chasing the animal liberationists, an arm with an old blue bull-horn tattoo holding a gun. The cop starts writing this down furiously. "You shoulda called me over."

"Sorry, she was talking so faintly," I say as an excuse.

"It's a hit, alright," says Fran, kneeling and shining her torch on the bodies. "Clinical."

I avoid looking into the car. Ernst and Dee were better off as shadows.

"Big money in rare wildlife," says Rosa brightly.

"Hey, you shouldn't be here, sweetie pie. You're a child," says Fran. "These are corpses."

"I want to go home now, Benji," says Rosa, catching the cue, in a little girl voice.

"Sarge ... the kid needs to go home," said Fran. "This is a crime scene and they're messing it up. We can follow these two up in the morning."

"Yeah ... take her home," says the sarge. "This is big organized crime stuff. What's your address? We'll need to follow up and get a proper statement," says the cop, his mind now on greater things.

I give him our real address. We are on a roll and I knew they'd track me down if I lied. The cop nods and writes.

"Thanks, buddy. And thanks for the info."

I add: "She said their names were Ernst and Dee. They worked for the Wildlife Liberation Army. Dee said there was a contact in the farm called Barnabas who tipped them off about an illegal shipment. It's such a terrible waste." I suddenly get goosebumps of sorrow and start to choke up. Rosa slips her hand into mine.

"We can arrange a lift," says the cop, looking at Rosa.

"It's okay. I'll get an Uber," I say. "You got a lot to do."

And that was almost that, although Rosa fetched her bag from the police car, found her drink bottle, said bye to the pangolins and gave them each a squirt of water.

"Sit tight," she whispers to them. "People are on the way with ants!"

*

Next day, Rosa turned 11. I'd been stumped for how to mark the moment. No direct family now. She didn't seem to have any friends her age. Yes, there were her tutors, and then me and Mrs Cimbalom, and Miloš the Prague ratter dog, and that seemed to be it.

So the week prior to her birthday (and the pangolins) I took a big plunge. I crossed the road to the house where the boy Rosa's age lived. Somehow she knew his name was Lionel. They'd probably talked as toddlers in the little park down the street. I'd seen him and his dad hang out in the park, play football, and watched him head to school of a morning. He'd looked reasonable, tidy (not like me), same age as her, a little bit brainy and studious.

So I'd borrowed one of the late Judge's tweed jackets and knocked on their standard door, and was met by a standard maid, and was ushered into the vestibule (not unlike Rosa's, but without the stained glass). Lionel's father appeared, sporting a sharp haircut, ironed chinos and a lambswool jumper. He gave me a quizzical look.

"I'm Benjamin from number 26 across the road and I look after young Rosa," I said, and got straight to the point, suggesting Lionel attend Rosa's 11th birthday party "as neighbors should be neighborly."

"Oh, Lionel's 11 as well, and hitting A grades in everything, and he's been put up a year at school," said his father proudly, and we shook hands.

He told me Lionel's mum worked in the national parliament and was "in and out". Then the father summonsed Lionel to personally accept the invite, so he appeared in the vestibule with a puzzled face. He wore glasses and was a stringy whippet of a lad, around the same height as Rosa. When I issued the invitation he said: "I'd love to come. I've noticed Rosa in the street."

That was a good start.

When I told Mrs Cimbalom what I'd arranged, she approved.

"Good idea," she'd said.

The following Saturday, we went swimming and found the haul of hungry pangolins. And Elodie went to France.

*

Then at three in the afternoon on Sunday, birthday party!

After a sleep-in, we have a special breakfast of maple syrup scrambled eggs, hot chocolate and dunking churros, and I give her some books – novels aimed at kids a bit older than her to help her understand the puzzling, enraging, engaging human condition. Rosa and I blow up some red and gold balloons and tie them around the vestibule and the downstairs living room. Mrs Cimbalom has baked a massive Romanian cherry cake, and on a previous shopping expedition, Elodie had helped Rosa choose a beautiful new dress which makes her look great and grown-up.

The door chimes ring daintily, and it is Mrs Gamelan, the music teacher, who brings a present of French piano scores she wants Rosa to have – Debussy and Satie. Next is Mr Zither, who brings a bunch of flowers which we fuss over to find a worthy vase.

Then Lionel arrives with his perfectly groomed mum, who is dressed head to toe in mulberry – casual jacket, exercise pants and trainers. The chime the house chooses for them is simple, but still musical, which indicates general approval of Lionel. Rosa and I usher them in and they gape a bit at the stained glass and the art, and Lionel's mum hangs around for a few minutes to make sure we aren't monsters, before telling Lionel she'll be at home across the road and to come back any time.

Rosa immediately takes a shine to Lionel, and he to her. Apparently, they'd both "noticed" each other while growing up in the same neighborhood, and were "intrigued". At least, that last bit was what Lionel told me the previous week. "She looks like an intriguing person," he'd said, when accepting the invitation, and his Dad patted him patronizingly on the head, which is where I assume the word "pat" comes from.

When his mother releases Lionel to the party and leaves, Rosa says, "I'll show you around my house," and they head for the lift, while I entertain the others.

There's a long absence from the two kids which starts to constitute rudeness, so I go to find the birthday girl. Neither has strayed far – they are in the kitchen talking about why Rosa doesn't go to school. Lionel is looking puzzled.

"My father's wish was that I be homeschooled," Rosa is explaining. "Those are my tutors downstairs."

"Okay," Lionel says.

"Hi, you two, come on down and talk to the other guests," I say, somewhat sharply. Lionel jumps from his stool and immediately looks embarrassed as if he'd committed a huge social *faux pas*. Rosa just says, "Come on," and I follow them downstairs. In the end, the tutors don't hang around for very long. We sing happy birthday, and after eating a piece of Romanian cherry cake they leave.

While Rosa and Lionel talk about something brainiac – Arabic mathematics and the development of algebra – the doorbell rings again, this time a very unenthusiastic scratchy sound, so I duck out of the party to the vestibule and gaze at the bulky shadows in the glass. Crowding the door are the cops from the night before.

"How are the pangolins?" I ask the sergeant as I take a deep breath and usher them in.

"Being cared for at the zoo," he says, and looks past me into the house. Constable Fran is gazing around, too, at the opulent candelabras and paintings.

"We've typed up your statement reflecting what the victim told you ..."

"Ah, yes, poor Dee."

"Can we come in and could you read through it? Add anything you might have missed."

"Sure, sure," I say. At that moment Rosa and Lionel come out of the front lounge.

"Oh, hello officers," she says. "Are you here with Mr Benjamin's statement?"

"Yes," says the sergeant, looking surprised at her legal acuity.

"Do you want to me to read through it as well? I spoke to the girl, too," says Rosa.

"No, no. One witness statement's enough – better the adult than the minor."

Rosa doesn't look pleased at being called a "minor" when she was the one who'd conducted the interview with Ernst and Dee.

"It'll be fine," says Sergeant Duke.

"How are the pangolins?" she asks.

"Comfortable. At the zoo."

"Good. I'm so glad. I have a guest, so if you don't mind … let's go, Lionel," she says, and they head upstairs as she explains to him why the police are here, hopefully not in too much detail, like her gathering evidence from talking corpses.

"Come through," I say and sit them around the big oak table covered in crumbs, while I read through what is an excellent report of the explanation I'd made in the small hours of the morning. "That's really good," I add. "You got everything." The sergeant doesn't smile at my compliment but nods his head.

"Thing is," says the sergeant uneasily, "Dr Louise Fraiche, our police surgeon, says the victim would have been dead instantly when shot, so she contends that the victim would have been unable to impart this very detailed and, I might add, accurate, information. As I said. Last night."

"Well, she talked to us," I say.

"I'm not doubting that the information is sound," says the cop. "We have a team up at Albrecht and they've raided the farm the deceased witness identified, found rare animals, and the two motorbikes, a stash of weapons, and they've made arrests, including one of the suspected killers, but we just don't understand how you …"

"I've got no explanation," I say, and I don't. "I just heard the girl tell her story."

The cop shrugs. "Well, we checked to confirm you were nowhere near the scene of the killing when it happened … you were at the pool, just as you said."

"What do you mean?"

"You're off the hook."

He sighs in exasperation and looks as if he'd rather arrest me there and then. I grin, remembering Rosa's advice about "just being cautioned" last night.

I observe the sergeant's afternoon face. Bags under his eyes, a no-nonsense mouth, little bit of scurf in his dark hair. This guy just manages to look after both his work pressure and himself. Constable Fran is older than I'd imagined. The dark of the previous night had given me a false sense of her age. And she looks kindlier.

"I'm really happy to help you out on this case," I say, "and so is Rosa. I'm sure she could give you a statement too. She's wise beyond her years," I add, reassuringly.

The sarge says, "Thanks."

"How long have you two been working together?" I ask, signing the statement.

"Two and a half years."

"Like a marriage sometimes," says Fran with a laugh. "Anyway, it's clear the kid is well looked after here."

"Yeah, it's her house, and her dad's. And we're in the middle of Rosa's birthday party. Would you like some cake?" I point to the half-cut cake in the center of the table.

"Naw...we gotta go talk to the barman as well," says the sarge sadly, looking at the mountain of cherry yumminess. I say, "Oh, come on, I'll fix that."

As I show them out the door with a box of takeaway cake, there's a shriek from above and Lionel descends the stairs in some haste.

"Are you okay," I ask, and see Rosa at the top of the staircase looking worried and shamefaced.

"A tail ..." he says. "A tail ...?"

The cops are immediately engaged.

"Are you okay, son?" says the sergeant noting Lionel's distress.

Lionel suddenly realizes there are police.

"Ah ... er, yes ... Rosa played a trick on me. I'm fine."

"A party trick," Rosa says. "I'm really sorry, Lionel."

Lionel tries to mask his hyperventilation.

The cop waits for a moment, and when Lionel doesn't say anything he replies, "Okay. We don't investigate party tricks," and moves toward the door. Then turns to me one more time, looking huffy.

"And Benjamin, no more nocturnal outings to the pool. That's not a request. It's a legal direction." Finally, Sergeant Duke and Constable Fran walk down the steps. I close the door.

"She's got a tail ..." says Lionel, his teeth chattering slightly. Rosa runs up to him and holds his arm.

"Its okay, Lionel. It's ...vestigial. I just thought you'd be interested."

I immediately ponder what Rosa, in her party frock, would have had to do to show Lionel her tail.

"Did you ...?" I start to ask, somewhat in shock.

"Only a little. The top of it. For a peek. We were talking about being different. Lionel feels different at school too, different from the other kids ... he's a class ahead of the others, and even then he's top of the class, but the older kids ignore him."

"Lionel," I say in a kind voice, "come with us. You have to trust us. Come to the kitchen." I press him gently and he follows us. In the friendly kitchen, in this calming house, I pour us three glasses of party lemonade and find a plate of jellybean kebabs. I notice that Rosa still has her yellow Bono-style glasses firmly on her nose, so there's been no eye reveal.

"Rosa doesn't have many friends. Some things about her that are indeed different. And you are a highly intelligent young man. I invited you because I thought you could be her ..."

"Friend," Rosa says, looking a bit anguished. "I want you to be my friend. I was so glad when Mr Benjamin invited someone my own age. I don't have school friends, or any close relatives. I didn't mean to frighten you."

"I wasn't frightened," says Lionel. "I was shocked! It's not normal for people to have a tail and I have to admit it looks somewhat … reptilian. If I were to have a tail, I would expect to have a mammal tail, with hair."

He really is pleasantly geeky. Rosa grips him by the arm. "Me too. I'd rather have a squirrel's tail, but that's … just how … I ended up."

Lionel has another think and twiddled with his glasses.

"I did get a fright, actually. I do want to be your friend. But whatever you do, don't let my mum and dad know about your tail, or they'll never, ever let me visit, or for you to come and play at my house. Dad said I was to invite you to lunch next weekend, and I'd like it if you could come. But please, please, please, don't show them your …"

"I promise I won't," says Rosa crossing her heart.

"I think you are … an angel," he adds quietly, "but devils have tails like yours."

"So do innocent lizards," says Rosa quickly, "and our human DNA shares many points with lizard DNA. You know Mum was a scientist. I showed you her lab." Lionel nods sagely as if Rosa's explanation is satisfactory, and off they go, chatting about DNA like embryonic nerdlings.

At 5 p.m., I call time, and Lionel departs. I hadn't realized how desperate Rosa was for the company of people her own age until her passionate declaration of friendship. Her father and mother probably hadn't realized either, keeping her quarantined from the "follies of the world". Only when she was confronted with the possibility of an actual friend had desperation bubbled to the surface.

It's clear to me that despite her golden eyes and lizard tail, Rosa is all human.

So when the door closes on Lionel and she immediately turns to me with a worried frown and asks straight out, "Am I a devil?", I'm able to answer honestly: "Absolutely not!"

BILLEON

Strangely, for a kid who grew up on the streets, I am now settled as the "man of the house" (permit me the little gloat). To be fair, though, I am the <u>only</u> man in the house unless Lionel comes visiting. Miloš is male, but he's a dog.

A few days after the birthday party, Lionel's formal father and Lionel are rewarded with a sweet tinkly chime at the door. The house is clearly warming to the boy and his friendship with Rosa. I graciously invite them in and we engage in neighborly small-chat in the sunny front lounge, where Lionel's dad finally gets to the point and asks for the phone number of Rosa's maths tutor, Mr Zither. He says that Lionel is flagging behind in some areas of study and that Rosa had told Lionel that Mr Zither is *inspirational*. Rosa hovers in front of one of the other chairs and winces at Lionel's father's speech.

"Of course, I'll pay him a decent fee," the father says. Lionel sits beside his dad looking embarrassed until Rosa invites him upstairs and they disappear.

I know Rosa is something of a maths genius and Mr Zither has all the time in the world for her. I'm doubtful he'd give Lionel a chance, but I provide Lionel's dad the number anyhow.

Later, Rosa chides me for doubting Lionel.

"I thought you were a champion of underdogs," she says, judgily.

"Well, what maths level is Lionel?"

"Being a professional nerd, and a year ahead of the rest of his class, he finds it a little difficult sometimes. Especially with advanced equations. He's aiming for early entry into university, so he's actually tackling some university level maths. I will tell Mr Zither this myself."

"Thank you Rosa," I say. I've been snobby about her friend and feel bad. Usually I'm only snobby about people who are clumsy or don't keep themselves pumped and fit. Chaz has turned me into a fitness freak and like him, I did look down on fatsos and sloths, but really, that's not okay either. My attitude is very unfair because people should always be allowed to make their own choices, or so Rosa tells me.

Still, later that day, when the urbex crew are spooning delicious banana sundaes into their mouths at the elbow park kiosk, Chaz laughs at my tale of snobbery.

"You are becoming a full snoot, bro," he barks and I laugh too and decide to put in a good word with Mr Zither as well.

So that's how Lionel came to be at the judge's house after Rosa's lesson on Thursday for a "maths tune-up" with Mr Zither, and then afternoon tea with Rosa, and it was organized for every week during school term.

*

Lionel to both his great delight and deep concern finds that Rosa's home is different. Very different. He's a nondescript lad, this boy with the black-rimmed square glasses and thick, black hair cut neat. He wears good cotton trousers and shirts, never a t-shirt, with shoes, never sneakers. But he's sharp and observant. Early on, he noticed the door had separate chimes for different people; spotted the weird friarbird in the roof garden; and discovered the whole vibe that leads to rarified thinking and the telling of truths, like when he had to admit he was indeed frightened when he saw Rosa's tail.

On the flip side, what hasn't been revealed to him are the very real dangers of the otherworldly townhouse.

One Thursday afternoon in mid-December, during a stretch of cold, clear days with watery sunshine, I'm in the study, reclining in the Judge's chair reading the second last chapter of *Beyond the Rule of Claw* and trying to understand the difference between the balance of probability and burden of proof. Miss Shecklestone wrote that: *the proof is in the pudding once you determine the nature of the poison.* This makes me laugh and I look up through the doorway to see a shiny shadow in the reflected glass of a hallway painting. Only a brief glimpse, but ugly. The eight-legged shadow had smoothly dropped down the reflected stairwell.

Woah! Madam C is at the shops. The kids are at risk in the kitchen. I run to the study fireplace and grab an iron poker and carefully stick my head out the door. There is a fine vertical web, single and silvery, dangling from the high ceiling down the middle of the stairwell cavity, to what looks like the second floor, where the thread deviates onto the landing. I can't see the spider. I hurtle down the stairs, my first instinct to protect Rosa.

Silvery web covers the stair steps and I see Billeon's shiny black butt disappear in the corner of the first-floor landing, as she creeps silently on her hairy feet into the dining room.

You stay away from Rosa, I think, gripping the poker hard.

I slide through into the kitchen silently, and motion to Rosa and Lionel who come over, faces creased with concern at my hushing motions and the poker being brandished in my hand.

I hiss: "Get into the atrium garden and lock yourselves in. Siddley must be here. With Billeon," I whisper to Rosa. "Billeon's in the dining room."

"He's after the tau," Rosa whispers back, ignoring my instruction. "Come on."

Instead of obeying me, she hurries out the kitchen door, and I have to grab Lionel and hustle him onto and up the stairs.

"Rosa!"

We rounded the corner and there is Billeon on the landing behind, bobbing malevolently on her eight black hairy legs.

"Oh, hello Mz B," says Rosa standing on or about the fifth stair up. "You haven't been invited into my house."

The spider flickers her front two legs at Rosa and waves her sharp jaws at us. Instead of shrinking in terror, Lionel is emboldened by Rosa's pluck.

"What a monster," he exclaims. "A giant *latrodectus* from the black widow family. Could be an Australian redback actually. There's a flash of color on her abdomen. Toxic bite, everyone!"

"She's a hench-spider," says Rosa angrily. "Her master is a nasty troll who is upstairs trying to steal some property we put away for safekeeping. This is a diversionary tactic."

"A hench-spider," says Lionel with some amazement.

And then Billeon charges at the two kids as quick as anything with eight legs can charge. Lionel squeaks, but I'm in between the spider and Rosa in the twink and hold the poker up so her poisonous fangs snap on the iron with a *kajing!* as my arms take the strain. Billeon and I are matched – I had two thick legs, she had eight skinny ones, and we start shoving each other, but with the dangerous stabbing of her sharp mandibles on the poker, close to my face.

But then, Billeon has an advantage – web.

"Run," I shout, as Billeon's two hind legs start their weaving movement, twisting sticky web around my legs. "Uh, fak," I say, pressed backward by both her weight and the driving power of the eight legs, as we stand, head-to-chelicera (that's her smelly, hairy, snapping mouth parts). Billeon stinks the stench of dead detritus. Her smell is foul. Luckily, her fangs stay jammed while I hold the poker in place. I see the malevolent hate in all her eyes boring into my mind, while poison starts to exude on the fangs. Somehow, the house helps me focus and I stare back. She is trying to bite and envenom me with her snappers, and a front pedipalp, or mini-leg, as well as her front right leg and its sharp bristles are inserted against my neck as she starts to prize me and the poker away from her head. Her eight eyes bore into my two, trying to psych me into submission and I feel the front leg on my neck starting to press harder and harder as the web thickens around my ankles.

Suddenly, there's a gush of sweetly smelling oil over my head into Billeon's eyes.

"Hold her up!" shouts Lionel behind me. Another gush of moisture.

The spider hisses horribly and immediately wrenches backward and spits the poker out. Another gush of spray sails over my head into the spider's underbelly. My ankles are wrapped in sticky web and I trip back on the bottom stair, buffering with my elbows as I fall, while the spider retreats and Lionel charges past me with a spray bottle of what smells like peppermint oil. Amazingly, the kid attacks and starts squirting more spray under the spider.

One flailing spider leg delivers a whack to Lionel who tumbles into a hall table, but he keeps squirting from the ground until the great blob of arachnid retreats into the dining room. Lionel jumps up and slams the door shut.

"My legs," I shout pointing to the bundle of web around my ankles and calves. Lionel runs to the kitchen, finds a huge knife and saws the sticky web free within a few seconds.

"Rosa's gone upstairs," he says, breathless with excitement.

"Peppermint oil, Lionel?" I shouldn't have asked. Lionel gets all explainy in the middle of the crisis.

"Spiders hate it. Rosa said there was some in the cleaning cupboard and I aimed for the book lungs under her belly ... through which spiders breathe." (The nerd). "Rosa told me to deal with Billeon while she dealt with the troll." (The brave nerd).

I groan. Rosa was facing off the fireball throwing troll.

"Come on, Lionel. The laboratory," and we sprint up two stories of staircase.

The laboratory door is blasted open and papers and objects are strewn everywhere. Rosa is inside looking at the open odds and sods drawer.

"The tau is gone. He needed time to crack the door lock."

"That's the last tau."

"Why is he stealing them?" I ask.

"Don't know," replies Rosa.

Only then did Rosa and I notice Lionel. He'd come off his adrenaline rush and his teeth were chattering. "That spider is still downstairs."

"She'll be gone. She stays with her master when he's on the loose."

"Loose from where?"

"That is a complicated question, Lionel," says Rosa.

"This is a complicated house," I add.

We go upstairs to the Hall of Justice and find one of the doors turned into charcoal. The friarbird is poking its head fearfully out from the pomegranate tree.

Clonk! it exclaims.

"Yes, a big one too," Rosa replies. "Madam Cimbalom will fix the door. She's a whizz with carpentry."

Downstairs, we gingerly open the dining room door, but instead of being gone, Billeon is still there, crushed under the suit of armor which had toppled as the spider passed. Clearly, the spider had burst like any squashed spider does. There's yellow spider goop over the furniture, the rugs, the paintings and the walls, goop-splat which must have sprayed from her body when the armor crushed her. Like custard, the fluid dripped in globs from the tabletop onto the floor. The spider's legs are stilled , the eight eyes now empty of malice.

The suit of armor must have fallen suddenly and heavily from its plinth, on top of Billeon – the house itself had defended its inhabitants.

I look at the mess and say: "Madam Cimbalom will not be pleased."

THE RETURN OF ELODIE

Just before Christmas, Rosa and I are late at work in the study, checking several new legal briefs, when a jaunty rendition of "The Wedding March" chimes though the house, a cheeky joke courtesy of the doorbell. We both know who is at the door, and Rosa gets there first and throws herself on Elodie.

Elodie hugs Rosa, dumps her fat backpack with a thud on the mosaic tiles, then turns and gives me a big kiss and warm hug and asks: "Can I stay?" Underneath a delight at seeing Rosa and myself, Elodie looks tired and drawn and wouldn't say much except that she's hungry and, "How are the rest of the crew?"

Then, after Rosa goes to bed, Elodie gives me a present. A painting that had hung in her mother's apartment when she was a child. An exquisite little painting of a cat and a bowl of fruit in swirly color.

"It's yours," she says. "We had two matching paintings in our lounge room on a dresser. On her deathbed, Mama admitted she painted them. I have the other one."

"It's beautiful. Thank you."

As we drink tea, she wants to know what happened to Rosa and me the night after she disappeared on the train on the metro platform at 2 a.m.

We sit, side by side, leaning on the big square kitchen island bench, and I tell Elodie how the police put us in the car, the surprise diversion to the terrible murder scene and how Rosa helped find the killers of Ernst and Dee. I tell her also about Rosa's new friendship with Lionel, and our battle in the house with Billeon, when Siddley stole the tau. She is most concerned about the spider's size.

Then we shift to the big couch, and with Elodie stretched out, her head on my lap, she breathes deep as if summoning courage, and starts talking about herself, her life, her mother's death.

She talks and talks. All the pain she's been chewing on for months, years, comes out in rapid-fire anguish, caused by the twilight time she's just experienced in France. Her mama had spoken to her in a regretful, dying mood, and Elodie discovered a whole new story about her childhood, and while she is usually guarded, she needs me to listen.

(Often, she would accuse me of not listening, and not understanding her, but tonight, I keep my mouth shut for most of the time.)

"I cannot be an aimless floating particle any more," she says. "I sat there with my mother in the hospital and looked at her as she gasped for breath, and thought, is this how it ends? Why are we made for this?"

I say: "Well, we are human, that's why, and in the end, our warranties run out and we ...."

"Ach, don't be glib, Benji. What do you know of life? You are even younger than me, and I'm just a kid. I am only 22 years old. My mama was 55 when she died. She was connected to horrible tubes in a hospice! She was cheated by life, and ... I never knew who cheated her, and why, until we spoke last week. I should have asked earlier. I would have understood her then, but I'd been a little bitch."

And then she shifted and sat beside me on the couch and told me her mother's story, which had spilled from the dying woman's lips as Elodie held her hand.

"Before I was born, Mama worked in the fashion industry in Paris for 15 years, as a clothing designer. She started very young, still studying, and worked for the same boss all that time. When she designed a fantastic bunch of patterns this boss, a man she called Apo, stole her portfolio and claimed her work as his. She protested, and Apo turned on her, accusing her of plagiarizing his designs, which was a massive lie.

"The dispute became *très* acrimonious. Mama said she threw things around the studio and totally lost it and attacked this Apo with a pair of scissors and she would have cut his throat if other staff members hadn't held her down, and the police then dragged her away, so Apo helped himself to all her work.

"The whole design team knew the truth, as Mama had been showing her colleagues her sketches and drafts over many years, but they said nothing. Apo fired her, but gave her a large sum of money, also – maybe he was pretending to buy her work, and assuaging guilt? Anyway, she moved to the mountains and met my father, a ski-instructor. That bit I knew, because I was always nagging her about my papa's identity. Their romance, if there was one, lasted for only a few months, but there I was made! Made in the mountains, born in the Alps. Mama just turned her back on her great talent so big was the betrayal. This I never knew. This was her deathbed confession to me, to explain her risky behavior, and the terrible hepatitis that killed her and, *mon cher* Benjee, it explains a lot.

"So, for years, Mama worked in ski resorts and raised me while her beautiful art – it was an extensive portfolio of designs, which I've never known about – became worldwide sensations, off-the-rack sales by the millions. She didn't get a cent from the royalties. The money went to this

Apo who took the credit, and other big fashion boys. She said she always wondered how many other talented people Apo stole ideas from, especially women.

"My mother, I now understand, was destroyed inside, and became hooked on alcohol and drugs, while meeting random men in clubs and bars I suppose, including my father who I've never met. No relationship was ever permanent for her – in fact, she was hard to live with because of her addictions.

"More and more she neglected me. I, on the other hand, went to a good school, thanks to Apo's money payoff – this, Mama made sure of. Apart from Mama's moods, I loved where I lived. We had a small flat in the main square of Albertville, and I could see the pine forests from my bedroom, and the snow-capped mountains, and I had lots of friends who I skied with. In my teens, I learned alpine and ice climbing, became an alpinist, guiding tourists in the mountains during the school holidays, and skiing in winter. The open air, the clear views, they were an escape from my mother and her problems.

"I wanted to do more for her. Help cure her, but she wouldn't listen. I have discovered she was on a crusade to wipe out the memory of her artistic promise and the betrayal. As she was dying, she asked: "Why didn't I stand up to that man more? Take him to court? I let myself down so badly."

Elodie cries for a little, and I feel my eyes go moist, too, but I keep my mouth shut and gently stroke her hair. She sips water and continues.

"And then she died with me holding her hand. She is dead! I wasn't there for her earlier, on her horrible downhill slide, because I was in prison for a year and then expelled from France! I, too, got hooked on bad things. Robbery and crime. Mama's money ran out, of course, when I was about 16 and by then Mama was in no state to earn a wage. I was recognized for my stealth, ropework and rappelling, and promised big money. My gang was breaking into a bank in Lyon one night, and the police turned up. One of my co-robbers had a gun, and shot at the police. We didn't even know he was armed! The police returned fire and he was shot in front of me and died in a bloody mess in my arms."

"In your arms?" I gasped.

"Even at 16 I knew inside here," she tapped her breastbone to indicate her heart, "you need someone with you when you die," she said simply. "That's why I returned to see Mama when she wrote and said she was dying. She had no-one else."

Then Elodie gets back to her story.

"So, the judge at my trial discovered from my birth certificate that my biological father came from this city, and immigration authorities were alerted, and after two years in juvenile detention, and even though I'd never met my father, I was thrown out of the country. My mother visited me only once in that time and it did not go well." Elodie shudders.

"Yesterday at the funeral were only three mourners. A pathetic ceremony. Me, my mother's landlady, and a passerby, some farty old man, who said he just wanted to be warm. Hah! I asked him why he was there and that's what he said – *It's just too cold out there, mademoiselle. Sorry about whoever has died.*

"After the funeral, the police were waiting for me outside the church. A police car. And they just arrested me, took me to collect my stuff and the little paintings that were my inheritance, and put me on a train at the border. I sat on the train and wept. Wept for hundreds of kilometres into my plastic cup of terrible, terrible coffee, and all I could think of was this: if I indeed have a family, it is you, Rosa, and the crew – well, at least my Sukki. You are the only people I know in the world and have love for."

Elodie paused.

I declare: "Well, because of your misfortunes, I met you."

She turned toward me on the couch and looked at me with those hazel eyes.

"Ahh! You are my big consolation prize," says Elodie, a bit too bitterly. "Benjee, this is not a case of misfortune. I brought this all on myself, being a stupid bandit." And then she apologizes. "I'm sorry to sound so angry. After the last few weeks, I am very tired. I am so happy to be in this house and have somewhere permanent to stay."

I like the way she said "permanent."

"I'm the same," I say. "After leaving home, I never stayed in one place for so long. The Judge's house is a luxury."

I wrap an arm round her shoulder and she draws in for a hug, her soft hair against my cheek.

Do I hear the house holding its breath? Maybe it's just me.

"I'm glad you're here," I add.

"I don't know what to think," she says.

I look up at the clock – it is five to midnight, and although I feel happy, I'm frightened for Elodie at the same time.

*

Elodie makes herself at home. We hang the cat paintings together in our bedroom. For a wonderful while I wake to the touch of her warm skin. She is as enthusiastic as me about the huge dressing gown collection, and we disport ourselves in different ones, day and night.

One morning soon after her return I go to the rooftop to do push-ups and squats, and find Elodie hiding from Rosa to smoke a sneaky cigarette (smoking was banned in the house). Elodie is dressed in a red and gold Chinese silk dressing gown with frilled cuffs, and sits cross-legged on the slate slab in the garden. I flip out – not about the fumes, (she is French after all) but because I don't understand the strange powers of the slab.

"Please don't sit there!" I say and tell her about the disappearance of Rosa's father who was one day a corpse on the slab, and the next day, gone.

"Vanished, you say? Like *poof*?" She clicks her fingers.

I nod. She is amazed, and promises instead to use the little table as her sneaky cigarette spot.

Elodie also moves into the kitchen and cooks wonders, and bonds with Rosa like a big sister. A lot of laughter prevails.

With me, sometimes she's different. Sometimes she is distant, but somehow she is there. Disconnected in her thoughts, and then passionate in lovemaking and conversation. Helping me understand how relationships work, mostly with a soft loving edge, and sometimes with a rasp.

Still, because of her past she has deep wounds and is looking for answers which I cannot provide. I know this now.

THE BLACK TAU

Rosa and I sit on the rattling tram. Seven o'clock, with bursts of icy evening rain that sting the face and threaten snow. Reflecting street Christmas decorations and car lights the round and oval puddles in the street shine green, red, orange, and blue, like fruit jubes, glossy and bright.

Elodie stayed home to scour her collection of fashion magazines, looking for hints of her mother's art. We invited her along, but she was in a "don't talk" mood and said she didn't want to get cold and wet. I didn't push her and we left her cross-legged in front of the roaring lounge-room fire downstairs. She was wearing tights with a holly and mistletoe pattern and a comfy t-shirt and her blonde hair and pale skin glowed red against the flame. She had a pair of scissors by her side, searching the magazines for fashion by Apo, though we've looked and haven't been able to track down any fashion designer named Apo yet.

Now I sit in the tram seat beside Rosa, who wears a raincoat, beanie and her little smile. I'm not sure who or what the smile is for. Maybe it's because she now has Lionel as co-conspirator in the house, successfully dealing with giant spiders no less. After the battle of Billeon, she'd shown Lionel her golden, crocodile eyes and he declared: "They look weird, but who cares!" That's it! Lionel cares/doesn't care. Judge Rosa is difficult to read sometimes, but Rosa the 11-year-old isn't. I'm only a handful of years older. I remember 11.

We have been invited to Mrs Heloise Simply's apartment downtown, in one of the very fancy new tower blocks. Chaz had rung and invited Elodie and me, and added, "Can you bring Rosa as well?" I'm not sure why Chaz rang on Mrs Simply's behalf, but I knew they'd been in contact after the brutal death of her boss. Mrs Simply steered the police well away from us, and for that Chaz and I were very grateful.

We haven't hung out for some time. While Chaz has stopped blowing his top about the busted-up crew, on the phone there was still a residual crankiness in his attitude so I was worried about spending an evening with him.

*

The tram stop in the boulevard is directly opposite the fancy tower block. We run through the rain to the building's big brass and glass doors and entering into a lobby with mirror-walls and lots of gold trim. We walk up to the concierge's desk and a snooty man in a uniform raises his eyebrow, then rings Heloise Simply's apartment. Once she gives him the nod, he opens the lift for us. Floor 23.

The lift croaks "Floor 23", the doors slide open and we look for apartment B and then, from habit, I look for the fire escape sign just in case I need to pull a sudden exit – ridiculous, I know. Apartment B's door is ajar. I knock and Mrs Simply shouts: "Do come in."

The apartment is plush and spacious, and in the middle, on a huge brown couch cluster, Heloise Simply and Chaz are in a cuddle. My jaw drops.

"Hi, Benji," says Chaz, bouncing up. "Hi, Rosa. A beer for you, Benji? And some cordial, Rosa?"

Chaz certainly looks at home in jeans and some kind of grey blazer, brown loafers on his feet. No urbex gear visible, and his beard is a tidy razor cut which enhances his jawline. Heloise looks like a princess. She is wearing a red and green African maxi-dress and sandals, and her copious braids are looped up in a stupendous red headscarf. She walks over and shakes Rosa's hand. Jazz music (jazz!?) is tootling faintly in the background which is amazing - Chaz is wholly and solely a hip-hop guy.

"Chaz has told me about you, Rosa, and your adventures. Welcome." She flashes a warm smile and Rosa said a polite, "Thank you."

"Please do take those orange glasses off. Chaz has told me about your beautiful eyes as well."

Rosa hates wearing them, so immediately whips them off. She looks up at Heloise, who looks momentarily disconcerted, then smiles another warm smile.

"Beautiful, as I'd imagined," she says. "I wish I had eyes like that!"

How incredibly polite is Heloise.

Behind her, the view from the balcony window is magnificent, across the old part of the harbor to the bay. You could just catch squall cloud shapes in the dark sky, scudding along.

I'm most amazed. Heloise is much less snooty than the day we bowled into Mr Dawson Kennedy's place. She oozes charm and warmth, while Chaz .... well, Chaz has turned into the drinks guy.

"Are you two ....?" I start.

"Seeing each other? Well, yes, bruz," says Chaz. He is looking very pleased with himself, as is Heloise. "I've moved in here for a while."

By now we are sitting on the excellent plush couches, and Rosa, with her usual quiet intensity, is watching Chaz and Heloise while she sips the lime soda. Chaz's arm stretches along the couch behind Heloise, who holds a glass of red wine. They are a striking couple, and though Chaz is younger, they don't look much different in age. I sip my beer.

He explains: "I've helped Heloise out with finalizing Mr Kennedy's estate and transferring his company, making sure everything was okay – gratis, of course, as a friendly gesture after she'd protected our identities from the cops. And we got even more friendly." They giggle at that, which is not very Chaz nor princess-like.

"And then," Chaz presses on, "after the will was read and the family inherited Kennedy Inc, Heloise was sacked. It was terrible."

"I was expecting instant dismissal," says Heloise. "The family were jealous of my close association and friendship with Dawson, which I might add was entirely platonic whatever they say. He was a lovely friend and we got on famously, but Dawson was much more interested in male lovers, though his dimwit family never guessed. We'd worked together for almost a decade – after I left university – and he bequeathed me money and a parcel of shares from his fortune. You must understand, first and foremost he was a collector of antiquities. Everything he did was to buy quality pre-Christian pieces. Sadly, his collection is of no interest to his family and will be auctioned, and it's expected to attract millions."

"Even the dodgy objects acquired by people like us?" I ask.

There's a pause as Heloise glances nervously at Rosa. "As you well know, Mr Dawson Kennedy sometimes reverted to unconventional methods when collecting antiquities. I have a background in archaeology and one of my roles was to assist Dawson in refining the provenances of a few of his acquisitions."

"Altering authentication documents?" I ask.

"Something like that," Heloise said with a naughty smile. Now I knew why Chaz had fallen for her. Meanwhile, Rosa's gaze dropped to her drink. She didn't want to hear that bit.

"That would be …" Rosa begins in a judgey vinegar tone.

"How long have you two been … cohabiting?" I interrupt, and Chaz's wide smile broke out.

"A month," he says definitively. "You went to care for Rosa, and Sukki and Yusif moved in together, Elodie headed off for France. So … I didn't have a crew" he said. "NOT that I'm complaining any more. So there you go. Our crew has disbanded – we've all gone our own ways." And he smiles at Heloise as if to say, "It's fine".

"After five years of close combat," I add.

"Yep," said Chaz. "Seven for you and me, Benji-man!" We do a little fist bump across the coffee table which perplexes Rosa, so Chaz does one with her as well, which makes her giggle.

I gesture to Chaz with a can-we-talk hand signal, and he and I go to the kitchen and pretend to get refills and chips.

"Hey, are you serious with Heloise? Is this it?"

He says: "Benji-man, this is it. She's real fine and we made a connection. A great connection! We're good for each other. I'm learning a lot from her about the antiquities and art biz, and she's into a new fitness regime with me."

Chaz can't help himself when it comes to physically tuning people up – me, Elodie, Sukki, Yusif have all been beneficiaries. In a normal world, Chaz would be a world champion fitness coach. Girls have always liked him, too. The old Chaz was back with the additional bonus of good clothes and grooming.

"So I got lonely and went to see how Heloise was going and she was snowed with work on Mr Dawson Kennedy's estate with the lawyers banging on the door, and she had to sort all of his chattels – that's like his art collection - and documents and accounts and whatnot, and then very quickly, like, I am her up-close and personal trainer," he says.

I laugh. "You dog! But she's buff anyway, isn't she?"

Chaz shakes his head, "She's lovely, but not so fit."

Not so fit means fit, but not supercharged, in Chaz lingo.

I know from the goofy look in his eye that he'd met "the one". I look over his shoulder to where Heloise and Rosa are talking, somewhere in a serious zone from the looks on their faces.

They are both very serious girls.

"I'm so glad for you, man," I say. "This is only good." We shake hands this time and go over to the couch while I think, *I wish it was that easy with Elodie*.

Heloise looks down a wrinkled nose at the chips, then stands and pulls a platter of cheese and pickles from the fridge and we start grazing. The beer is cold and delicious and I think things have turned out okay. Until Chaz says: "There's just one thing. And we need your advice, Judge Rosa Somberly."

He walked over to a bureau along the side of the wall, and pulled out a leather satchel and I think, uh-oh.

"And so," says Heloise, "while we were listing and logging everything for the solicitor and the estate, I found this in Dawson's safe, in a box, tucked up the back. I'd never seen this item before, but then I'd never actually emptied his safe out." She smiles. "It is a big safe."

Her long fingers (with mother-of-pearl nail extensions) deftly throw the cloth off the tau without her touching the object.

"This one's a live one," says Chaz. "And Dawson Kennedy clearly knew it had powers, hence the care he took to cover and hide it."

"He was an antiquarian of some note," says Heloise with pride, "but there is no record of provenance for this little bull. I don't know where it came from."

Both Rosa and I crane over the object. It's bigger than the other taus. About the size of Chaz's large fist. A black bull this time, not coppery green. As we crane closer, some small sparks start popping between its horns and we draw back immediately. I check its eyes, and they look very lifelike, almost as if the beast is watching me back.

"This tau senses us," says Rosa.

Heloise tilts her head and looks at Rosa. "I'm convinced that none of the other bulls in his gallery cabinet had this potency, or energy, or battery life, or whatever you want to call it. They were just small heavy objects. No sparks."

"Hmmm. I think this is the one Siddley's been looking for," Rosa says. "He broke into my house last week with his hench-spider ..."

"Hench-spider?" asks Chaz.

"A giant black spider from the *Latrodectus* genus," I explain, nerdily.

"Benji forced it back with a poker," Rosa explains, and Chaz nods in approval.

"Horrible experience," I add.

"Benji, and I, and Lionel, fought it off and it was finally squashed by the suit of armor. Exploded gunk everywhere," says Rosa. "We spent hours on the cleanup. But by then, Siddley had robbed my mum's odds and sods drawer of the original tau you guys," she coughs, "stole."

"How big was the spider?" asks Chaz, impressed by the story.

"Almost two meters long by two high," I say. "Including leg length."

Heloise Simply starts to look around nervously.

Rosa points. "This tau could possibly take Siddley back to the era of the Minoans, somewhere he appears to want to go, with his mayhem and damage. This tau is strong. You can feel the *pull of time* within it."

Even I feel the *pull of time* from where I sit. Rosa sweeps her hand over the statue and there is a fluster of tiny blue sparks as her palm passes over it, like blue fur, covering the bull's back, plus bigger sparks between its horns.

"The pull of time?" asks Heloise.

"Time doesn't always flow in a straight line," says Rosa calmly, as she makes the bull sparkle. "There can be time sumps and time ramps and occasionally," she points at the tau, "sinkholes. Happens when the atoms are out of whack with the space-time continuum. This probably wasn't meant to be a sinkhole when it was forged, but you can feel that it's in the wrong place."

There's a puzzled silence.

"What was the other tau that we saw? The one in the cafe?" Chaz asks.

"I spoke to Madam Cimbalom after the cafe ... event ... and we think that tau was a connection to one person. From a funerary offering. This one is different. It may have been forged or owned by a person of power – it has already burned up and turned black."

"So what should we do?"

"This tau must be kept secure. More secure than any that Siddley stole, for sure. We will take it, and then we should call the crew together to make a plan to dispose of it. The job may take the whole team," I say.

"Gives us time for some research," says Rosa.

"One more gig!" says Chaz, delightedly.

"Why don't you both come over next Saturday. I think we can hold Siddley off until then," Rosa says.

Heloise Simply wraps the bronze creature up in its soft leather, gently drops it in a special box and places it in the leather satchel on the bureau.

"How very exciting," Heloise says, "but no spiders, please."

*

We make our way home, Rosa sits nervously beside me on the tram with the satchel.

"Is Mrs Simply a forger?" Rosa finally bursts out, as the tram slid through the late evening traffic.

"Hmmm, possibly," I say. "She may adjust documents slightly to falsify previous ownership. But on the bright side, she's also an archaeologist and a very good business manager."

Rosa seems to lighten up when she considers the "bright side". I notice she holds the leather satchel tight and watches the people on the tram with a wary eye.

"Do you want me to hold that?" I ask nervously.

"Would you? I can feel the tau buzzing on my knees through the leather."

I take the satchel gingerly, wrap the strap round my shoulder, and place the bag on the seat, slightly away from my hip. This tau was a live one!

As we walk up our street, every shadow seems menacing, and my senses are alert for Siddley, for giant spiders with sharp fangs that go *snick*, for big black cats, or for whatever else may be thrown at us. I case each tree for movement as we pass under them, but there's nothing.

We arrive home damp as the late winter rain starts to go slow-mo and morph into snow. This time we go straight to the laboratory safe, rather than bothering to wax the object, and lodge it in the odds and sods drawer. We lock up the satchel, spin the combination wheel and only then do we start to breathe properly again.

PART 2 KNOSSOS

ARIA IN THE OX-COACH

Hot, hot, hot and the heat seems to dial up the colors to hyperreal dream shades. Reds are redder, blues are bluer, greens quiver in front of my eyes. There's a vibrancy of color that is hard, almost, to behold. I hadn't fallen asleep, but I felt I was waking up in a bright lucid dream.

Waves roll in from the ocean, a deep-blue green. The wind is whippy, but warm, coming in ocean gusts, and foam is blown sideways. Rainbows are captured in the refracted waterdrops, rainbows which glow momentarily and fade. We're lying in warm sand on a long, long beach.

I ask, *Where are we?* but I know the answer already. We in ancient Crete, which we now call Minoa. A kilometer along the beach to my left is a small town and a harbor with boats. I can see two boats nearing the harbor at speed, triangular sails being furled by sailors in quite difficult gusty weather, and oars being extended for more precision. I learn later this port town is Amnisos, the port town of Co-no-sos, or as we know it, Knossos.

Behind, on a gentle hill that rises to a line of trees, is a field full of black cattle. A huge bull with long horizontal horns chews the grassy side of the dune close by.

"Why, it's our bull!" says Heloise, noticing the animal as she rolls over and props herself on her elbows. The bull ignores her and keeps chewing its cud.

"Or his big bro," answers Chaz.

"He's ours," says Heloise, sleepily.

Still we lay on the warm sand near the field. Rosa who has been bustling about while we wake up, brushes sand off her sneakers and is especially keen to go, but I say, "Let's all recover from our journey first, Rosa."

Rosa nods, then takes her dress off, and wearing only her knickers, runs down the beach, little crocodile tail wagging, and plunges into the water. She starts swimming strongly into the surf. Heloise and Chaz nudge each other, strip and do the same, and I follow, letting a cold plunge in the water wake me and center me. I dive into an icy wave and it splashes across my head in so many green bubbles.

Better than actually dissolving, which was how we got here in the first place.

*

Where to begin?

That first Saturday in March, the crew gathered for dinner for a last planning meeting to rid ourselves of the black tau.

For some reason, the crew didn't like the dining fare Rosa and I had planned – cheesy noodles, schnitzels, and fried peanut butter sandwiches. Instead, Sukki came early to teach Elodie to make a Japanese dinner delicacy, helped by Rosa, who was wearing her new pink beanie. Elodie has told me before that French people are endlessly fascinated by Japanese stuff, and vice versa. I could hear Rosa laughing out loud, a sound that made me inexplicably happy. Yusif and I were drinking beers in the dining room, and I was trying to explain to him the intricacies of the house, while he joke-scoffed at my observations.

I suddenly said to him: "I know you're a bit older than us, but don't you think we might be morphing into adults? Throwing a bougie dinner party no less, old friends together?"

"Don't throw away your inner kid," advised Yusif, looking gloomy. "I almost did. Being an adult can feel important, but don't forget fun. That's why I hang with you guys."

"I think we're having fun."

"Yes, my friend, fun is good," he said. "All good, so long as we ignore all the spooky mumbo jumbo like magic bulls and ghosts."

I grinned at Yusif and he grinned back. The friction from the crew break-up had passed and we were now good friends.

Chaz and Heloise Simply then arrived. They were *really* bougie. Chaz, sleek in his new blazer and chinos, and a pair of smart new leather boots I'd never seen before, Heloise wearing a camel coat and a tight-fitted red woolen dress, She wore a pendant necklace with a big blob of silver on the end – so chic. What a couple! She put the coat on the gauntlet of the suit of armor where it hung like a moulted skin.

They were also looking forward to the promise of something fancy like miso-saturated salmon and cured seaweed.

Mrs Cimbalom joined us at the table, an ex-officio member of our ex-urbex crew, looking prim and proper. She wore a long peach chiffon gown and elbow length white gloves having "dressed for dinner" as she called it.

As we ate, Heloise went official again and explained to the others she'd found yet another small tau in the personal effects of Dawson Kennedy. Yusif went white as a sheet, Sukki and Elodie were immediately interested.

"It crackles!" she added.

"Show us," Elodie demanded. So, putting on a pair of thick leather gardening gloves Heloise pulled the parcel from the satchel on the sideboard and brought it to the table where she unwrapped the object. This black tau sat in the middle of the table, sparking blue because so many people, including a couple of Elementals, surrounded it with their bio-electric energy. I poked it with my dirty fork.

"We need to get rid of it permanently," said Rosa.

The blue sparks were producing a mist now, and the crackling sounded louder, like popcorn cooking.

"Yep," I agreed. "We must work out where to hide it from Siddley, so no-one gets hurt or killed."

But the crackling intensified quickly until the tau and the tabletop were almost obscured in a blue electric mist, speckled with white sparks. Mrs Cimbalom jumped up and ordered, "Stay there," and everything went weird as the little bull started to grow on the table. The metal creature ballooned out, and a sudden bovine poo smell blew around, its head was shaking and it became a live animal, standing mysteriously through the dining table, while the dining room started to go hazy and white. The bull then dipped its head into the bowl with the green leaf salad and took a munch of lettuce while I began to see bubbles floating up and around me.

"Hold on," ordered Mrs Cimbalom, who was smiling faintly in a hazy doorway halo. "Hold hands!" and she threw a big floppy hat like a frisbee to Rosa who automatically stuffed her beanie in a pocket and replaced it with the hat. Then my hand found Rosa's hand, and Elodie's, who were sitting on either side of me.

"Bon voyage," I heard Mrs Cimbalom say her voice fading: "It's one of those time sinks. You've ignited it somehow ... come back whenever you feel like it ... I'll stay and mind the shop ..."

I hadn't enjoyed the sense of dissolving in the white haze, like I was one of those effervescent pills you put in water and you suddenly turn into these bubbles, lots of white bubbles rushing around, and you disappear, so many molecules of yourself, somewhere light and airy and the pill dissolves. Some weird ethereal amniotic fluid rushing us somewhere else. The bubbles are your particles, they pass in front of your face, your friends are dissolving around you as well, their faces and arms and legs turning into bubbles, and then in a few seconds, the bubbles start solidifying in a bright light which turns out to be the sun in a blue sky, even though shortly before it was night-time in a big room lit by lamps. And as you solidify you see your friends around you lying on a strange shore, some unconscious, or fainted in fright, and some shaking their heads in a mix of fear and amazement, for a hazard unforeseen and a recovery welcomed.

*

Now cold saltwater was around me with face-slapping waves. A real reviving swim among the green bubbles and foam belonging to the ancient Aegean Sea.

Chaz is already drying himself with his t-shirt and dressing in his chinos, looking up at a road, and Rosa is keen to go, but I point to the prone figures of Elodie, Sukki, and Yusif still lying in the boundary between the sand and the soft grass and heath herbs. They are awake, and while they lie peaceably, they're properly discombobulated.

"Have a swim," Chaz advises the others, sitting next to Heloise on the sand.

I smell the herbs. I don't know which herb or herbs, but the air is warm with their beautiful scents.

"Thyme," said Heloise. "Wild thyme."

"We must have wits and senses about us for the next stage," I say. Damp Rosa bites her bottom lip and nods.

We sit and dry ourselves, watching the others splash their faces in seawater, coming to terms with our emergence in the land of the Minoans, the crossroads of the old cultures, centuries before the iron makers with their fiery forges and hard metal.

Finally, after an hour or so recovering from bubbledom, we pick ourselves up from the soft warm sand, and walk through rich-smelling grass, and the herd of cows, and past the huge black bull that ignores us. We climb to a rocky road, up the slope, with rough paving, shaded by big trees, palms and cypress. On the other side a barley field, the hint of a house of some sort, and a great green forest beyond. The mountains in the middle of the island rear up like craggy green prongs into a blue cloudless sky. We find ourselves under a wide tree, branches extending outward. The field of barley is now behind us, as well as cows, and that bull – still creating a munching rhythm of contentment. Happy bull.

Further down the road there are small mud and stone houses, some with little gardens, but no smoke rising as yet. It's a hot day and not time for cooking. I can see lots of little houses around the bay. This scented air is unbelievable, with occasional cooling gusts blowing from the blue sea at the bottom of this long hill, and a better view of the harbor.

Bobbing alongside the distant jetty are 10 or 12 long, pointy-prowed sailboats and a bunch of smaller fishing yachts. I want to go to the harbor where bigger whitewashed buildings sit landward of the stone jetty to check the boats out and talk to the fishermen, but the others say no.

We have a task ahead.

This discombobulation makes a strange mark on all of us. We are in the wrong place and the wrong time. I pinch myself, and wonder if it's the same as when I was a dream-bat, taking a dream flight to some new hallucination, or if I'm just a projection of myself like the old man of the forest, but into the past. My self-administered pinch hurts; the air is purer than I've ever smelled; and the sun is hot on my skin. So, no. We have been inserted into an ancient reality. Both Heloise and Chaz are looking at each other in wonder. Elodie and Sukki are already stretching and facing the walk up the hill to Knossos.

A herd of goats or sheep is coming down the road, the animals flowing fast like a white and black river contained by low stone walls and olive hedges. There's a man at the rear of the flock in a straw hat, bare chest and woolen loincloth, his skin deeply brown. He flicks the animals with a leather switch. As he passes, he glances at us strangely, our little justice party wearing early 21st century clothes. He stares at Chaz and Heloise even harder.

"Hello," says Rosa, but the man, as he passes, turns his head away and mutters, "Foreigners."

So! The presence of The Judge still allows a heightened understanding of language, even in the wrong place and wrong time. The farmer said something like "Xenochs," but we all understand, anyway. The farmer had seen us and was completely indifferent behind his grey black beard and dark eyes. Indifference is a thing. We must be real.

"Xenochs," I say to Sukki, who is beside me, stretching.

"That's us," she says with a smile.

"Okay. We good?" says Chaz.

"Yes, let's go," says Sukki, looking around. She looks the liveliest of all of us, drinking everything in. The man with the strictest worldview of reason, Yusif, looks the most stunned.

We start walking up the hill and turning inland. Chaz leads, with Sukki and Heloise. I follow, Rosa's alongside me, and with her big floppy hat and her short stature I can't see her face. It's like walking beside a lolloping sunflower. Then behind us are Yusif and Elodie. I sense their foot-treads, and Elodie is now beside me too.

"I am, what you say, flabbergasted," she says.

Rosa looks up at her, squinting past the sunhat with her dark glasses. "We cannot know how this will turn out. Just remember that. Only Mrs Cimbalom would know, but you have to ask her to find out."

"I don't want to know. Destiny is something that should never be written," Elodie answers.

"Destiny is not written, but it can be read," adds Rosa and I feel a cold shiver run down my back. The same shiver I felt when I first saw the Caiman's eyes, or when the Minoan ghost tried to grasp the tau in the dark gallery, or the shiver of dread at the half-glimpsed shadow of Billeon in the picture glass.

Rosa looked up at me this time, clearly sensing my mood. "Father always said you must use your judgment as you look for the truth. The laws were forged long before even the time of ancient Keftiu. Inviolable laws of nature and humans. Don't shiver, Mr Benji. Enjoy the fresh air and sunshine. Don't be swayed by unreasonable feelings."

Unreasonable feelings were always part of the human package – even folly – but I had to smile at the 11 year old handing me advice from some metaphoric judge's bench and I tried to lighten my mood.

"At least Mrs Cimbalom knew you'd need a sunhat, Rosa."

"She's like that," Rosa said.

After a while of walking in silence, in and out of the shade along the roadway, we stop for a break and I ask Rosa what happens with diseases. All our horrible modern diseases. Couldn't we alter the course of history by giving the Minoans some plague?

"Have you been vaccinated?" she asked.

I shrug and say I suppose so, but being vaccinated doesn't mean you won't catch some ancient lurgy.

We continue the steady pace and realize Heloise Simply is neither a fitness freak like us, nor an Elemental like Rosa. Heloise finds the pace set by

Chaz too hot and hard, so she slows to walk at the back with still-stunned Yusif and Elodie who are ambling along. Chaz and enthusiastic Sukki are well ahead now, and as we go, we pass groups of people who look at us oddly, farmers herding goats, or carrying chickens in baskets, merchants with handcarts, or just kids walking from one farm to the next. The main throughfare between Amnisos and Knossos is slow going.

And we are catching up to a large, slower party on the road ahead. They have a group of men in short kilts at the rear, and a number of women in skirts and bodices, wearing straw hats. The party follows an ox-drawn cart and sings a lilting song, the strange tune trailing towards us in the breeze. The cart is covered in red and gold tasseled material, so I assume someone important is aboard. The rear guard finally hears us coming and looks around, surprised.

Chaz slows up as the obstacle of the cart and the guards slow him down, and we catch up. There's a villa-sized house in the middle of some olive groves beside the road and a trickling stream and bridge in front of the cart. As we get too close, the guard puts out his hand and says, "Stop", and the women look around and stop singing and stare. The ox-cart rolls on ahead leaving the rest of the party behind. But we obey the guy with the spear.

The guard wears a short kilt with some sort of codpiece over his groin, and a woolen shirt, and wears multi-strapped brown leather sandals. He's not armored, but there's a knife in his woolen woven belt and that spear in his hand.

"You foreigners who've arrived at the port?" he asks.

"Yes, we're headed for Knossos."

"Where?"

I'm confused. I thought it would be easily understood – Knossos.

"The palace," I explain.

"Ah ... the palace. *Co-no-sos*." The guy looks reasonably friendly and not at all officious. "Yes, you can go there and be dumbstruck and awestruck, and make your votive offerings. That is fine, but you can't ever pass the ox-coach of the High Priestess of the Great Goddess. She has precedence, *xenochs*. So just stay behind us a little."

And helpfully the guard falls in with us and starts walking and talking at the same time and we soon catch up with the other two guards and eight or so intrigued women who glance back at us.

"No-one has precedence over the High Priestess, not even the Minos," he says. "This is our way."

"Of course not." I agree. Then I ask: "Do you get *xenochs* here a lot?"

"Mostly Greeks." He said. "And some Egyptians, like you two ..." He points at Chaz and Heloise." Chaz nods in agreement. And Heliose says in her gracious voice, "Yes," playing along.

"Keftiu always has a few visitors, as does the palace," says the guard. "I've been to Greece with a trader, and it's not a nice place. The Greeks are a hard people, don't respect the god of the wind and water. That's why foreigners find that reaching Keftiu is difficult. Easy enough for us to sail the great sea to Egypt, or Lydia, or Cyprus, but numbskull foreigners don't have those fine skills, scuse the oath – but you people obviously know how to sail. And us, obviously, and some on the islands to the north, but they're family, know what I mean? The mainlanders, not so good with boats. Sink. Scared to come. Specially the Greeks."

"Handy," I say. "You are protected."

"Yes. Keeps us safe. The day those bloody Greeks work out sailing proper, we're in for it," says the guard. "I'm Iomas."

"I'm Benjamin. And this is ..."

Iomas the guard looks at my guiding hand to Rosa's upturned face poking from the floppy brim and suddenly looks aghast.

"Ahhh! I know who this is! You're The Judge!"

We've all stopped, and the guard looks pale and shaken.

"That's me," says Rosa. "Pleased to meet you, Iomas."

"How do you know who she is," I ask, but the guard only has eyes for the 11-year-old kid in the hat and dark glasses and completely ignores me.

"I am begging your pardon, Judge. I shall inform the High Priestess," and he starts dashing after the ox-coach, or cart, or whatever it is shouting, "Wait up, wait up," almost shoving the parade of women aside.

Rosa looks at me thoughtfully. "If you know what you are looking for I'm easy to spot in a crowd," she says. "In this eon, everyone's hyper-aware of us, as many gods and godlets are worshipped, some being the projection of Elementals, though I understand there's not so much worship of the Judge. And a good thing too given my ... job," she adds. Still, Rosa chews her lower lip and I'm sure she's a little shaken at being recognized so easily.

The guard walks back, looking much more formal.

"The High Priestess requests the Judge's company in the ox-coach. Her retinue can follow, of course."

"Can this man – my Associate, at least – walk alongside the ox-coach," says Rosa brightly, indicating me, and I know she's nervous to hang out by herself with a High Priestess, and needs a wingman. I turn and wink at the crew who look nonplussed.

"Of course," says Iomas bowing, and we are led forward to the waiting ox-coach, and discover there are two carts ahead of us. And lions. Two lionesses are being led by other retainers. There is a man on a horse between the two carts, with a hooded hunting eagle perched on his long leather glove. The rear cart is pulled by an ox, hence the slowness, and carries two old women, comfortably arranged on cushions. One of the women is playing games with a pet monkey. I nod to them. We pass the big lionesses gingerly, but they seem pretty tame and resigned to being led. We reach the front, where a long coach is pulled by another ox with horns decorated in gold tips and ribbons.

The coachmen have pointed hats and bow slightly as we approach and they help Rosa climb in beside a most gorgeous older woman, the only occupant of the cart. The priestess looks slim, has high cheekbones and long, black Minoan curls, which trickle down her shoulders. Her eyes are sharp and black, and she wears tons of makeup and a flouncy open bodice that reveals and lifts her bare breasts. The red and purple skirt, which looks like it's made of cotton, tumbles down to her calves to what look like quite modern brown leather boots. The bodice and skirt are embroidered with bright blue and yellow lily flowers and little birds. I search her face and decide she is not the same woman as the ghost who revealed herself to us, back in the city diner, but a more forceful, older person. I look at such finery and sophistication and yet here we are in 2000 BC? Four thousand years before I was born?

And she's so hot! Immediately, I hope she can't read my mind, but the High Priestess only has eyes for Rosa.

"I greet you, Judge," the priestess says in a lilting voice.

"High Priestess of the Great Goddess," says Rosa, dipping her head in acknowledgment and sits beside her on a cushion.

"Oh no, no, no, that will not do. No obeisance from you. You can't be my follower." The cart driver, standing on a narrow rim in front of the cart, twitched his whip to get the oxen walking and the guy then sits down and the procession commences again.

"You are The Judge," says the priestess. Now eavesdropping is difficult, because the road has a stone surface and the clop of ox hoofs and rattle of the cart are noisy. There are a few bells on the bridle, too. But I hear enough.

"High Priestess, I was merely thanking you," Rosa says. "You invited me into your ox-coach."

"Ahh. This is my pleasure." She gazes fondly at Rosa. "You are so young, yet my retainer did well to see your eminence," said the priestess.

"He is a sharp fellow."

"I have sent another retainer running ahead to let the palace know of your manifestation here in Keftiu. The Scion of Theus, the Minos, will greet you in the throne room on your arrival. I have given orders."

"You ... outrank him, of course," Rosa said.

"On religious and social matters, yes; on rivers, oceans, wind and fire, gardening and harvests, yes – the overwhelming power of nature courses through me from the Great Goddess. Life and death. I look after the rituals for both, as you know. But, on more lowly business and political matters, it is the Minos who guides this island, making alliances with the great Pharaohs of Egypt and our island cousins. But you know that, too."

"I do," says Rosa with a smile, and so do I.

I'm getting used to Rosa's world, and understand this woman, whose name is Aria, is as close to an Elemental as a human can ever be. She is the link to the Great Goddess, the giver of light and life, fertility and fecundity, and the taker of life as well. Before we humans complicated things, inventing new gods and goddesses, pantheons of demigods, and hemi-demigods, and the many religions since, there was only the Great Goddess worshipped for tens of thousands of years, sometimes in the shape of a woman, sometimes a creature. This Aria was a real woman, but almost a demigoddess herself. Existing before the original knowledge faded and the man-made politics of the gods began. I glance up and now see the waves of power on her skin and in her eyes, reverberating with her link to the goddess.

Somehow, maybe from living in the house with Rosa, I too have the ability to recognize some things. The lilies on her embroidery appear alive and there's a gold snake necklace which dips into the top of her breasts. The jewel shimmers with life. Bright gold ducks fly under her earlobes in the shape of beaten earrings.

This is a hyperreal woman. The High Priestess is mortal, but a link to something that exists in Ancient Crete and has existed for a long time into the past. She looks down at me and I smile and bow my head, a devotee. No denying it. She's a real High Priestess and deserves respect.

"Your name?" she asks me.

"Apologies, High Priestess," Rosa says, "this is Benjamin, my Associate."

"High Priestess," I murmur in what I hope is an exceedingly respectful tone.

"You have a chief counsellor?" she asks Rosa. "I would have thought The Judge needs no-one to help make her decisions."

"I am a child, High Priestess. Sometimes people fail to see through this ... Benjamin sets them straight."

"I find that hard to believe. Your unadorned eminence is obvious."

"It happens," she says, grinning at me.

"And this device hiding your eyes?" The High Priestess points at the sunglasses.

Rosa removes them and the High Priestess looks at Rosa's crocodile eyes without a hint of surprise.

"Hmmm. You have a touch of the wild," she says, pleased. "This is gratifying."

"I have to tell people – who might be gratified by my wild streak – that I also have a touch of the tame." The High Priestess gives an infectious laugh of recognition and invites Rosa to eat one the figs that she has in a basket.

"And you too, Benjamin," she adds, idly tossing a ripe brown fig to me with a beringed hand. I catch the fruit and thank her, and as I bite into the juicy delicious fruit, lulled into a false sense of security, I think *These Minoans, or is it Keftians, are very warm and friendly.*

*

After some slow progress, we stop, right in the middle of the road, and cool beer from the rear cart is distributed by the guards from clay pots that are decorated with gaudy octopuses. More figs and dates are shared. Our crew merges with the priestess's retinue behind the cart. While the priestess and the Judge stay secluded, the Minoan women immediately home in on our three female travelers to talk about the cloth they wear (the female retinue were very stylish and colorful), the fashions of the foreigners and whether they are also priestesses. They touch Elodie's blonde hair and Heloise's dark cheeks and red dress, but very respectfully. The female retinue tell our crew they assist the High Priestess in her votive and ritual duties, as well as her personal care.

Heloise and Elodie do well, not claiming too much, nor presenting new ideas into this strong ancient culture, but Sukki is all over the Minoan design and jewelry asking questions back. She obviously adores the embroidery and the beaten gold and silver, the bracelets and religious finery.

Behind our crowd, other travelers are stopped in their tracks, because they are not allowed to pass the priestess, but they don't seem to mind and a couple of travellers behind us find some bread in their pockets to chew, or they drink from waterbags while they wait. Further down the hill herdsmen sit on the verge among some goats, and a merchant waits patiently with his laden horse.

I don't join the throng at the rear but stick close to Rosa and as far away from the lionesses as possible. At the back I hear Chaz trash-talking the Greeks with the soldiers, and Yusif pretending he's a Hittite rather than from Athens, but Yusif engages only halfheartedly, not his usual boisterous know-it-all self.

Then the man with the eagle gets the nod from Aria and calls for the procession to form up again and we proceed at a slow pace up the long hill.

The trip by cart to Knossos is not a massive distance, but slow going. Folk coming past the other way stop and raise their arms in a form of supplication, like they are giving the High Priestess something. Their upraised hands waggle.

The assistant priestesses move into a formation of two lines, and are harmonious in their singing. The combination of notes in their singing scale are strange, but attractive too. The women sing and they sway their skirts as they walk, which is quite a skill, almost hypnotic. I look back and see Sukki laughing as she was being shown how to walk, though she wore prosaic pants and sneakers, and the priestesses beside her pointed at her hip and helped Sukki sway in time.

"They are preparing for the spring ceremonies," Iomas said to me. "The offerings are to the goddesses for bounty later this year, as Persif coming to us now."

I wasn't sure what he meant unless Persif had something to do with the Greek goddess Persephone who, in the myth, emerges from Hades at springtime to bring life. But Persephone was a later Greek mythological figure. I knew this from my deep dive into books on Egyptian and Greek religion in the first weeks at the Judge's house when I thought Rosa was a mythical being too. Of course, I found nothing.

Thing was, I'd never found an actual "judge" in the Greek or Roman classics. There was no solo mythical figure like Judge Somberly to balance right from wrong. There were gods of justice as some sort of metaphor, but not a judge that presided over disputes.

Yet here, Iomas and Aria the High Priestess knew exactly who Rosa was.

All I found as I had read into the night, were horrible judgey gods and kings, taking offense, blasting their enemies or turning them into trees or monsters. But I knew Persephone. Was she Persif? Spring was a Persephone thing.

"So these junior priestesses dance at these ceremonies?" I asked the guard, who held his hardwood spear, tipped with a bronze point, lightly over a shoulder as he walked. "Oh, yes. Dance and sing. It's beautiful. It's beautiful now. Guarding these women is a joy."

I watch as Sukki, Elodie and Heloise start to get the swing of it, singing and swaying along with the priestesses. By the time we approach Conosos the women in our crew have learned a couple of songs by heart and sing along in Minoan, clapping at the right spots.

*

There it is, on a rise, like a giant iced wedding cake of red pillars and white roofs, holding up the power and prestige of the Minos and the High Priestess, the greatest palace of its age.

Surrounding the massive architectural marvel, a large town. The priestess's wooden ox-cart clacks and rolls up the stone roadway, past huts and small stone and mud houses whitewashed in lime, past more stately villas and shops, through a market packed with people.

The Knossans along the way raise their arms to the priestess, women ululate in great pleasure and men cheer, as she and The Judge sit quietly in their cart on the approach. I can see Rosa not just taking in the scene, but watching the faces of the populace as they adore the high-Priestess who attends their Great Goddess. By now it's early evening and there's smoke coming from charcoal braziers placed outside people's front doors on which to grill or bake their evening meals. A slight brown pall sits in a band above the town. There's an intense orange sunset like I've never seen before.

I drop back from Rosa to walk with the rest of my crew who are receiving as much interest as the priestess herself, these *xenochs* in strange clothes. Our jackets and boots. Sukki's Japanese eyes, the fact Chaz and I are tall, that Chaz and Heloise are black, and her long braided hair and red woolen dress. Elodie's blonde locks. People point at us.

Only Yusif with his big Greek beard looks vaguely like the locals.

What is common between us and the mingling Minoans is that many looked as fit and trim as the urbex crew, unlike the grumpy citizens of my modern city. These people look fed and happy. I wonder at this level of brimming health – even older folk who would, in our world, normally have a paunch or flabby muscles. The Minoans work hard physically, no doubt. As we crunch up the main roadway, I see the guards in the High Priestess's retinue are trained for fighting, and have not a centimeter of fat.

The normal folk who raise their worshipful arms as the priestess passes wear very little clothing – it's warm even for early spring. Short colorful kilts or skirts on the women, some with loose woolen tops, but many men and women wear nothing up top. They wear sandals, or just as often have bare feet, and naked kids run around. But their hair is clean and combed and many people have leather bracelets, and a scattering of bronze or copper jewelry – again both men and women. Some call out to the High Priestess to send the mother goddess their blessing as she passes.

One of the priestesses on foot had to be in her late fifties, and although her bodice is not so revealing of her breasts, she is also lean and strong, with taut arms and a trim figure, as she waves her hand and explains the layout of the palace to Elodie. "We shall arrive at the processional hall, and I am sure that The Judge will be ushered into the royal reception. Whether the retinue will, I know not ... but you are all so strange, the Minos might want to assess you. The games have started, so you may be obliged to watch, and you women, you will lodge with us, at the quarters of the priestess, and the men, the barracks."

Okay, I think.

"As for The Judge, she may stay wherever she wishes."

Okay, I ponder.

The red sunset clamps the Palace of Knossos in a vice of color, a vivid sight that won't ever leave my mind: the huge white three-story structures, the staircases, the red pillars slightly shorter at the bottom than the tops, the carved decorations of dolphins, double-headed axes, and monkeys across the cornices. Then we rumble into the plaza at the front of the palace and the procession ends.

Soldiers swarm out to help with the horse and oxen, and the priestesses go to assist their leader (and Rosa) from the spacious front cart. The courtyard buzzes, and the High Priestess performs a delicate stretch to restore circulation, while her attendant priestesses ruffle her skirt to make sure it's neat, and then, between the two tame lionesses she leads us into the cool colonnades of the palace.

BOXING

Yusif is beside me and we walk together, although I keep a wary eye on Rosa who is still with the priestess at the front of the halted procession. Yusif's face is haunted. He's been walking at the rear, in what he'd imagined was a personal dream, but it just goes on and on. The logical progress of this enduring experience confuses him. Everything is too real.

"How is this done? This hallucination? We were playing a parlor game at your house ..."

"Wasn't really a game," I say. "We were examining the last tau that Heloise had found. No-one touched it, but it started glowing and Rosa warned us – told us to hold hands for stability. We all held hands ... remember?"

He ignores me.

"Was there some drug in the food?"

"No drugs. I bought everything from the supermarket for the dinner with Elodie. And the wine was from the cellar with a French label and an old cork. Nothing in the food. Remember, we all saw the same thing – the tau started to grow into the shape of a bull. A large long-horned auroch. Remember? It started to get shaggy, we were still holding hands, and things faded and I fell unconscious and here we are. We are in Knossos, 4000 years before our dinner party, and several thousand kilometers from our city. This is the Bronze Age. There is no such thing as iron or steel or glass yet, but look around, what a civilization!"

Yusif sighs in exasperation, a long frothy sigh.

"Is not possible."

"Rosa said it might happen and everyone, including you, agreed to it. Except Mrs Cimbalom who said ..."

"*Someone has to mind the shop ...*" Yusif intoned, mocking Mrs Cimbalom's strange accent. "Yes, I remember that. But I didn't think it could possibly happen. I was just playing along with the parlor game."

"Well, keep playing along and we might get home," I said curtly. "We don't know these people, or their ways. We are looking for Siddley. We need to find out what he's up to."

"Hmmm," says Yusif.

"Are you two having an argument," Elodie says, gripping my arm.

"No, no. Just a discussion about the nature of our reality," Yusif says, and I grin.

"That's okay," says Elodie excitedly. "We have to go with the women as the High Priestess must prepare for the meeting with the Minos. I think they'll feed us. Iomas says you guys are off to watch some boxing."

*

In the cool of the colonnade, the deep red columns interspersed with sunlight beating through from the courtyard, I walk over to Rosa and Heloise and say, "Rosa should go with the High Priestess, don't you think? As her guest – and Sukki, Heloise and Elodie can help you. Okay?"

"Okay," says Rosa, confidently.

"Chaz, Yusif and I apparently have to go and watch some boxing."

"Ew," says Sukki. "Not a fan of boxing."

"Don't even know if it's like our boxing, but that's what Elodie heard the retainers say."

Chaz, Yusif and I are guided by chatting soldiers through a bunch of corridors, one of which was large and where we were confronted with the most vivid image of a bull charging from a fresco toward oncomers. Not quite lifelike, but fierce, bunched shoulder muscles, wide horns down. I'm astonished at the artfulness of the image, as if the painted bull was challenging anyone who entered the palace to a bullfight. Then a little niggle began in the back of my mind. I know about King Minos and the Minotaur in the labyrinth, but weren't the Minoans also famous for bull leaping? Somersaulting over charging bulls.

Wow! I think. That would be amazing to watch.

We veer left up another passage.

*

The boxing hasn't started and Iomas is offering us brined-olive paste and cut tomatoes on a grain bread, and we drink more beer, which is cool but not icy. It tastes fine and it slaked my thirst and the olivey bread fills my stomach. Chaz asks for seconds and Iomas happily obliges. Yusif sits quietly sipping from a jug, eyes moving round carefully, watching the throng.

"Ok, this beer seems real," he says. "The vibe here is quite ... hard."

"Yeah, boxing, bud," Chaz says. "Blood sport and feels like this always, whatever the century, it seems."

"Yeah."

The three of us sit in the shade on a retaining wall between a couple of columns, along a large dusty rectangular courtyard. The courtyard is between the inner palace and some outer buildings. There's a big throng of peeps around the edge of the space. I'm beside Iomas who's become our host and guide. On the opposite side of the rectangular plaza is a long high platform with shade covers, and comfortable chairs with red and black cushions.

"Sun's dropped. It's cool now, so the fights will start," Iomas says.

To begin, the blowing of some long bronze instruments that did not sound like trumpets, more rumbly-deep in tone like an Australian didgeridoo. A group of five bare-chested kilted musicians are to the side, rumbling or droning, while a group of drummers, on a signal, start a beat. The drums sound and a large fat guy in leather vest and pants and a long colorful robe walks to the stage, followed by robed retainers with soft, pointed hats. The fat guy slouches himself on the biggest bench chair in the middle of the podium while a small man follows and hands him a skin of wine. This old gravitas guy has sweeping white hair, a similar beard, huge shoulders, and I see his black twinkling eyes from the other side of the plaza. He's searching for me, Yusif and Chaz. I tap Chaz and gave the man on the throne a head bow. Chaz follows suit, as does Yusif, even though he still regards the whole event as one continuing hallucination.

"Is that the Minos?" I ask Iomas.

"Yes, he is our king."

"And the queen?"

"She doesn't like boxing. Neither does the priestess. They stay well away. This is part of soldiering. Preparing for war, if it comes to us."

Fair enough. Though there are one or two women in the gathering crowd, it's pretty much man and boy heavy.

I observe the king of Keftiu . The king looks away from us as the competitors come in – older boys and men, lean, in loincloths, barefooted, hands padded up with leather boxing gloves. They move into the center of the square ... there must have been around sixty or so boxers, jiggling and jogging on the spot and warming up. Courtiers and townsfolk keep packing the edge of the piazza.

Some of the boxers are close to us, still jiggling nervously on their feet. Some are really young, only 14 or 15, others are in their late 20s. Their bodies are oiled and their curled black hair scoops down the back of their necks, which is clearly a fashion. Some younger ones have the back of their neck shaved.

The drumming and droning continues as the plaza fills, and then as suddenly as it started, it stops. Another retainer stands beside the Minos, also in finery: a glorious cloak, and gold bracelets.

"The Minos," he says. Everyone slid to their knees, boxers, spectators, and the courtiers on the podium.

The king stands and looks at the boxers. "I want to see how fierce you can be, how brave, how you can hold up your heads in your villages and say, I fight for the Minos, I fight for our people. And at the end, one of you will be able to boast, *I won*. Stand."

Everyone gets off their knees. We sit back on the wall expectantly.

"Face your first!" Opponents square off around the plaza. One or two punch each other's glove in recognition.

"Fight!"

And the melee begins. No Queensbury or Boxing Federation rules here. They are right into it, parrying and blocking, but mostly hard swinging thumps to bodies and heads. Dust rose in the setting sunlight, as figures dodge and duck and punch. Once an opponent is downed, the victor moves on to find the nearest available other winner. Admittedly, they did stick to fighting one-to-one, but sometimes that only lasts a couple of flailing moments.

A teenage kid would take five minutes to beat another kid, turn round and find himself faced with a burly 28-year-old soldier. Then the weaker opponent would dodge a few punches but be quickly pummeled into the ground, blood streaming from their nose, or cuts to the face, and there they'd be beaten, or kicked, until the loser surrenders by slapping the dirt. Very ugly. Their family members would scramble over and help the loser off the fighting area so they don't get accidentally stomped on.

The noise is huge. The crowd cheers their favorites as the drummers keep the beat – a thumping rhythm, and the bronze tubes parp in shrill blasts.

"Wow, this is crazy," I say. Chaz, who has boxed all his life, takes a keen interest. Yusif too is transfixed.

A brutal process, but methodical, as if on a crowded battlefield. A winner would find and face off with another winner, and they'd square up again. The weak are winnowed out until the best fighters are warmed up for the final few fights, occasionally being handed a skin of drink by supporters as they hunt for a worthy or not so worthy opponent.

Fifty or 60 fighters, 30 fights. Then 15 and then 10, and the contestants make sure they move always toward the Minos so he can view their prowess. The Minos is enjoying the sport, calls out to the fighters, exhorts them to "show no mercy," and other mad slogans.

"Take him clean," I hear him shout to one pair of contestants who were in a thump-fest in front of his throne.

At one point during the melee, right in front of us, a soldier's bloodlust has him knocking a weaker guy down, and repeatedly punching his opponent's prone body in a sickening fashion, and Chaz shouts, "Hey," and leaps into the square and whacks the aggressor on the shoulder.

"He's down," Chaz shouts. "Stop it."

The soldier looks up, swinging a punch at Chaz who ducks and says, "Fight someone else," and bangs the man hard on the shoulder again until the soldier recognizes Chaz, in his modern clothes, as a non-combatant (and also someone to be reckoned with) and so searches for another opponent. Chaz sits with a grunt, while the prone man's people nod a thanks and pull the unconscious dude over the wall into the colonnade behind, splashing his face with beer.

I was glad Rosa was with the women. She'd be perplexed and upset to see so many unconscious and injured bodies being dragged from the square, but this was how they trained for battle in the Bronze Age and how a king picked his champion fighters.

I stare hard at one of the two final fights where a tall young man, with long black hair, is toying with his older opponent, fisting some fast jabs into the man's face. *Bang bang*. The face of the younger man is cut with a cruel smile, a smile I'd seen before. The resemblance to Tau al-Gorz is striking. It is him! Him as an older youth, maybe early twenties, an awesome physique (not the slumped bundle of flab I'd seen) and no Siddley or Giddley playing across his chest.

"That's a very young Tau al-Gorz," I whisper to Chaz.

"What's he doing here?"

"He's one of them. An Elemental. He can pop up anywhere and everywhere," I try to explain, but it sounds stupid.

From the young warrior, there is certainly no mercy. He moves in, elbows bent to deliver a blow and his opponent is literally punched off his feet and lands square on his back in an unseemly winded heap. Tau al-Gorz doesn't even look down at the clearly unconscious man. He moves fluidly round, plays with his glove, and waits for the other semi-final bout to end.

This takes longer as two big burly guys, with thick stumps for arms and tree trunks for legs, conduct a bashfest. One hits the other in the face or chest, and the other would recover and swing his fist back. Tau moves forward waiting, I think, to see who'll triumph, to judge his opponent. There's a lot of yelling and catcalling from the crowd, they obviously know the two guys – probably soldiers – and I guess wagers of some sort had been placed, even though money hasn't yet been invented.

A blonde fighter gives his opponent quite a blow to the jaw and the man staggers toward the young Tau al-Gorz, who just steps in his way and cleans him up with one punch. The crowd gasps at this intervention, but the Minos actually laughs and shouts: "Cutting to the chase, eh, son?"

The drums fall silent for the final bout.

The young prince holds up his fist, acknowledging his father, King Minos, and then spins around to face the finalist who comes into Tau al-Gorz's fight space before he's ready, and proceeds to slam al-Gorz with an uppercut. Tau falls back, but doesn't fall over. He steadies himself and shakes his head, a snarl on his face. The burly soldier is much beefier than Tau al-Gorz, the prince, and he punches his glove a couple of times indicating no quarter will be given. The youth might be the son of the king, but he is up for a proper fight.

They circle each other. The crowd is hushed. "Come on," shouts the Minos impatiently, his voice cutting through the darkening space. The prince does a little dance to the left and right, the burly guy charges in with a roar and strives to deliver another roundhouse punch but the prince dances out of the way and as the bloke flies past (he'd put everything into the missed punch) Tau al-Gorz thumps his opponent on the side of the head, in the ear.

The burly guy had a thick neck and hard head for sure. He staggers, much as Tau had, but turns quickly and lands two pretty heavy blows on Tau's body. The prince had not been expecting such a quick recovery. Tau punches back. A flurry of punches in the face, while the big guy tries to kick him and locks his right arm in a half-wrestle, but Tau just goes *bang bang* with his left fist, and that hurts. The burly guy moves back, somewhat stunned, and Tau al-Gorz again shows no mercy, delivering an uppercut that I hear from the other side of the plaza, which sounds like the crack of the man's jaw. The burly guy sags to the ground on his knees and slumps onto his face. There's a brief cheer, marking the end of the tournament.

"Wow," says Chaz. "What a punch."

"So cruel," says Yusif, sadly.

The prince bows once to his father and walks over to a huddle of retainers, one who hands him a jug of beer which he swills down.

The tournament, if that what it was, has lasted almost an hour, and it's almost dark with the lamps and flares casting both licks of orange light and wavering shadows about the square as people file homeward.

The prince has won, as he should.

*

Now I'm sitting with Rosa in the Bronze Age dark, on the roof of Knossos palace where we've climbed some sturdy vines to find quiet. The palace is still bustling beneath, but fires around the city have died down. Cooking braziers fill with dying embers, distant candles glimmer, and the stars, those constellations above, are bright as hot sparks. Stars 4000 years out of place, but still recognizable. Orion the Hunter is there. So's the bright half-moon rising, illuminating Rosa's small face clearly.

Rosa leans close, keeping warm. Her little hand is in mine to indicate we are talking about deep things, and she wants the reassurance that I'm on her side, and to reassure me also that she's got my back. The essence of handholding, really.

Rosa's face is serious. "I think people have a half-understanding of so much, and just fill in the blank bits with their ideas, visions, words. If there's a dark space, they see a ghost. They look at stars and see heroes in the shapes, and then invest the shapes with some power over their lives! That's what my mother said, and it's true ... it's true! People make meaning out of nothing."

I nodded. People were always grasping for meaning. I know I was, especially around Rosa! Somehow Rosa means something, and I'm always going to guess.

"And Papa, he would say: *You have to read between the nonsense humans have invented to find the facts, and come to the right judgment.* And take nothing for granted. Things get made up all the time to fit a situation. But right now, here we are at an important moment in history and this is no invention. *We are in the wrong place at the wrong time.* You, me, Elodie, Sukki, Mrs Simply, Chaz and Mr Yusif. Our atoms are in the wrong place in the spacetime continuum. If we stay here, things won't end well, and that's not something that's written, Benji, that's just what happens."

I shiver. It's just the cold making me shiver because her words are strangely soothing, like they explain a feeling I have already. I know what she means, and I am prepared for bad things.

"The women in our crew," she goes on, "are already in love with Aria, the High Priestess. All three clearly have understood her strong female power, and bonded. They've become her women. Acolytes. That's the Greek word, isn't it, Mr Benji? Funnily, I think they were already acolytes before they even met her, and now they have been accepted."

"What, Elodie, and Sukki?"

"And Mrs Simply."

"How?"

"Aria embodies the spirit of life in nature, the most powerful force in the world. High Priestess Aria is human, but a projection as well, a hybrid. She's a presence, a teacher, a power and a drug. After the journey in the cart, we returned to the temple within the palace, but the Minos was too busy with the boxing to meet with me. Aria was furious about this. But her women went about their business – they ritually bathed in the goddess's pools to purify themselves, and ate, and sang, and the High Priestess has spoken to the women about the spring rituals in Keftiu, and how our crew will be involved."

"O...kay," I say warily.

"It may change the way they think. I'm a child. I'm not allowed, because I'm a girl, I'm not yet ... fertile. You must be a woman to take part in the devotions."

"I understand."

"And as Judge it would be wrong anyway. I am independent of every-thing."

"I know."

"Worst thing of all about the temple, it was filled with baskets and baskets of fresh crocuses, reminding me of when Mama died. That spring when I was six. Crocuses, with their saffron, are the priestess's important offerings gathered in the hillsides for these rituals. I saw the horrible flowers and started to cry and everyone was shocked that The Judge would ..."

"Even judges cry."

"I'm not supposed to cry ... in their view. And I couldn't explain why I cried, but I think I have now come to terms with crocuses. I decided it wasn't the fault of the flowers that Mama died. That's a fact, not a feeling. Crying at crocuses is a reaction to a feeling."

Rosa pauses for a minute and stares at the dark land speckled with the little orange home-fires. Just below, a line of pitch torches lights the boundary of the palace. The velvety dark is humid, and there's a mild breeze bringing the smell of the fields and the herbs in the forests.

"The next few days will be a big test for all of us." She now looked gloomy.

"This whole trip into Keftiu is a big test."

"I'm working on an escape mechanism to get us out of here. We can't stay long."

"I agree," I said. I could feel that in my bones. They were in the wrong place, along with the rest of me.

I told her about the boxing, or really, the fight-festival or battle practice, and the presence of the young Tau al-Gorz, and that there was no sign of Siddley or Giddley. Rosa scowled at the whole idea of an unpleasant boxing battle but kept listening. I told about Chaz entering the fray, briefly, about Yusif becoming more withdrawn and bewildered. She shook her head.

"We're here because of Tau al-Gorz, I'm sure. Those little bulls that Siddley was trying to round up. He was desperately trying to find them," Rosa said.

"That's true. He killed Dawson Kennedy to steal taus. Was his plan to stop us from coming here?"

"Possibly. We must find the truth about the taus, and Siddley, and why he was after them," said Rosa grimly.

We stared toward the ocean. This tug of war between humanity and nature – the Prince of Knossos and The Caiman. Does the Judge mediate between the two? What was to fear? Out there in the dark?

*

Ten days now, in this rocky otherworld. Hot and ancient. People are courteous, because we are guests of their beloved High Priestess.

Chaz, Yusif and I sleep on straw pallets in barrack-style halls with soldiers and guards. Thin woolen blankets keep out the early morning chill. Chaz and I absorb the experience, but every time he wakes in the morning Yusif is surprised that he's still in Knossos and not his house.

The latrines down the back of the barracks are foul and I can't get used to squatting over a ditch with other men. That's the only downside. Basic community hygiene hasn't been properly worked out. Every so often there's a stink around the town.

Mostly, we are apart from the women in our crew and I don't see Elodie much, as she and the others learn to be priestesses, and Sukki, a priestess artisan, is hanging with the Minoan craftspeople, learning their skills in jewelry and fabric dyeing.

Because Rosa is too young and too Elemental to be a priestess, she hangs out with Chaz and me, exploring the palace and the town, hunting for Siddley and explanations as to why we are here.

We quickly realise that in the cities of Minoa, the palace is everything, and Knossos is the greatest palace of them all. From miles around, farmers bring excess produce to storage chambers and this is distributed in time by palace officials to citizens who need food. There's no such thing as money – currency will come to the Mediterranean in a few centuries. The Minoans keep detailed records about who brought goods to the palace and who took what from it, so fairness plays into the deal. Officials use delicate ink seals on papyrus paper to mark food deliveries and barters. Cloth, pottery, jewelry, cosmetics and leatherwork are made in the palace grounds. The palace is the hub of Minoan society. It is not just the home of their king, and the temple of the goddess, but also the major provider to the people.

We are located in a doorway of human history between a life of nomadic herding and foraging, and the beginning of a civic society, nations, and technology driven by iron – nails, ploughshares and swords. Forged iron's not quite here yet – the Chinese and the people in Mesopotamia, the Hittites, are just starting to smelt iron. Here, in Minoa, the hardest metal known is bronze, so the weapons haven't that iron edge, that hardness.

We are in an ancient place where people still understand and communicate with Elementals in ceremony and rituals, and where the new hardscrabble life of early farming creating villages and towns and a formalized trade, are developing. As Rosa reminds me, the most powerful force in the world is nature, but the second most powerful is the human imagination.

"Mum taught me that," she said with a little wistful smile.

In the city of Knossos, young Rosa doesn't cover her eyes, because people look at her in awe, not surprise or fear. They know she is The Judge and think she is some demigod, though I know better – she is also just a girl.

*

A few days on and I'm sitting on the colonnade wall in the almost empty boxing courtyard, yarning with Chaz who is relaxed and has come fully back to me as his friend since his new romance with Heloise. He grudgingly admits it was time for him to move on from the crew too. Maybe even in ten years' time he'll thank me!

Like me, he's thrilled to be on this adventure, and can't stop talking about the Minoans. Yesterday, we rose before dawn and Chaz and I walked with Rosa back down the hill to the port of Amnisos to check the amazing boats and talk to the seafarers. Chaz was wanting to find an Egyptian, who looked like Chaz, to ask what Africa's like, but there were none around the docks, although a couple of sailors had been to Egypt said it was hot, green and beautiful.

We were given some grilled fresh fish and hot pepper sauce for lunch by a bunch of fishermen who had called us over and said they'd cooked too much. That was cool, sitting on the stone jetty around a charcoal brazier eating spicy, hot fried fish off a leaf with our fingers. Still, I was sad Yusif wasn't with us to enjoy the experience.

Two wooden fishing boats bobbed in the dark Aegean waters beside us, ropes to the jetty and the fishermen talked of shoals of sardines they were netting out to sea. The sky above, light blue and cloudless with a gentle sea breeze warm to the cheek.

*

Yusif is missing all this. If the time-sinkhole experience wasn't so unsettling for him, he'd be fascinated too by the fishermen's tales, but unfortunately, he spends most of his time hiding indoors and we can't lure him out. Today, Chaz and I sit on the colonnade wall, talking about getting Yusif out for some exercise and sun on his skin, at least, when Rosa comes running up to us, and hands me what is a thin silver ring. She hands one to Chaz too.

"Should fit your fat fingers," she says cheekily. "Put them on. I asked Heloise if she would sacrifice her silver blob pendant so that Sukki can make us each a ring. Actually, she made herself and Heloise earrings instead. Elodie has a ring too. They all came from the same lump of silver."

I slide the filigreed ring onto my index finger, as does Chaz.

"Why? What's doing with this?" asks Chaz.

"Well, they are from the same piece of silver – but this silver's our link to The Judge's house. The silver has been down the time travelling pathway with Heloise. When we leave, this silver will act like a compass to take us home. The atoms in the metal are out of their timeline. To go, we can <u>will</u> ourselves home, but we need the atoms in the metal to take us to the right place."

"I don't want to go yet," says Chaz. "This is way too interesting."

"The pathway will know when the time comes. So will you."

"I see. The pathway?" I ask. Chaz is twirling the ring on his finger.

"It's the slab on the roof, and the slab in the basement, I'm sure. The dining table sits between the two. They're like … big battery terminals … but different … in the right circumstances they shift our polarities … our atoms. The atoms in the silver. It's complicated." She sighed in exasperation. "Mum was going to explain it sometime."

"I see," I added.

Rosa raised her hand and I saw a small ring on her finger too. "Yusif objected to the ring, of course – claimed it was hocus-pocus – but Sukki made him wear it 'for her'. Sukki has beaten and rolled the metal beautifully, don't you think?"

"She's an artist," I said.

"Sure is," says Chaz.

"Sukki loves this place too much," said Rosa, a tremor of worry in her voice. "She may not want to leave."

*

Next morning after boiled eggs, olives, cheese, bread, tomato and thin beer, we join the women and process into the mountains along with a winding crowd of priestesses, palace officials who run Knossos, and their attendants, and ordinary folk dressed in their best robes, kilts and woolen hats and women in flouncy skirts and blouse-bodices. The lionesses are not far from the front, a symbol of Aria's power.

Our cavalcade winds up a track through forests, many places showing the scars of timber-getting, as people harvest the wood for charcoal making, and for cooking, but the further we go, the more primordial the land becomes: forested ridges with steep open gullies, fronds, creepers. The land is very green and lush. There's a lot of rainfall in 2000 BC Aegean. There are monkeys in the trees. Priestesses sing and chant, as on the first morning, but there's less fun in the melody. A serious procession with serious devotional music. Drums accompany their voices.

At the top of most of the gullies along which water trickles seaward, is a shrine to the Great Goddess. There we stop to allow the priestesses to make offerings. As we make our way uphill, the way they pick plants and flowers, and at one point we stop at a long rectangular structure hung from a branch which turns out to be a beehive made of woven fronds and wood. The hive contraption is lowered on a rope, and a priestess fires up a ceramic smoking vessel with holes in the end where the smoke pours from, including a faint perfume that stuns the bees. Another priestess reaches into a slot and pulls out a trellis structure and harvests some, but not all, of the honey. This is classical beekeeping.

"These bees are the armies of the goddess. They keep the forest alive," one young priestess called Xeniu tells me. She offers me some honeycomb from a ceramic pot she holds. It is sweet and utterly delicious. Having flown as a bee, thanks to the Old Man of the Forest's mushroom, I know the heaviness of pollen on my legs, but I don't pass that memory on to Xeniu. I, too, want to keep a low profile.

Elodie, Heloise and Sukki are at the head of the procession singing, already wearing some of the regalia of a junior priestess – earrings depicting dancing dolphins, leather armbands, colorful skirts with the open blouses. The uncanny ability to converse with the Minoans eases them into this world of nature worship and ritual.

The young priestess Xeniu is slim, small and pretty, with a dark olive complexion, and thick dark eyebrows. Her face has dimples and she has a mane of black frizzy hair. She gives me the sweetest smile as I suck every last speck of honey out of the wax which she finally takes from me.

"For candles."

She puts it in a dilly-bag she carries.

"We dream. That is where the Great Goddess lives. In all of our dreams," the young priestess says to me. "Dreams are where we come from. Bees dream of flowers and their queen too." Xeniu walks beside me for a while talking about her village in the hills, and then hurries forward for the next devotional when a shrine comes into view.

As the long line of people ascends to the limestone plateau, the ocean below is azure blue. I can just see the High Priestess, sometimes carried in a ox-coach by her male retainers, but often walking at the head of the procession with her lionesses. The wind from the distant ocean is cool and Aria comes to a mountain pass where there's a big stone stage. An open air temple. She ascends a flight of steep steps and sits on a limestone throne, with carved walls and plinths with stone cups. She holds life-sized bronze sculptures of snakes, one in each hand and she sits very still, head high, hair rustling in the wind, her full breasts thrust from her bodice, while the singing and drumming continues.

Petals from spring flowers, such as crocuses and lilies, are thrown over her becoming shards of light and color. The snakes which she raises slowly above her head appear to shimmer and writhe. An aura of colors forms around the priestess, and the honey is poured into cracks along the back of the altar by senior priestesses, and into horn shaped cups that line the altar. Still, the petals are scattered over Aria who continues to chant. Elodie, Heloise and Sukki are still there, chanting and passing petal, honey and wine offerings to more senior priestesses, all three very engaged in their work. I have been missing Elodie while she's learned to be a priestess.

I don't understand the words of the chanting. They are from a much earlier language, apparently. One that allegedly came from the place of the gods that made the world, but more likely from older civilizations we know nothing about. More petals are scattered into the earth through cracks and crevasses around the altar, along with small ceramic tokens, much like the taus. Honey drips from votive jars. They are summoning Persif. Craving spring, life, rebirth. Tempting the goddess with honey and wine to emerge and fertilize the earth.

Over the next hour, the chanting and singing intensifies after the offerings are made and libations poured from bull's horns and triton shells, and then the priestess stands, looks to the sky and lifts the snakes up – what were once bronze sculptures seem to wriggle in her hands now, and I feel a heat emanating, weirdly, from the altar and then suddenly the songs and chants end, the drumming stops and the priestess staggers back into her seat where senior female retainers provide her with reviving wine.

"We can go now," says Xeniu, who returns from the chanting ceremony. Maybe she has taken a shine to me, or maybe she has been appointed as my guide. She is very earnest and sweet and more to the point, businesslike. There is no flirting, but maybe these transactions are different in Ancient Crete. Maybe she is flirting, attracted to the tall xenoch that is me. Who knows. Elodie is still up with Aria the High Priestess, learning – I glance across at her, wondering if she notices the attentions of this young priestess.

"In a few days, at the full moon, is the ceremony of the bulls," Xeniu says, "so there will be favor from the goddess, and also her son. Crops will mature and the harvest will come. The High Priestess has to be cared for – she has implored the Great Goddess for a beneficial harvest. Now we must impress the goddess's son, Theus, so they both remain kind and giving. These are important days."

JUMP

The midday sun is like warm honey on the skin, so Rosa wears her floppy hat. She sits on a huge red cushion on the royal podium between the Minos and the High Priestess, who occupy their thrones. Beside Rosa and The Minos, is Queen Itone, the King's wife. I see for the first time, a tall woman with long tresses, a slim nose, and dark searching eyes, also in gold-thread finery, fine purple cotton robes and a broad-brimmed felt or wool hat. I know the Minos is generally gung-ho, but he's very cautious around Rosa and uses his wife as a buffer to keep her at a distance, this visible presence of an Elemental.

Having a so-called "demigod" in his palace worries him (he told me, at the feast at the palace the previous night), because he is unsure of why Rosa is here. ("Do you know why you're here?" he had asked me and I shrugged and answered, "No, Lord Minos."). Like all leaders, he doesn't appreciate surprises, and our arrival is a surprise. Maybe he's worried Rosa will judge him over something or other, though he appears to be a fair-minded, if tough, man. Queen Itone seems up for a chat with The Judge, though. As Rosa had told me, they've met several times in the women's quarters and "got on quite well". As queen, Itone is forbidden to be a priestess, but seems friendly toward Aria, unlike her husband who resents Aria's power. Aria, Rosa and Itone are hoeing into a basket of honey cakes.

*

At the feast last night, we were celebrating the final ceremonies in the great hall in the Knossos palace, with movable panel walls thrown right back to enlarge the room. Braziers were lit in the chamber's fire grates and, from the kitchens came a banquet of grilled lamb, chicken, and spring vegetables, spiced and herbed.

Unlike the previous spring festival events, the king's retinue mingled more freely with both the palace officials and warriors, and the High Priestess's retinue. Everyone was feasting and drinking. Tomorrow is the big final day of ceremony to summon spring and fertility to the land.

At this banquet, the Minos calls me over to sit by his side on a comfortable bench. The bench is carved with swirls and lions' heads, and clearly it's where he conducts more informal discussions and laps up the palace gossip. He wasn't as fat as I thought. Muscled, with deep-brown skin, and that cagey old face that had brought much prosperity on his people. The beard is white and voluminous, eyes deep brown and eyebrows grey and very bushy. He rests on a pillow with a goblet of wine in his hand. And he is friendly to me, even charming. We chat and he finally gets to the point.

"Ben Ja Min, your judge's people attend our spring festivals to summon Persif from Hades to hasten the harvest. It is fortuitous. I ask you that The Judge's champions participate in tomorrow's test. I know The Judge cannot. She is who she is, and a child, and it would be unseemly, but I can see that her retinue have the powers."

"To what?"

"Participate in the bull jumping, Ben Ja Min. With the godlike powers given by your judge, you shall be tested against my son and his retinue. As will the priestess's champions. This is a great day."

"Bull jumping?"

"This is my decree."

I sit in this warm hall with wine in my belly, and a hunk of lamb in my hand, looking at the Minos's hunting dogs splayed under the table waiting for scraps. His men sat around in their robes, making drunken conversation and leering at the priestesses from the corners of their eyes, and my head spins.

Chaz could possibly jump over a bull – he'd try any feat of daring. Sukki also has lift. Me? – the gymnastics and parkour we've mucked around with over the years could help, but an 800 kilogram bull at full charge? Possibly Elodie at a pinch – she's foremost a climber.

Yusif has tangled himself up in exasperation, believing it's an endless bad dream, and keeps insisting again and again that he just wants to wake up, while Heloise wouldn't stand a chance with a charging bull – she's not urbex. Those two are out.

"You ask a lot from strangers not trained in this ritual," I say to the Minos.

"Agreed, and you will be rewarded by the goddess, and by me, in either this life or the next, whatever the result. The Judge must have champions. You, for one. The Egyptian," he points at Chaz, "the small woman ..."

Yes, the Minos has been appraising us under those grey bushy eyebrows, as warriors. He wants us tested. He wants to test Rosa's power.

"You perform as a trio to satisfy Theus," he rumbles. "You must form a trio of champions – that's the way. You can do nothing other."

The bulls I've seen in various fields while walking around have been big, but docile, but this means nothing. The palace officials may prepare highly aggressive animals, twisted and tortured for bloodsport. I wouldn't trust the Minos to play fair.

He'd want his son's team to be victorious, surely?

"I will convey your wish to The Judge for her assent."

"She will look very weak if she does not agree," the Minos says casually in his low rumbly voice. He's playing politics with the Elemental. He doesn't understand why she's here so, yes, we're being tested.

I nod. At least I've raised the possibility of a caveat, Rosa forbidding the sport, though in the end it will be a decision for Chaz, Sukki and myself, because we're the bull-jumpers and always Rosa's champions.

*

"Yep," says Chaz with a flashing smile. "Whatever happens, bro, I'm in."

He's in. Can't help himself. That's why I love Chaz.

When I find her in an antechamber to the feasting hall, deep in conversation with some local girls, Sukki also nods with a sparkle in her eyes. She's not one to shirk. Yusif, in his state of disbelief, protests that it is "a madness", but we ignore him. The goddess's women gaze on little Sukki with awe at the prospect of her leaping over giant bulls.

We can't let Rosa down, even though, when I convey the Minos's request, she immediately forbids us to jump. We've seen plenty of frescos and decorations on pots of bull jumping over the past few weeks. For Minoans, it's a thing. The main thing.

"You haven't trained!" Rosa blurts in horror. "You've never jumped over a bull!"

"Your credibility as Judge will be in tatters if we don't offer up a team," I say.

"I agree with Yusif. You are all mad."

But I certainly didn't feel mad – just grimly determined.

"It'll be like flipping over the handlebars of a bike," I said. "You'll see." And across the room, standing in flickering flame and shadows, I spot beautiful Xeniu.

*

The bull field is long, maybe 50 or 60 meters, but not much wider than a basketball court. The arena is a pit, lined with stone walls about 2 meters high so that the spectators are protected from the possibly enraged animals, but can easily look down, close to the action. Heat is trapped in the pit, so it's a sauna. At either end are entrances, and behind one entrance are pens with large bulls, both brown and white and black, all, to my relief, looking quite docile. We come down the ramp at the other end with the other champions. As it's a long-walled pit, there's no escape for the participants from an out-of-control bull, except the narrow alleys at each end, so this jumping field could well be a death trap.

There's a large crowd surrounding the arena, and perched on a variety of stands and podia, and watching from high windows in adjacent palace buildings. Two thousand people, at least, from the lands around Knossos. Yusif and Elodie sit near The Judge. Elodie's in her 21st century clothes. She's a retainer of The Judge today, not a trainee priestess. Rosa looks very concerned, having suddenly inherited champions who might get hurt.

Sukki, Chaz and I are pretty much stripped down and bare-footed. Sukki is in her sports bra and undies, Chaz and I are bare-chested and dressed in embarrassingly small and inadequate loincloths, borrowed from Iomas. Did I mention the Minoans don't like to wear much?

Like the jumpers in the two other teams, which are bigger – four or five persons in each – we've wound cloth around our hands as quasi-gloves. Chaz, being a black man is, as usual, attracting interest, and he's enjoying the attention. Sukki has her hair in a ponytail. I am almost at the point of hyperventilating, but Sukki, for a warm-up exercise (and stress relief) performs a series of 10 forward flips alongside one of the walls to the cheers of the crowd and it makes me feel calmer. The drummers and droners are back with their brass tube-trumpets, and flags flap on high thin poles amongst the crowd.

It's very festive.

*

The evening before, Xeniu assured me that the animals were seldom aggressive. She is super impressed that I'm going to try and vault a bull. We are standing beside each other by a long bench laden with food. Elodie is, as usual, over with the High Priestess.

"But be careful," Xeniu warns, "after some handling and jumping the bulls can get angry. If the team completes their three jumps quickly then that is enough. The more handling and prodding the bulls get, the angrier they get. The trick is to complete the jumps as quickly and lightly as possible. You will be well regarded for lightness of touch on the beasts."

"And then what happens?"

"The bulls are taken and sacrificed by the priestesses ..."

"You?"

"Yes, me among others. They have been vaulted by Theus's champions, and blessed."

"Theus?"

"The son of the goddess."

"Ahh," I said, suddenly working it out. "Zeus!"

"Who?"

"Never mind. Just someone I know of."

"The sacrifices ensure that spring will lead to summer and that Persif is among us to allow the harvest," Xeniu says. "She will have emerged from the depths of the underworld. Our people have performed this ceremony since before the time of planting, when the sun first passed across the sky. This is the most important time of the year. The planting will begin immediately after the sacrifices of the bulls. If we get the great songs and rituals wrong, we could be in trouble."

"Have you ever been in trouble?"

Xeniu smiles a bright smile. "Not in my lifetime, or my mother's or my grandmothers', but calamity happens. The ground can shake, and the stores can crumble onto the grain, or the rains come and not relent. This is the reason to be kind to our earth and succor the soil."

Then Xeniu stands on her toes and reaches up to kiss me, and I waver. I sense a luscious succulent, delicious thing, this going-to-be kiss, and I smell the honey balm on her skin and I bend toward her. We shuffle into the shadows and kiss, and I taste her honeyed lips. The spell of spring, the goddess. Whatever it is, she grips me and tightens against me, and I hold her soft curly ringlets in my hand, between my fingers, as we press together in a burst of uncontrolled passion, my blood pounding. We explore each other's warm, soft mouths as she kisses me urgently, and I see her closed eyes and big black eyelashes enhanced with fine kohl, and I'm washed through with a feeling of pure joy in these flickering shadows of the Bronze Age. A mystical kiss.

But what was it that Mrs Cimbalom had said? I was Loyalty. And I had a loyalty to both Elodie and Rosa.

Heart and head.

Suddenly Mrs Cimbalom's face appears in my mind, with her wise eyes and mocking smile. I stop and draw back. I extend my fingertip and place it on Xeniu's lips and I say, "Sorry, I can't do this," and she looks very disappointed (as am I), but I now know what has to happen. Kissing and then loving this young priestess is so wrong, and the fun of making a baby – which was where we were heading – would be a disaster. Human folly! I am not supposed to be here. I love Elodie.

I hug her in a tight apology, and then say "goodbye" and hurry into the light and back to the group to talk bull jumping tactics.

Heart still racing from the sharp physical passion I'd felt for Xeniu, I walk into the hall with the moving wall panels, and the great fresco of bulls and birds. Then I stop to recover my mental balance, hand against one of the red pillars, steadying myself.

If it hadn't been for Mrs Cimbalom's mocking face …

I watch the crowd in the bright firelight, stretched out eating and drinking, talking, laughing – the warriors, the priestesses, the servants (none seem to be slaves that I can make out, but maybe they are), the peaceableness of the place. Calmer now, I stride up to benches and cushions where my crew are, intermingled with new friends. We are all being seduced by Knossos.

"Elodie," I say to her as I reach our crew and the huddle of new friends. She stretches a hand out to me and smiles. I stretch out both hands and hold both of hers tightly, thinking, *What a close thing, that would-have-been seduction.* There's a sudden flicker of concern on her face as she looks at me, but I launch into my speech. "Elodie, I love you. I know this place is a treasure, a mystery, and a revelation for the crew, and you've found a beautiful belief, but we all have to leave Knossos, or we will fail. All of us. As soon as possible after we jump these bulls we must go. It's important."

"I know," she says, with a smile. "It's okay. I will come back with you. After the past month, I know I will always have a connection with the goddess wherever I am. Just don't get killed tomorrow."

Rosa is watching us talk with her own little smile, which disappears when she hears Elodie's last request.

"We'll be careful," I promise.

*

In the bull pit with us are the High Priestess's jump crew: three women, and two men, one of who is Iomas. Further along the pit wall there's the young Tau al-Gorz and his crew, four men and one woman. Their crews are in huddles. Also, near the two stone arches that form exits, stand support people. Heloise is on the field at our end ready with jugs of fresh beer and first aid – bandages and stuff. She's our only support. The other crews have several.

Clearly the people of Knossos love their rituals, spectacles and festivals. The crowd keeps building and people jostle each other to get the best vantage points to watch the jumpers. I wave to Rosa to reassure her. She waves back. Elodie and Yusif are now beside her. Elodie smiles as if she wants to be on the bull-floor with us. Yusif looks despondent.

I copy Sukki and her acrobatics and stand on my hands and take a little walk on the granular hot sand, just for a stretch. Chaz and I have always been fans of gymnastics, but we'd never been that attentive to technique – a couple of crazy untrained show-offs who risk breaking their necks. That was us. We could leap and maneuver ourselves easily over the vaulting horse or the parallel bars. At the gym though, there were thick mats in case we crashed out. Here there are no mats. And pairs of long sharp bull horns between us and the ground. For this ceremony the other team members are obliged to catch their bull vaulters, or at least impede their accelerated descent.

Sukki is slight, so she'll be catchable, but Chaz and I are big men.

Then the music stops. The Minos and his retinue arrive and sit on their podium close to the High Priestess. Neither acknowledges the other. The Minos waves his hand and the excited crowd hushes. His official cryer stands to say: "The straws have been drawn. Champions of Aria, High Priestess of the Great Goddess who is mother of Theus, will leap the first of his bulls." I'm relieved – we can watch theory being put into practice before we have to jump.

The first bull is released into the ring. A man and a woman stand before the beast and call it in, waving their arms, and the bull focuses. It snorts and briskly trots further into the jumping area. Another man slips behind the bull, and our friend Iomas, wearing only his tiny loincloth, moves directly in front. He has a magnificent physique, muscles popping everywhere.

The two callers move a little further out of the way. No-one is really going out of their way to taunt the animal – rather, they call it over it so that the Minos, his queen, the High Priestess and special guest Rosa can view proceedings easily.

The crowd starts clapping in unison along with the drumbeat and Iomas starts sprinting and before the bull catches his eye, Iomas dives over its head, without touching the horns and, with his hands uses the beast's shoulders as a springboard to flip over the other side as the huge bull passes underneath. It's a beautiful athletic feat. The man behind the bull catches him as he made an almost perfect vertical landing. Within moments one of the lesser priestesses, who is minimally clad in a band of cloth holding her breasts and a tiny strip of cloth around her hips and thighs, sprints at the beast and it seems her mane of dark hair becomes wings which lift her over the bull – she doesn't even touch the beast, but folds herself into a spinning ball and then she too lands safe on two feet, held by Iomas. They both turn and the first catcher has looped in front of the animal and runs – by now the animal is somewhat aggrieved and it switches its horns in an angle and starts to accelerate forward at a trot, but the third jumper, another priestess, reads the beast's move and lifts over the lower right horn, landing her palms on the bull's back much like Iomas. She alights with some acceleration, but is caught through the elbows by the first woman and Iomas, and though the bull has a kick out with its back legs and starts turning to go after its tormentors, it's over and the crowd is impressed.

They cheer and some wave little flags. The droners and drummers create a celebratory racket, those on the brass drone-pipes puffing their cheeks and creating bursts of sound on top of the sub-harmony.

Pretty Xeniu is right.

"Guys, that was textbook," I say to Chaz and Sukki. "Quick turn-arounds and speed between the jumps is the key. Be ready to jump as soon as the other person lands – before the bull knows what's happening." Sukki nods sharply (she's going first). Chaz says "got it."

As I'm talking, men with poles rebuff the huffing bull and prod it back up the ramp toward ritual slaughter.

The Minos cryer stands in his long robes and shouts in a deep bellow, "And now, the champions of Ro Sa Som Burly, The Judge!"

We are on. We fist-bump one another. Not having bull callers, as the first team did, Sukki and I (I'm to jump second) have to call in the new bull, a beautiful brown animal with some white patches and magnificent horizontal horns. We call out and the beast switches its head from one side to another until it is focused on us. Chaz stands behind as per the plan. Chaz is big and hard-muscled. I have total confidence in him, and also in Sukki's remarkable skills. As for me, I'm crapping myself. I am a fake gymnast.

Sukki first. The clapping starts again in time with the drums. She's featherweight, in her undies and sports bra. The more naked you are, the better, Xeniu had told me, "As we are all of nature … and there's less cloth to get caught in the horns." A practical hint, there. My little loincloth is almost not there and I feel the hot sand between my toes.

Sukki grins from ear to ear in excitement, and turns and winks at me before she faces her monster. Sukki, I understood, was fearless. Or maybe filled with courage, because Rosa watches on. Perhaps Rosa has the power to inspire?

A vertical leap to start her run and arms and legs pumping, Sukki launches across the bull, and it's over in a flash. A somersault with a featherlight connection, fingertips on the beasts back, flinging her over, onto her feet and into Chaz who holds her with a delighted laugh. He gives

her a big bear hug and she waves to the whooping and cheering crowd –
obviously they love a good mystical clearance.

Now me. I angle in front of the bull that, basically, hadn't noticed Sukki
at all – except as a blur and a breeze. The beast sees me though. We eye
each other and I'm somehow drawn into its mind and instincts. I'm saying
to myself just go! But I feel its resentment, and belief in its strength. I try
to calm the beast with my mind, persuade the beautiful creature that I'll
inconvenience it for only a couple of seconds. But bulls are bullish, and I
can see my pleas are futile. The beast even paws the ground. Snorts. I've
taken too long.

I trot back a few steps as it lumbers toward me ... 800 kilograms or so
of auroch. I have only urbex instincts and my body mass to work with. I
mutter, "This is for you, Rosa," and run as though I was going to complete
a high jump. Adrenaline drenches me as I vault across the bull's big head
and stretch out to its shoulders for a flying handstand, one eye on the
thick yellow horns. A handstand will clear it, and acceleration will do the
rest. But the bull jerks its head round to watch me, and its horn tip flicks
up toward its tormentor – maybe it picks me as a novice. I swerve and
bend midair, and only land one hand on its spine and somehow twist off,
but not cleanly, only enough to avoid the sharp sideways horn. I hear the
crowd vent a loud *"ooooh"* as they see the bull's attempt to gore my leg
and I suddenly realize this whole thing was stinking dangerous. I land in
something of a somersault and miraculously flip to a standing position.
The crowd likes that, but when I crash into Sukki and we both fall to the
ground there is muffled laughter.

"Sorry, Sukki," I say to her as she lay pinned under me, her face against
my shoulder. I feel blood trickling down my leg, leap off her and she stands
quickly.

"That's okay – it got your leg!"

"I know," I say. "I think it's a scratch though." We brush ourselves down, getting rid of the sand that's stuck to our sweaty skin. The bull starts to dance around and view us, but Chaz has already positioned himself in front of the now quite angry beast.

"Oi, bull!" he shouts. "I'm here."

The bull shakes its head from side to side, confused, in the middle of the noise and action.

I hear the crowd chant "E-gyp-tian! E-gyp-tian!"

Sukki and I are poised, ready to catch Chaz's 90 kilos of muscle. I feel blood trickling down my leg, but I'm too focused to look down. Chaz's run is indeed textbook. Or text-fresco. A long sprint up, eyes fixed on the bull's back, I hear his grunt as he leaps and upends, legs straight up in the air, both hands pressed on the animal's shoulders as the bull charges under him, and he flexes his elbows to power a most amazing flip onto his feet. An upright stop, Neither I nor Sukki are needed as catchers, fortunately. The crowd cheers wildly and over in the stands I see the Minos nod approval and Rosa blow out a held breath.

The bull turns and sees us, but decides against further action as men arrive to prod it away with sticks.

The Judge's champions have vindicated her position as an important entity up there on the podium, and another bull is vanquished.

We trot over to where Rosa and the rest of the crew are seated and give her a champion's wave. Rosa waves lamely back, shrinking into her voluminous red cushion. I can see she isn't enjoying her godlike fame. Elodie grins madly at us. The Minos catches my eye and nods again.

We get out of the way as priestesses and cowherds maneuver our rather confused bull out of the ring toward its inevitable sacrifice. The cryer stands and bellows: "By order of the straws, the final team, the champions of the Minos."

Young Prince Minos and his retinue hit the center of the bull pit and bow to the Minos, while we slug fresh beer and rinse the taste of dust and bull sweat from our mouths. I sit against the wall while Heloise wipes the gash on my leg with a wet rag, but luckily it's a deep scratch more than anything worse. Heloise tuts and mutters something about serious risk-taking. I can she she's suddenly displeased with our jumping venture. She washes it clean with some form of stinging grappa the priestesses gave her and plasters it with a honey poultice and a cotton bandage. Bull horns aren't the cleanest of items. Heloise hands me the last of the grappa in a jug. I swig the wine.

"That was risky," she says, looking me in the eye. "Risky, but amazing."

"Chaz and Sukki were amazing. I was the klutz."

"No!" she says. "You did this amazing twist to avoid the point of the horn. I don't think anyone would mark you down for that. But in hindsight, why put yourself in that position when you've never worked with a bull. Still, you did well."

"You're too kind. I flattened poor Sukki."

"Would take a lot more than you to flatten me," laughs Sukki as she leans against the barrier wall, arms folded, watching team three, now with extreme professional interest.

Rosa is perched forward now, the first time she's seen the young Tau al-Gorz. The prince looks up at her searching stare and nods a greeting, and she nods back with an unreadable expression on her face.

Young Prince Minos and his team are warrior class, so they're really fit and agile. Fighters who train and practice for the bull leaps.

Their bull is a big black monster as befitting warriors although it seems pretty docile for the first guy, who goes over extending just one pivoting hand like a show-off. He does a Chaz landing too, needing no catchers. After this indignity the bull sparks up a bit though and wheels round looking for the jumper. The second jumper is a tall woman, Myrina the Lydian, who wears a short kilt, breasts strapped with a cloth band, bedazzling in gold bracelets and a mane of red hair. I know she's a warrior because her physique was super strong. She is also, as palace gossip has it, the prince's lover.

She calls it out, clapping: "Hey, bull – over here, big boy", and the bull refocuses, finding its tormentor. It takes two or three steps toward her working itself into a run, but she charges too, and is over the beast before it knows it, but instead of a flip, she jumps almost two meters high over the dangerous horns, one foot on the shoulder, a second on the rump and a running jump from its rear end. What's impressive is the reach of her first leap over the bull's head as it charges her. And what really fires up the bull, just in time for the prince's turn, is the kick in the rump as she dismounts. By now the bull is wheeling round, looking for its tormentors, hoofing the sand angrily.

It's Heloise, leaning against the wall beside me, who says, "This isn't good." The beast is about 50 meters away, but she looks frightened as it thrashes angrily.

A couple of Prince Minos' retainers clap and wave to bring it round toward their master, who is stripped down except for a loincloth. The bull charges one of the retainers before he can step out of the way and is headbutted to the ground and trampled. The other retainer bravely pulls the man out of the way as the bull passes. Then the snorting beast focuses on the prince himself – he's in the middle of the pit, his back to us. His team members run to position themselves behind the rampaging animal.

"Hoi," shouts the prince, "you are mine!" The bull turns to face him and I can see confusion and anger in the beast's eyes. The prince, a mighty figure of sweaty muscularity, beats his chest with his fist. Prince Minos would look weak if he doesn't jump the angry beast. He prepares for the double-handed flip off the shoulders and starts his run, but the bull has other ideas and pulls up short as it sees the prince pelting toward him.

Without any time to adjust his leap the prince flies smack bang into the bull's turning horn, gored through the stomach, pinioned. His blood sprays into the air as the bull tosses its head sharply, and the prince's body barrel-rolls off the back of the bull into the dirt with a dull thud. I've never seen anything more sickening.

Then mayhem. The crowd screams, an eerie wail of mass anguish. This was not what should happen, their prince gored. Then the blood-crazed bull slews to one side of the pit and crashes into a man who is leaning against the wall, and who sags to the ground as the bull spots our group at the end of the run next to the slipway, and comes charging toward us, enraged, violent, and mad, its right horn stained and dripping with Tau al-Gorz's blood.

Before we have time to move, a small figure lands in front of us from the wall behind, and raises her hand at the bull and says, "Stop". And the bull stops in its tracks and starts to back off. Rosa advances slowly, hand up. The bull snorts once, and retreats. The crowd hardly breathes.

"Calm," she says. "Not your fault. These people. Did this. To you." The bull trembles from the panic and adrenaline running through it like a freight train. "Slow, slow, slow," she says. "Stop!" And the bull ceases moving and is frozen to the spot. Then Rosa, Heloise and I run across to Tau al-Gorz, who lies flat on his back in the dirt.

The young prince is surrounded by retainers and his team, but Rosa burrows her way in between Myrina and a couple of men trying to pour beer into the prone man's mouth. They move out of Rosa's way.

"Dead," she says to me, eyes flashing angrily. Then she says: "So, THIS is why we are here!" And more loudly, "NOT FAIR!"

Blood flows from the deep gash in the young prince's stomach. His mouth hangs slack, unswallowed beer dribbling out. The bull's horn has pierced his organs along with arteries and he's bleeding out. Rosa's golden eyes glow like a fire being fanned. The sound of the crowd recedes as I watch her – she glances at me once again, an almost pleading look, and then puts her palm gently on the wound. Tau doesn't move except for his closed eyelids, which start to quiver as if he is having an active dream. Slowly, slowly, the wound starts healing. Around me, time is paused, the crowd behind and gathered fighters hushed and still. The Prince groans, his torso shudders and his arm moves – Rosa is monumentally silent, concentrating, channeling whatever Elemental pressure and bioelectric force she is creating into the skin as it knits. The blood disappears around the narrowing gash, and then it's over.

She stands, wipes her hands on her Minoan kilt, leaving a red stain.

"He's lost blood," Rosa says to the tall woman. "Make sure he drinks, and rests. And eats when he can." Then she looks at me in consternation. After bringing Tau al-Gorz's life force back into play, Rosa is drained and tired, her skin a little pale, hands shaking slightly.

"Oh, dear," she murmurs.

I desperately want to know whether Tau's eyes had changed color to that of a crocodile, but then I remember his beady black eyes staring at the chessboard on that fateful day in the Hall of Justice 4000 or so years from now and realize they hadn't changed over those years. Rosa is a different Elemental to the Caiman and this, a different occasion. Most likely, different side-effect.

The Minos has jumped down the two meter wall and he strides to our huddle around the fallen Tau al-Gorz. He's flanked by his retinue, and we move to let him tower over his son, casting a sharp shadow. He looks like a force of nature, and he rubs his voluminous beard.

"The Judge brought him back to life, highness," said Myrina, looking up, while Tau splutters over the beer being dripped down his mouth. The Minos nods briefly at the woman's words. He then looked at his son and looks at Rosa and says, "Thank you for sparing my son's life, Judge. His leap showed weakness, and now he can ... consider and learn, rather than be eaten by the Great Goddess's foul worms."

Rosa regards the king and says, "This had to be. In return, spare that bull. He was not at fault."

"That is all you want as a reward?" The Minos is astonished.

"That's not a reward," she says simply. "It's a matter of life and death."

"But we need three bulls for the ceremony," says a minion.

"Slaughter another one," snaps the Minos. "The bull that killed my son shall live to remind him of his weakness and failure."

"Wouldn't be fair to kill that bull," says Rosa quietly, to me. "Wasn't the bull's fault. The beast pulled back, startled by Tau's charge." I had to agree. She's still The Judge.

Somehow, Rosa and Tau al-Gorz are connected in a vast loop across four millennia. How and why, I can't understand, but because Tau died and lived, Rosa died and lived.

I stare up at the crowd, hundreds of people craning their necks as Tau al-Gorz is finally hauled from the ground by Myrina and Iomas and limps off to his retinue.

Having seen him gored, the prince's departure provokes a mixed response from the onlookers. Some people cheer, others stare in silence at the man's chest, where there had been a horrendous wound but now nothing. Many eyes are fixed on The Judge as well, and she knows it.

We walk off through the ramped alleyway, out of the pit. The people in the stands and the alleyway gesture in supplication to Rosa, arms in the air.

Others kneeling. Rosa tried to look important and grateful, but is not very good at it. Instead, she looks embarrassed.

"We need to leave here now," she mutters to me. "This is wrong. The polarity here is between the Minos and the goddess, and I can't become part of it. You understand that?"

I understand very well that this is Elemental, and Rosa had done something miraculous to the king's son, just as Caiman had done to her. She can't replace either the Minos or the goddess in the mix though. Somehow she just needed to be here in this moment, to ensure that Tau al-Gorz lived. I wasn't even sure that such life-force revival was a duty of The Judge.

"Also, I want to go home," said Rosa, "And play Monopoly with Lionel."

I looked down at her. "We can go now, can't we?"

"I think so. We should tell everyone." I turn and watch the crew straggling behind in the walkway, talking about what happened. But not just the crew. Elodie is talking animatedly to Myrina the Lydian and Iomas. Sukki is laughing with two of Tau al-Gorz's warriors, tiny between Minoan statues. Chaz and Heloise are talking, too, to another priestess. Yusif follows at the end, sullen and alone.

We are forming relationships. We are becoming community in the wrong place.

We have to go.

*

Rosa and I looked at one another as our procession entered an elaborate outdoor colonnade. I could suddenly feel the same lurch in my being I'd felt when we'd dissolved around the dining table into the past. I turned and waited for Chaz and Heloise who were walking, smiling, together.

I shout to them. "We're going back to the house now. Just decide to leave, picture the house and ..." I could see the effervescence of time start to form around me. Those opaque bubbles. Chaz nodded and held Heloise's hand and I looked further back at the rest of the crew. "We must go home!" I shout again, Rosa's hand in mine. I lift our hands to suggest they, too, hold on.

Behind us Elodie, Sukki and Yusif see what's happening. Elodie looks sad while Sukki's face is devastated. I see Elodie talk to Sukki, who shakes her head vigorously, and Elodie says something back, animatedly. They are having a heated conversation when an unconsciousness overwhelms me.

Not this time was it the pleasant, effervescent, free-form bubble travel. I'm out cold.

*

I feel hard stone under my back and through my closed eyes, there's no sense of light – it's pitch dark with a cold, dry smell. Then I hear the tinkling of glass.

Glass! I hadn't heard or seen glass in weeks and weeks.

Carefully, I open an eye. Beside me was a sweetly sleeping Rosa (thank goodness) and I see the elegant arm and hand of Heloise Simply flopped beyond Rosa's head.

"Tea, Benji?"

Mrs Cimbalom in her red scarf looms above me, with a brass tray and glasses, like some bizarre flight attendant. I close my eyes again. A mirage?

"Oh, Madam Cimbalom ..." I say. "it's been a long time."

"Take your time, Mr Benji."

I am still dressed only in the small loincloth round my waist and a woven leather wristband, and feel slightly embarrassed. Still, I adjust the cloth to a modest angle and sit up and dear Mrs Cimbalom hands me a Turkish tea cup filled with the most aromatic tea I've ever smelt, fruity and warm. To my left, Chaz, also unconscious. No Elodie. No Sukki. No Yusif. I sip the tea and am instantly awake.

It is obvious, now – we are in the cellar of The Judge's house, on the big stone slab. Light spills from an open door, one of the strange locked metal doors in the basement wall that I'd spotted months ago and through it I see some red froufrou. Clearly, an entrance to Mrs Cimbalom's flat. Of course, her flat is a basement structure. Mrs Cimbalom looks concerned and relieved at the same time. Lashings of red lipstick, her dark pupils twinkle.

"Did The Judge go well?"

"She was awesome ... Elodie? Sukki? Yusif? Have they arrived."

I can't see them on the big slab. My heart is sinking.

"Maybe later," Mrs Cimbalom says with a doubtful *moue* of her lips.

"All the girls are acolytes ... of the great goddess. Except Rosa," I add.

"Let's wake the others, and you can tell me about it," Mrs Cimbalom says.

I poke Rosa gently with my finger.

"Hey, Judge, wake up," I say.

*

We recover in the downstairs lounge with its comfy chairs and couches – me, Chaz, Heloise and Rosa. The recovery takes a few hours of napping, cold and hot drinks, and Mrs Cimbalom's sandwiches. I'm pleased to see Rosa is equally as affected by the journey – she is just quiet and cute.

As Chaz and I had arrived on the slate slab in our bull-jumping state of minimal clothing, Mrs Cimbalom brought us wooly dressing gowns from the collection, pajamas for Rosa and a kimono for Heloise. She also patched up my leg which had started bleeding again and dresses it with goo from the purple first-aid kit. Rosa disappeared to change out of the bloodstained kilt and is back on the couch in warm pajamas.

So we just lie on cushions and get used to the diffuse light coming through the window, filtered by new-growth leaves on the tree outside also celebrating the arrival of spring.

"This is like the worst ever jet lag," I eventually groan.

Chaz says, "What you get from extreme time tourism."

Rosa says, "It's more than just tourism. I set something in place with Tau al-Gorz, like an inexplicable chess move."

Heloise reaches out to pull a small bronze tau from the bag she always carries.

"You stole it?" asks Rosa.

"*I* didn't. Chaz did," says Heloise.

He can't tell a lie in the house, of course, and says, "It was lying on one of the walls at a votive ceremony. They threw it into a crack in a rock and it got stuck. I like the little cows, I thought we might need one. Surely it could be a path back if we need to go."

Rosa looks unconvinced.

Chaz looks at Rosa his eyes shining and continued: "That journey you took us on, that was a blast."

"I'd say it was ... wonderful," agrees Heloise.

"Wasn't sure about much when we first arrived," Chaz continues, stretched out on a couch, gesticulating at the ceiling, "but those people we met. What they did. Iomas, Aria, the Minos, and his peeps. Seemed like a simple life they had farming, and all those ceremonies all the time, and then I realized it was *so complicated*."

"Being there, I found some answers to my own life," says Heloise, "and I've many more questions."

Rosa looks at Chaz and Heloise carefully. "First impressions are good, but you must try and see the whole picture before you make a judgment."

"I got first impressions and second impressions," says Chaz enthusiastically. "I'm getting to my judgment, Miss Rosa Cat's-eyes."

"And I could write a great book on the Minoans …. but I can't really cite personal experience as the source," Heloise adds with a smile.

"Stay here tonight, you two," I say to Heloise and Chaz. "We'll do up the top bedroom and we can take turns checking that others arrive safe."

*

But Sukki, Yusif and Elodie fail to materialize over the course of the night. Clearly, you have to want to return to materialize, and for some reason they hadn't yet decided to leave Knossos. I promise Chaz and Heloise I'll check the pathway slab downstairs regularly and let them know if anyone turns up.

CONSEQUENCES

T he pen.

I gave Yusif a pen once, a present for teaching me the art of deep reading, and that's how I knew he'd returned. A week went by, then I find the small black microball on the basement slab. Yusif and no doubt Sukki had effervesced back during the night then sneaked out the front door and left silently in the dark. Yusif didn't want to face me. Or perhaps Sukki didn't want to talk? No, Sukki was always up for a chat. Yusif had gone. Why did he return my gift? To sever our friendship? My stomach lurches.

Worse than the rejected pen, I also know that if Elodie had arrived with them, she'd have woken me or Rosa. Her absence upsets me even more, and over the next few days I become frantic.

*

I ignore the crude symbolism of the pen and catch up with Sukki and Yusif a couple of weeks later. After failing to find a trace of them in any of the old haunts, Mrs Cimbalom gently suggests I go to Gilberto's. It is a small boutique jewelry shop downtown where I find beautiful beaten-gold snake earrings, exactly like the ones Sukki, Heloise and Elodie wore in the devotional ceremonies, when they fell into their trances and their faces were suffused with love for the High Priestess. Then, Sukki's eyes were alive and bright.

But when I find Sukki (her address came from the jewelry shop's owner) she really does look flattened. Squashed and miserable, living in a little fourth-story unit with a tiny kitchen. Yusif is a shell. He can't even speak, his eyes are deadened and he sits staring at his fingers.

At least she makes me a cup of tea.

"Why didn't Elodie come back with you both?" I ask.

"Benji, it's true. I loved everything in Knossos. I wanted to stay … and after you disappeared in front of our faces, I felt brave, being there with Elodie, although she was telling me again and again that we should leave too. We had an argument that I won … for a while. I wanted to stay forever in the palace. But everything was overwhelming. Then one night he," she points at Yusif, "was crying like a confused baby. I was tired, he couldn't sleep. But Yusif would not return without me. He'd never do that, and staying in Knossos was killing him. I held him and listened to his wailing and it just broke my resolve. I decided okay, we'll go. I was heartbroken. And we woke in your house in the dark. I was so disappointed, I lay on the rock downstairs and couldn't face anyone, and Yusif only wanted to escape into the street and run as far from your house as possible. He's shattered."

"And you didn't tell Elodie you were leaving?"

"When you decide to leave, it just happens. I had no time to tell her. To be honest, I wanted stay at the temple serving the goddess and learning everything from the High Priestess and," Sukki says, bent over her workbench making intricate jewelry based on the Minoan patterning of dots and abstract ocean waves across bright silver, "I am serving her now, but it is not the same."

"It's just a religion," I try.

"No," retorts Sukki angrily. "This is being ... as close to the natural world as humans can be. You know that ... you know how the ceremonies connect with the earth and its cycles. You know your place in the scheme of things, where you come from, where you will eventually go. You know the stars whirl around you for a short lifetime, but also forever."

I nod. I know.

"I feel this in every fiber of my being," Sukki goes on. "The elements, my ancestors, the life around me, the sea, the earth, the air. Can't I go back?"

"I don't know."

Yusif sits at the end of the table and makes a strangled noise and looks terrified. His hair is matted. He is acting like a madman. But he can't speak. He just keeps tapping the tabletop in a scattered pattern with his fingertips.

"He's on strong anti-depressants," Sukki says. "They don't really work. He doesn't talk to me, to anyone, but he panics if I leave the room. I take care of him ... but I don't really know what to do beyond that."

She sounds so sad. I tell them to come for dinner, but Yusif shakes his head vigorously. The Judge's house terrifies him and I know they'll never turn up.

And I was now desperate about Elodie. She promised to return with me. Sukki and Yusif abandoned her, in the past. Where was she?

*

After Rosa hears middle-of-the-night noises upstairs, she shakes me awake and we cautiously walk up the short flight of stairs to the Hall of Justice. It's 3 a.m. in the morning, no sign of streaky dawn light yet.

And there he sits in dull lamplight, a large figure, slumped on a chair in the gloom: the Bull, the Sweeper of Change, Rosa's murderer, prince of the Minos, Tau al-Gorz.

Tau al-Gorz sits where I'd first seen him, in the attic room armchair. Still with dank black hair, wearing a voluminous, dirty, brown robe, front sliding open to reveal his saggy grey skin, somehow incorporating Giddley and Siddley, his freeloading trolls. Almost a year back, he'd been immolated by Rosa's father. This night, a week after my visit to Sukki, the ogre sits shamefaced.

Rosa welcomes him, but her voice sounds dry and strained, and she watches Siddley nervously. "You know Caiman still craves justice for her rivers and forests," she says. "When the time comes, she will bring her case here. Is this why you've come?"

"Pffft, no. Not this time," grumbles Tau al-Gorz. "I know Caiman is my enemy. She never stops trying to halt my projects, my opportunities, my progress ... she never leaves me be ... I will ultimately defeat her, in a just manner, when she finally brings one of her spurious cases to you, Judge. But no, this is not about Caiman." And then there's silence. Silence and brooding observation – of Rosa and me. The silence filled with a menacing energy that reminded me of the night I'd hidden behind the curtains over in the corner, just before I bore witness to Rosa's murder.

We quietly regard each other for some minutes, enough light in the room to read one another's faces, Tau al-Gorz' hard eyes, Siddley and Giddley as tattoos, immobile, staring out.

"I remember now," he finally croaks in his deep rumble, "I remember you in the bull-jumping pit."

But he doesn't point at Rosa. He points at me.

"You were there."

I nod.

"In front of my father, the Minos. You did a half-decent jump over that brown one."

I nod again.

He points at Rosa. "And then she brought me back from death, didn't she? Reversed Charon's boat over the Styx and tipped me back onto the shores of the living?" Asking me. Maybe he found it tricky asking the child he'd murdered, about his own life-after-death.

I nodded.

Tau al-Gorz has caused much destruction since that day, almost 4000 years ago, but his face is stricken as he pieces together this very distant memory. The bull's horn, clean through him. The humiliation of the goring, and the brutal sarcasm of his father, all those millennia ago, the crowd hushed by the death of their prince by the black bull's horn. That's what he remembers.

And after waking, he remembers me standing over him, shading his face from the Aegean sun, and remembers Rosa wiping her bloodied hands on her kilt, and then Myrina, the red headed Scythian woman, and Iomas picking him off the sand, and his team dragging him across to his retinue.

Here in this time in the Hall of Justice, Tau al-Gorz is the old, mature Elemental. On his saggy chest is a kinetic tableaux: Siddley (the evil one), crouches with his arm over his face, for this minute rejected by his master, while Giddley, his good conscience, listens carefully, finger curled under her chin. They are both impersonating colorful tattoos.

Instead of her lurid disco-queen jumpsuit, Giddley wears a dirty little kimono covered in magnolias. Her forearm is bruised and she stares outward with her golden eyes, just like Rosa's.

"That was when we met, father," says Giddley. "In the bull pit."

"That was when you arrived within me, Giddley," says Tau al-Gorz. "I was pierced by the power of the black bull, and then the Judge placed her hands on me and brought you forth."

"I'd not yet projected into the world," Giddley says.

"You were a seed. My calming one. The Judge found you in me."

Rosa stares at Giddley, perturbed by her role in the fiasco. "Not really my job," she mutters. "It just happened."

Tau al-Gorz looks at Rosa in an almost fatherly way. "There's no such thing as coincidence, child."

"Siddley tried to stop us coming to Knossos," Rosa says. "He murdered a man."

"As Siddley would. He hates his sister," said the ogre with ominous calm. "Without your champions arriving on the scene, I'd have jumped a different bull. The brown one! There would have been no accident, and I would have gone through life with only Siddley. And what a total wasteland the world would be!" Tau al-Gorz then smiled at the thought, a horrible grin.

"I can hear you all," says Siddley, head still shaded by his arm. "That Judge spoilt it for us both, father. I remembered those two from back in the old time, so I tried to stop the meddling Judge coming back and creating HER."

Pointy teeth in a jealous snarl, Siddley unleashes and takes a swipe at Giddley, who dodges out of the way.

"SILENCE!" shouts Tau al-Gorz. "I know exactly what you tried to prevent, SIDDLEY!"

"You killed her once!" shrieks Siddley pointing at Rosa. "She should have been left for dead!"

"SILENCE!"

As Tau al-Gorz yells at his bad conscience, the friarbird, perched on a windowsill, shrieks *Oichh!* for added effect.

Siddley sneers at us and then lifts his tatty sleeve, covering his face again, turning into a tattoo.

"So that's how it worked out," I gasp. "Giddley was created when you brought Tau al-Gorz back to life. That's why she has your eyes!"

"Siddley was balanced by Giddley," Rosa says. "But honestly, I had no idea."

"Balance is a difficult thing," says Tau al-Gorz.

Rosa smiles. "But balance is wonderful when you achieve it. When you stand on your hands, swinging over a raging bull, or when all things are equal."

"I try."

"I know you do, Tau al-Gorz," Rosa says.

Best to encourage the ogre to love his good conscience when he's in a meditative mood.

Tau al-Gorz then looks at me, with his beady dark eyes buried in mounds of wrinkles. "I'm sorry about your friend. The one that came to Conosos with you and who stayed behind," he says.

"Who?"

"That fair-haired woman who stayed to tend the goddess back then."

Given I'd only seen Elodie a few weeks ago, and was worried sick, I shake my head.

"I'm waiting for her to return, like all the others have."

"What was her name? She, your friend, will not come back," Tau al-Gorz says. "She stayed in Conosos for many years, but later died in an earthquake, in a temple south of the island. She was the temple's guardian, a very old woman, who lived a quiet, chaste life. I tried many times in her youth to romance her, but she wouldn't have me. She told me that men could never be trusted, and she'd been hurt once too often. Which is true, isn't it?" Tau al-Gorz looks at me searchingly.

I inhale sharply. I feel sick. Rosa looks upset.

"She was wedded to the goddess," Tau al-Gorz says simply.

"We're sorry," says Giddley, aware of my anguish. Siddley peeks out behind his arm looking pleased at my sudden discomfort.

My Elodie, gone. Wedded to someone else – an Elemental. No need for me to wait now. Her fate was never written, but was blurted out by Tau al-Gorz. I think he was trying to be helpful, but tears started to stream down my face. Tau al-Gorz suddenly looked uncomfortable.

"I'll go, Judge. I have many projects and much to achieve. I didn't realize you'd healed me in that bull pit until I remembered his face," says Tau al-Gorz pointing at me again. "I came to confirm that memory."

The ogre heaves himself from the armchair, and squeezes through a French door onto the roof garden in a gust of stale air and decay.

I'm weeping now. Rosa is not sure what to do, but she too is upset. We'd both hoped Elodie would return, as she'd become something of a confidante to Rosa too. Rosa put her hand on my arm to try and steady me – as a friend.

"It's okay. I'll be myself in a minute," I say.

"I'll make tea," she says.

"You did warn that going back would involve consequences."

Then, The Judge's house drew a kernel of truth out of me, as I look at Rosa's sweet face. "I almost cheated on Elodie that night before the bull jumping. I fell for the junior priestess, Xeniu, momentarily. I don't know why. But I didn't cheat. We kissed, yes, and I felt for a moment I loved her, but I realized doing something like that was another human folly. I knew nothing about her except that she was beautiful and kind, but I was being disloyal in the wrong place, wrong time. I searched for Elodie and told her I loved her. I was loyal. She said she'd return with me."

Rosa nods and looks at me sadly.

"Maybe after we left, Elodie found out from Xeniu, and thought the worst?" I add.

"I'll make some tea," she says again, and she heads downstairs, leaving me to my misery.

*

After that meeting, which lasted into the early morning, my worry suddenly expanded into full panic and I ran out the front door, and through the little iron gate on the street, down Madam Cimbalom's steps, and rang her front doorbell which jingles like a normal doorbell.

She opened the door in a waft of Chanel No. 5, and I blurt, "Did Elodie die in an earthquake? Is she really dead?"

Madam Cimbalom waves me into her flat with a look of glee. Miloš, the Prague ratter, stares up at me with his ogo-pogo eyes, but stays mute. In her narrow hallway, there's a cabinet with trophies in it.

"My late husband's. He was a magnificent archer. Now, if you sit in the parlor, I'll make some breakfast tea and then we can cast the greegrees!" She sounds very excited.

I note that some of her archery husband's trophies went back to championships in 1811 which makes my head swim a bit. And there was an ancient, brown, Greek pot featuring an archer, with a pointy beard, drawing his bow. And a large gold medallion which looked worn with time, a similar bearded archer imprinted on it. Can Madam C be that old? Or was she a child bride? Down the corridor I could see the kitchen beyond, and a closed door which I expected was her boudoir, because you'd expect Madam Cimbalom to have a boudoir instead of a bedroom.

Her parlor is cozy, with a crackling fireplace.

"Be seated," she says to me at the coffee table. I sink into a high backed Windsor chair. Miloš, the Prague ratter, bounces onto the couch and is told sternly to get down and sit in his basket, and I think I hear a grumble as he curls up. Madam Cimbalom sits in the opposite chair and pulls out her little velvet bag from her skirt. She handed me the greegrees: the triangular dice, the hazel twig, the shriveled mouse, the finger bones, the emerald and the black onyx.

"Isn't this fun!" Madam Cimbalom adds.

I put the collections of items in my palm and throw them on the table gently so they won't skitter off the edge and she stretches over to have a look.

"Not getting much signal from that throw, Mr Benji! Pick zem up again and throw properly! Remember, she's a long way away, in a long time ago. Best shot!"

I threw the greegrees with some force. The desiccated mouse's head bounces off the table and ricochets off the bronze fireguard and lands on the windowsill. The finger bone lands in Madam C's teacup, the twig in her saucer, and the gems and dice remain on the coffee table. One triangular dice reveals a picture of a half-moon, and the other a spider.

"Better. Yes. As we speak, she is still alive in the Bronze Age," she points to the bronze fireguard, "and looking for something." She pointed at the mouse head staring out the window. "She is well fed," she points at the spider, "but she is confused. The half-moon shows that she is halfway through a cycle – possibly a journey. And the bone in the tea says she is in a body of water, while the hazel twig in the saucer says she's beside the water. At a beach on an island, perhaps?"

I sit back and sigh in relief, and though the reading sounds really, really, hokey – especially the Bronze Age fireguard bit – I trust her.

"Does this reading mean Elodie's true lifespan is continued in now time, rather than the Bronze Age time?" I ask. "Because, surely, if she'd been crushed in an earthquake, the bone would have said something else. Snapped in two, perhaps?" At least that's what I hoped.

"Take it as you find it," Madam Cimbalom says gently and sympathetically.

"Well, your surname is Fortune," I say.

"Ah, that's my married name," she answers mysteriously. "I once married a Mr Fortune."

"And your maiden name?"

"Ah, Mr Benji, I've forgotten. It's been a long time since I was a maiden."

I smile even though I feel depressed, again recalling my wrong-kiss with Xeniu.

"I saw you, in Knossos. I was about to do a stupid thing, and you appeared in my mind. To warn me, I think," I add.

"Did I warn you? Or did I remind you of something?"

"I took it as a warning."

"I have no recollection of being in your mind, Mr Benjamin," she says, a kind smile this time, without mockery. "I am sure you made the right decision without me."

THE CASE OF THE OILY PENGUIN

"Benji ... Benji. I really need your help. Cheer up, please!"

Rosa stands by my bed while I try to sink under the soft quilts forever. Where I've been sunk for several days. I want to bury myself deep into my misery. A forever wave of quilts. I want the bed to swallow me. I want to say, "Go away," to Rosa but can't. She looks too upset.

Instead I say, "Urgh."

"Caiman has finally brought the witnesses for her case against Tau al-Gorz. Like I told you yesterday! I can't do it without you!" Rosa starts to cry. "You have to help me. It's godmother's case. It's complicated. I can't think it through on my own. Please, Benji ..."

I slowly shuffle upright against a pillow. Last time I'd seen Rosa cry was the morning after her father died.

"I'm worried about you. Why are you always in bed?" she asks.

Rosa doesn't understand the human-folly-pain-continuum of the broken adult heart, but I realize she cares about me, which pulls me out of my selfish slump.

"I'm totally sad about Elodie," I say. "I'm sad that I'll never see her again. She's my girlfriend and she's still alive back then, whatever that means, and also maybe crushed in an earthquake." I gulp. "But you're right, I'm your Associate, and I must assist. So, Rosa, let me gather my thoughts."

"I'll make you a hot drink," she says with a relieved look, and disappears.

Yesterday, after a visit from the Caiman, Rosa talked to me about the case. After Caiman met with her, she'd sat by the bed while I'd mostly ignored her blather. I was depressed and there were so many cases. The Case of the Oily Penguin, she'd said. Something about a rig. Yesterday, her story went in one sad ear and out the other, but slowly, I remember the conversation.

Rosa returns with a mug of hot chocolate.

"Is the Oily Penguin here?" I finally ask.

"Yes."

"What time is it?" I ask.

"Midnight."

"What day?"

"Tuesday."

"Has Elodie come back?"

"No."

I know Rosa is almost as upset about Elodie as I am. Elodie is ... or was ... her confidante, especially in matters of Lionel relations and tail management. I was hopeless with all of that. Rosa had missed Elodie when she'd gone to Paris and was jubilant when she moved in with us. But now? It had been months and months of nothing. Mrs Cimbalom had hinted Elodie was still alive in ancient Crete. But if Tau al-Gorz was correct, she was never coming back – she'd been crushed in a falling temple.

If you want to travel up the pathway, you only need to decide it's time to leave, and you'll be effervesced home. Why didn't Elodie just come home? This fact drove me mad with sorrow.

I sit and take a deep breath, and slurp down the excellent hot chocolate. "Excuse me," I say heading to the wardrobe. I choose a particularly robe-like dressing gown with brown velvet cuffs, covered in golden golf clubs. Rosa is wearing her red pajamas.

"I'll just comb my hair before we meet the appellant," I say in a serious voice, trying to get into the legal spirit.

Upstairs we find two penguins, emperors, tall and stately with sleek, black back feathers, but shiny white in the breasts, and bright yellow beaks. Handsome creatures. The friarbird is attempting to converse with a series of *quarks* and *oichs* but they ignore him. If a penguin could look sad, they were looking very sad with their drooping beaks. They sadden me all over again.

"So you say there was a rig?" I begin.

"A rig," says a penguin.

"What's a rig, Benji?" Rosa asks.

"A floating platform used to drill into the seabed to explore for oil under earth's outer crust, Judge. How did the rig get to Antarctica?"

"The rig was built at Tau Base Delta in Coats Land, near our home, and they launched it last week," one penguin says.

"Terrifying," says the second penguin.

"We watched the ships arrive months ago in late winter and between storms they assembled it on the ice."

"And the ice melted and now it floats toward our peninsula. Where our babies are. To drill for oil where our babies are!" The second penguin is almost shrieking.

"And how did you get to the Judge's house?" I ask.

"The Caiman assisted us with the correct pathway," the first penguin says.

I look at Rosa.

"Oil and seabirds don't mix," I tell Rosa.

"But has a crime been committed? Has there been a spill? Has a penguin got oily?" she asks.

"The rig shouldn't be there. Antarctica is a protected place. Protected by the world," the penguin said.

But I scrolled on my smartphone and say, "I think you'll find Tau al-Gorz will have somehow persuaded countries to leave the treaty which protected the Antarctic. Hmmm. Here. Looks like several countries have dropped out of the big Antarctic Protection Treaty over the past two years using various excuses, and because not enough countries are signed up, the agreement to protect Antarctica is void."

"Voided," says penguin one.

"Voided," repeats the other sad penguin.

"So, let me understand. There is now no treaty protecting the Antarctic, but still no crime has been committed?" repeats Rosa.

"Well, there has been one," and the penguin ushers a fluffy baby from behind its back using a flipper. The penguin chick has grey downy feathers and a yellow beak and looks adorable. I smile for the first time in weeks. There were streaks of what looked like washed off oil down its back, but not enough to harm it.

"What actually happened to this fledgling?" Rosa asks. In the Judge's house, the penguin was unable to lie. "The chick tripped and fell into a puddle of oil spilled in the snow from a drum at Tau Base Delta."

"How big was the puddle?"

The penguin raised its flippers about a meter wide, but the house of truth-telling forced his flippers slowly in until they were 20 centimeters apart.

"Does that constitute an oil spill?"

The penguins can't answer. I look it up. An oil spill is, technically, the release of crude oil into water. Oil is lighter so it floats, sometimes in a centimeters thick band, and the feathers on birds on the surface of the water get slicked so they can't stay warm in the freezing water. In the Antarctic, a real spill would mean thousands of penguins would freeze to death very quickly, or drown.

"My baby was oiled!" says the sad penguin.

"Yes, but that's not quite the same as an oil spill," Rosa says. "Did you push the baby into the puddle?"

The penguin, with great mental effort, managed to keep its beak shut and ignore the question.

"We can't let an oil spill happen," shrieks the other bird.

"Would be a disaster," says the first penguin. "You don't know how fierce the wind gets in Antarctica. How crushing the ice can be. What are they doing putting a drilling rig in our bay?"

"How many oil spills have there been in the Antarctic?" Rosa asks.

She was being very logical.

The emperor penguin, which was almost as tall as her, looks Rosa directly in the eye.

"We've NEVER had one around our part of the world because there's *never* been oil drilling in the MOST HOSTILE ENVIRONMENT ON THE PLANET." The penguin's eyes flash with electricity and it snickers its beak in annoyance.

Rosa merely nodded. She'd got her answer.

"Can I borrow your phone, Benji, to text Lionel. I think we'll need his drone," she says.

*

Rosa looks up at the disc of the full moon and the moon looks as cold as I feel. The two penguins and the baby are patiently standing beside us.

Lionel is standing to one side looking gobsmacked and delighted at the same time, his first trip down the pathway. He is carrying his precious drone, the item Rosa wanted for her court visit. The drone is almost as big as Lionel.

"Antarctica," Lionel finally says in awe. "So cooold."

*

Earlier, after texting, Rosa confesses that she and Lionel were always sneaking into one another's houses. "We found a conduit that leads to Lionel's cellar, and we've been to-ing and fro-ing," she says.

Lionel was at ours within minutes after Rosa's text, carrying his drone. Apparently, he was still up wrestling with maths equations. I decide he can come, because it's just a reconnaissance mission and he was great in the Billeon incident. And I was ever the irresponsible adult.

"Don't you wake your household with all this to-ing and fro-ing?" I ask suspiciously.

"The trick is to move like a wraith," Lionel says mysteriously and Rosa giggles.

*

Now we are on the moonlit ridge above the Weddell Sea wearing about ten dressing gowns, plus scarves, wooly coats, and beanies. I found an extra fleece for Lionel from Rosa's mum's wardrobe. We shiver in the silence. There's no wind, but the temperature is minus-30 (I packed a digital thermometer from the laboratory in my utility backpack to help with gathering evidence). The two emperor penguins and fluffy chick stand with us in Coats Land, part of British, or maybe Norwegian, but definitely *penguin*, territory in the Antarctic. I don't know who Mr or Mrs Coats was, but I'm sure they got cold here as well. My breath is close to forming icicles and the cold is making my lungs hurt as I breath.

The rig and the ice are silver, though yellow lights illuminate the drill towers and cabins. It's a big structure, but some of the icebergs beyond are as huge.

Moonshine reflects on the snow and ice, like it's silver fire.

Lionel wanders ahead, over to the two blinking penguins and is further amazed that he can talk to them. "Ahem ... in the colony ... are all the chicks hatched?" I could hear him ask, and the penguins say, "Oh yes," and Lionel's mouth gapes open and looks at me in mild panic. I just shrug. The court is in session.

Rosa looks up at me, then looks at the oil rig sitting in the bay. Apart from the occasional faint clang or shout from the rig, there is silence. The water is still, semi-frozen, and ice floes sit like globs of white in the black. But the oil rig is lit up like a fun park and is surrounded by boats.

"The moon reminds me of my mother," says Rosa quietly.

I try it on: "Is your mother Artemis, the moon goddess?"

"Noooo, silly man. Mum and I used to look at the moon through a telescope when she was teaching me astronomy. She was a chemist," says Rosa. "The moon is the moon. The moon goddess is made up by humans to explain femininity ... and hunting ... and werewolves," she adds. "For some strange reason."

"Okay."

"I don't like that," she adds, pointing at the oil rig, "but it hasn't caused harm."

"Isn't there a thing in law called abundant caution? Where you prevent something before bad things happen?" I ask.

Rosa shrugged. Her breath was frozen.

"Not in law."

"But it's dangerous," I say.

"It's dangerous," she agrees.

"What can we do?" asks Lionel, catching on. He's a quick boy.

"Where is your colony?" Rosa asks one of the penguins.

"Just over the ridge there. Follow us." And it starts shuffling through the ice and dark, followed by its mate and the baby. The snow is deep and it's a big effort. I start to walk and the world disappears on me and I experience a sharp pain in my back. I'd just slid over on my bum and I'm staring up at a million bright pinprick stars in the sky.

"Ow."

Rosa and Lionel help me up. "Not very urbex," she says.

"Shuffle," orders the penguin. And so we shuffle off, up a long hill, in the chill air and the moonlight. An acrid smell soon catches my nose, and as we reach the top of the icy ridge, there's the colony, a HUGE expanse of ice, filled with large penguins as far as the eye can see. Thousands of them. The moonlight makes everything crystal clear. I can hear the noise too, honking and yarping, the sounds of an immensity of birds, not so far away. The stink of bad fish and poo is monumental.

"What's that smell?" I asked the penguin.

"It's the smell of home."

I'm glad I hadn't said, "What's that *horrible* smell."

A sharp night. Sharp shadows, sharp smells, penguin beaks (sharp) and the icy air is keen and cold.

Standing on top of some rocks on the ridge, I see the lit-up oil rig in the next bay. Lionel sets up his drone on a rock. It sits there like a squat black insect with tiny red leader lights like eyes, and six propellors. The plan is to measure the distance to the rig from the shore and video the construction. He pairs the steering unit with the drone and lifts the device into the air, sending it whirring. Firstly, high over the penguin colony and then after activating the GPS, Lionel aims it over the headland and out to sea. On the video screen attached to Lionel's control stick I see the flicker of white ice floes and black seas below the drone as it moves along until finally reaching the oil rig. Rosa and the two penguins also watch the screen over Lionel's shoulder as he eases the drone a little bit higher.

"Don't let the riggers hear it," I whisper to him, though I don't know why I'm whispering.

"There's too much construction noise. They won't hear drone buzz," Lionel replies.

The rig is small but it sure had a big drill tower and the men on the platform work under lights, assembling the drill tower with huge wrenches and robot lifters which whizzed around the deck.

"Looks like a jack-up rig," says Lionel, "a mobile rig."

How does the lad know all this stuff?

The penguin beside me clicks its beak angrily at the sight of the drill.

A boat moored to the platform's ladders is being emptied of scaffolding and drill parts by a crane, and men are guiding the hardened metal drill line up and over. The platform's well lit, so we can see the men moving around in their parkas and boots. On the back of their thick orange parkas is the Tau Corporation logo, the black bull horns with a thick drill for a face … or skull. Lionel is right – it's too noisy on the platform because no-one hears the mosquito buzz of the drone. It's clear the drilling is still in preparation and hasn't started.

"Battery's running out of juice, I'll have to turn back," says Lionel as he steers his drone back to the headland and lands it neatly on the rock in front of us.

"I've videoed that. The rig is very close – just over a kilometer from the penguin's beach according to the GPS," he says. "Won't be very deep there.

Rosa looks thoughtful. I inform the penguins that we'll be in touch soon and we thank them for their help. They waddle and slide down the slope toward their colony, while the world in front of me dissolves – very quickly

– and we somehow arrive on the slab on the roof garden and it's still night. The slab is hard and cold, but the air is warm and smells pleasantly of blossom.

I look at the moon – both this city and Coats Land share the same moonlight. Traveling the pathway in real time is nowhere near as discombobulating as time travel to the past. Lionel shakes his head in amazed delight. He tucks his drone under his arm and shakes my hand and Rosa's.

"I don't know quite what to say about that experience, including the bi-lingual penguins. I'll have to think about what just happened. I'd better go home to bed," he says.

"Stay warm," I advise and Rosa and he disappear downstairs.

*

We're in the comfy chairs in the attic room now, warming up, discussing the witnesses.

"The parents pushed that baby penguin into the oil puddle," says Rosa.

"I think so. And they knew the humans around would clean the little fluffer up."

"A bit mean," she adds.

"A bit desperate," I mutter.

"I don't know all the laws. The laws about these things. About unintended consequences. Father was teaching me all this when he died." Rosa sounds very frustrated. "I know Caiman thinks there's a big case here, but I can't see it. And sending me a slightly dirty penguin chick is not her style. There's something else underneath all this which I can't grasp. I'm sorry."

And she stomps out of the Hall of Justice to bed, clearly annoyed with herself.

*

Me? I stay up. For days I had been lying in bed with the glooms. And my lungs and eyes are still sore from Antarctic ice-air and I need a cup of tea to warm up my giblets, so I take the lift down to the first floor and put the kettle on and make a snack – a mushroom and pickled cucumber omelet sandwich. Then I take supper to the study. I shed my beanie and three of the dressing gowns and throw them untidily on the chaise lounge and for a while I sit in the Judge's chair chomping the hot sandwich and savoring the slightly bitter black tea that Madam C buys at the markets.

Then I pick up the Judge's massive magnifying glass and look over the big globe of the world on its stand. I crouch down to Antarctica and find the coast of Coats Land and looked through the clear sky at the ice sheet glinting in the moonlight. Further north, up into the Atlantic, clouds are gathering in angry sworls.

Then, for a sad few minutes, I examine the island of Crete, sitting in the wine-dark sea, just coming out of night, with pale dawn light on its beautiful high mountains and plateau. There are rain clouds to the north, but the sky over Crete is clear. I knew I wasn't looking at ancient Crete. I could see the glint of glass and tiles in the dawn light, of the cities and towns that stretched along the coast where Knossos once had been. I wished I could catch a glimpse of Elodie on the beach, or even on the side of a teacup, having a swim.

Then back to the Judge's chair. There was *Beyond the Rule of Claw*, on the last chapter. I picked the book up.

"*But back to first principles,*" Miss Shecklestone QC wrote.

There is nothing more damned than a civilization that sits and waits for the worst to happen. The law has a role there too. When laws are made by a government, they are often made in anticipation of the worst, and to stop harmful excesses. For example, our Clean Air Act. When it is found that a person or organization has invented a way to exploit something lawfully, but immorally, then you change the law to call the exploitation "stealing" and prevent it from happening.

I nodded in agreement.

Rules, like houses and promises, can be made.

Interesting, I think. And houses and promises can be broken, too, especially houses in an earthquake. Anyway, Rosa wasn't a rule-making government. She was the Judge.

As I concentrate on Miss Shecklestone's wise words there's a sudden enormous THUMP and a cloud of dry-paper dust. I almost jump out of my skin, and tea has splashed from the cup onto the desk.

There was a gold-embossed leatherbound book which had fallen, presumably out of the painted ceiling, in front of me, entitled *The Gods in the Machine*. I looked up for any more incoming, but I couldn't see the ceiling at all. The room was gloomy, with drawn drapes and it was shadowed above the reading lights. I gingerly pulled the new book toward me and opened it up.

*

FOREWORD

There are no such things as gods.

Well, that was upfront!

Only certainty that atoms and elements will act and react through the laws of nature. The earth will orbit the sun, the spring will kindle the green shoots, fire will consume matter.

Atoms remain the same, but always constitute change. Everything is dynamic. Earth, ocean and sky. Those slow motion rocks that move infinitesimally through time.

We are stardust and we are golden as is all plant life, animal life and rock life. All elements have their rules. And knowledge of those rules and what we do with them bind us to the destiny we choose. Chemistry is chemistry! Physics is physics! Biology, biology!

And choices are made by understanding those rules, and then following or ignoring them.

Goodness, I think. This is a very shouty book. I close the book to examine the cover to find out who the author was.

It says: *by Dr Ciara Somberly.*

Rosa's mum!

"Okay, Rosa's mum," I say, and take a slurp of tea, and a munch of sandwich, while I open the first chapter. "Let's go!"

THE TRIAL OF TAU AL-GORZ

Tau al-Gorz is enraged. I can feel his hard Elemental energy bouncing off the walls like an emotional drumbeat. A fury-vibe. He's hunched and seems poised to spring at Rosa from the defendant's bench and maybe strangle her. She sits across from the bloated ogre, behind the Judge's desk. Rosa is calm but hidden on my lap is the old metal fire poker, half bent by Billeon's fangs. A weapon, just in case I have to physically defend her, because, after all, Tau al-Gorz has struck out at Rosa before, with lethal consequences. I knew I'd lose the fight, but it would give Rosa escape time.

Siddley, in his stupid Italian suit and hat, is bouncing around his master's chest. Giddley is crouched in a corner, watchful.

Caiman, more relaxed, sits on the other side of the court aisle in her robes, clawed front legs crossed and tail wrapped round the back of the bench of the Appellants. She's with the two penguins we'd met a couple of days back. Beside me, but slightly higher at the Judge's bench, young Rosa is scribbling notes and sporting a Judge's wig! This is new. It was big, pink and stiff and made of coconut bristle. I thought it looked stupid, but

I'm not going to tell her, because she'd proudly told me at breakfast that, "today, I am going to wear a vegan wig."

Rosa finishes her scribbling, looks up and announces there will be no jury of peers because Tau al-Gorz and Caiman have no peers, being Elementals, and as Judge, she would try the case alone.

"And no games of chess either. This time the court will resolve the dispute between the Caiman and Tau al-Gorz with the evidence before it." She bangs her gavel. This is very brave. Her father had resorted to the chess game, either because he thought their dispute was too complicated for him, or through cowardice, though the reason why is never raised in the Judge's house.

Tau al-Gorz, Rosa's erstwhile murderer, speaks. "There is no case to answer. Drilling for oil is a perfectly legal activity and has been going on for a thousand years, from the time the ancient Anatolians collected naptha – their word for crude petroleum."

"Naptha!" scoffs Caiman in her growly contralto voice. "You know where that led the Anatolians. Greek fire and violence. Burned boats. War. Oil was nasty then and oil is nasty now. Nasty, nasty men's business."

"Silence in court, godmother and Tau al-Gorz," Rosa orders. "There will be no cross talk."

At least Caiman didn't call Rosa, "Egg", as she has done before. The giant reptile just shuts up, glowers and twitches her tail.

At the Associate's desk, I keep a keen eye on Siddley and Giddley who bob about on Tau al-Gorz's chest like a couple of ugly manboobs. Giddley still wears her dirty kimono and avoids Siddley, but she's alert and interested, a little bit awed by Rosa's pink wig. Whereas Siddley, in his tiny Zegna suit, is ballistic.

*

The furious Tau al-Gorz and Siddley, his bad conscience, inflamed one another's anger.

As he came through the doors earlier, the ogre had fumed, "This instant summons down the pathway is an outrage. I'm a very busy corporeal entity with a lot of projects. This is a mistake."

"You should be ashamed of yourselves," Siddley had shouted at us, head popping out of the ogre's chest.

The whole atmosphere in the room was dark and onlookers were nervous.

Rosa ignored his complaints as the friarbird bailiff led him to his bench. Tau al-Gorz had lurched and stomped in fury, rattling the room, and possibly the whole district. Caiman then slid in, and the friarbird hopped before her to the bench of the appellants. The court was filling behind-wise. I could see shapes, one being the fuzzy black shape of Bastqut, the cat "god", while the Old Man of the Forest had taken up a stool in the back corner. Other deformed projections were bobbles in the gloom, a range of Elementals and creatures I didn't recognize who were deeply interested in the outcome of the trial.

Again it's the middle of the night, when the Elementals preferred to do business, and the lights in the Hall of Justice are dim.

Chaz, Heloise and Sukki sit together next to where Mrs Cimbalom is, halfway down the left row knitting a scarf. Sukki had encouraged Yusif to go to a mental health respite center for the night so she could come along, and surprisingly he'd said yes. So, apart from Yusif and my absent Elodie, the crew are here. Directly behind Caiman are several more emperor penguins who'd hitched a lift up the pathway with the witness penguins. I believe this time Rosa was safe from the ogre, but violence permeates the air and I grip the poker with my hand, ready to defend. The courtroom is full. I'm on guard.

*

Rosa says to Caiman, "your submission please."

Caiman speaks. "Tau al-Gorz has again pushed his interests into a place where he has no business. The coast of Antarctica. A pristine place, where he is about to pierce the seafloor with a diamond drillbit, into an oil reservoir which may or may not be big, but which will likely leak and drown and murder the penguins that live beside this ice shelf."

"Pah!" says Tau. "The engineering is sophisticated and strong."

"Strong!" parrots Siddley.

Rosa chides Tau. "You'll have your turn, Tau al-Gorz. What do the appellants accuse Tau al-Gorz of?"

"Ignorance!" says Caiman.

"Not a crime, my dear girl. Never been a crime," says Tau al-Gorz to the Caiman.

"Hah, you think?" one of the penguins parps, and Siddley, already furious, loses it. In his pinstriped suit, he leaps from Tau al-Gorz's chest onto the floor in front of Rosa's bench and raises his little flaming fist, poised to throw a fireball at the penguin's head. Siddley's eyes are bulging and his back is arched like a bow, ready to hurl the fireball when Rosa bangs her gavel, the fireball pops, and a large piece of popcorn flies into the air and bounces off the roof. Siddley looks at the smoking stump where his hand had been, while the popcorn rolls in front of a penguin who munches it up and nods to his friend as if to say, "Yummy".

"Order in court. Sit down, Siddley," she says. Licking his burned stump he slinks back onto Tau al-Gorz.

"Explain how ignorance is a crime?" Rosa says.

"Certainly. Can I call my first witness?" Caiman asks.

The friarbird, who is clearly the court bailiff, says *oich!* and leads a portly man, who looks like he is wearing a giant, white knitted tyre, toward the witness stand beside the bench.

"And you are?" Caiman asks.

"I'm an 890 hectopascal low-pressure wind system currently off the coast of Coats Land, with destructive gusts up to 350 kilometers an hour," says the being.

"So you're a projection and not the actual wind system?" the Judge confirms.

"Yes. If I was the actual wind system, this city would be destroyed. I'm from the screaming sixties down in the Antarctic circle."

"Thank you for the clarification," Rosa says politely.

"And, as a storm, where are you currently heading?" Caiman asks.

"Well, I could be heading toward this entity's oil rig," pointing at Tau al-Gorz, "but lucky for him, I'm going to cross the coast of Coats Land further to the east."

"What would happen if you crossed over the oil rig?"

"The rig would be plucked from the seabed, like a soggy garden weed from a wet flowerbed, and thrown onto the shore and the hole in the ocean bed would be unplugged and belch oil. For sure."

"When your brother and sister storms cross the coast wouldn't the adjacent penguins be killed by the force of the wind anyway?" Rosa interrupts, suddenly concerned.

"Er, some penguins would, and that's the way of it, but these penguin what are here ..." he waves a knitted finger at the penguins on the bench, "them penguins are brilliantly engineered to deal with monumental storms such as me."

The penguins in the room honk quietly in approval.

"His oil rig is <u>not</u>. There is no oil rig that can be engineered to withstand me," adds the 890 hectopascal storm pointing at Tau al-Gorz. "His rig would snap like a pretzel."

"Thank you for your evidence," Caiman concludes.

"Cross examination," says Tau al-Gorz. Rosa gestures for him to speak. With a wheeze, Tau stands, and towers over the storm.

"But you are not headed for Penguin Bay in Coats Land, are you?"

"Not me, but one of us will get there."

"My risk assessments say that could be in ten years time which gives my minions a decade to explore for oil and exploit the reserve," Tau al-Gorz boasts.

The 890 hectopascal storm looks dubious. "That sounds like naive optimism. Should never be optimistic with the likes of me. We brush across the coast a lot more often than you think, sir. I wouldn't risk it. And then there's your oil tankers, bobbing about. They'd burst open and sink too."

"Pah!" says Tau. "You underestimate my engineers." And he sat down heavily.

The storm is dismissed and disappears in a whoosh, blowing a few pieces of paper off Rosa's desk. I pick them up for her.

"I'd say again, ignorance is not a crime," Tau al-Gorz says. "And I have …"

"You'll have your turn," said Rosa. "Next witness."

The Friarbird leads a rather gorgeous woman with platinum blonde hair and wearing a shiny silver-sequined figure-hugging dress into the room. She has a little mole on her left cheek above her ruby red lips, but otherwise to my eyes, she is flawless.

"And you are?"

"I'm Diamonds," she says in a throaty whisper from the witness stand.

"Your witness, Caiman."

"Do you constitute the drill tip of this man's oil rig?"

"Among other things, I do, though I'd rather focus on the jewelry."

"And you pierce the earth's surface?"

"In a rotational motion." She does a little twirl and pouts. "I may look gorgeous, but I'm very hard."

"And how do you feel when you drill?"

"Awful. Awful. I feel I'm betraying the mother who birthed me from carbon, with her crushing weight and metamorphic power. Here I am, bright and beautiful and then I'm made to turn on her by that entity, and hurt her." She points at Tau al-Gorz. "He's a mean, mean man." Diamonds starts to cry and I hand her a court-issued tissue.

Once she had composed herself, Caiman asks, "So you can withstand the pressures of drilling?"

"Of course ... as I said, I'm the hardest element of all. But the pipes above me sometimes snap under the wrong circumstances. Very flakey, those pipes."

"Has it happened before?"

"Oh yes, many times. That's why I prefer to think about Cartier ... or Tiffany. Not oil spills, which are never my fault."

"Thank you, Diamonds," says the Caiman.

"Your witness, Tau al-Gorz?"

Tau stands up, then goes "Humph" and sits down again.

"No questions. She works for me all the time, Judge," he finally says. "I'd like the court to note that she's a hostile witness."

"Hostile," hisses Siddley.

"Noted," says Rosa.

Diamonds blows Tau al-Gorz an ironic kiss, and then leaves. Chaz and Heloise watch the sparkly witness shimmy out the door in her tight dress and they both started to giggle like little kids.

I don't feel so cheery, but Diamonds had definitely been entertaining. Also, I can't see where this trial is going. It is all a bit mad.

"Next witness," says Rosa, staying very, very serious. She is slightly distracted when we both see the figure of Lionel sneaking in the landing door. He slinks into a seat in the back to sit next to the Old Man of the Forest. Suddenly Rosa looks really flustered.

I pass her a note. *Don't worry! Just be a nerd. L is here for you.*

She reads the note and gives me her little smile and bangs her gavel.

The next witness enters without the friarbird because she knew well the room and needed no guiding.

It is Elodie.

She is dressed in a long purple priestess dress and cloak, embroidered with crocuses and lilies, her blonde hair in Minoan ringlets on her shoulders. Her hair is laced with little flowers and her hand holds a triton shell carved with dancing dolphins. I am wonder-struck.

Rosa looks at me with a second little smile, as if she already knew that this witness would appear. Of course she did. She's the Judge.

I almost faint and realize I hadn't breathed from the time Elodie came in and made her careful way through the crowd to the witness stand. She is so beautiful, and stands in serene silence with her triton shell. Just once she glances at me with a smile and then goes very, very serious.

"And you are?" Rosa asks.

"Elodie, junior priestess of the Great Goddess."

Tau al-Gorz's face is complicated. He looks consternated, confused, angry and slightly enraptured, all at once. Siddley is aghast. Giddley is nodding sagely as if to say, "Good call." I notice Giddley has a puffy black eye.

The Caiman stands.

"Elodie."

"Yes, Ms Caiman," she answers.

"Where have you been?"

"I have been in Keftiu, also known as Kriti or Crete, looking for my dear friends Sukki and Yusif while I also traveled the island with the High Priestess bestowing offerings and blessings to the Great Goddess along the way."

"Why do you bestow offerings?"

"Because the Great Goddess needs to be strong and nourished and understood. To have the balance. To provide all life with a place, with food, reflection and laughter."

"Are you aware of this entity?" Caiman points to Tau al-Gorz.

"Yes, I once saw him being killed by a bull. But he lived again."

"So he got a second chance?"

"He did. And at the same time acquired something of a conscience. Which he often has difficulty listening to." At this, Giddley waved to Elodie and gave her a thumbs-up.

The Caiman asks: "If he listened properly, what would his conscience say about drilling for oil in the Antarctic?"

"Oh, I think he knows already," says Elodie. She smiled at the huge crocodile and then at Tau. "He ignores his conscience, which is worse than ignorance. I think his father, the great Minos, would also advise him to preserve what sustains you. And you don't kill things unnecessarily."

"Thank you," says Caiman sitting down.

"Your witness, Tau al-Gorz."

The Tau stands with his fearsome bulk and beady eyes, and leers at Elodie, face glowering after the telling off from the priestess.

"We rid ourselves of the Great Goddess 3000 years ago."

"No, you didn't. She's here in the court." Elodie points at Caiman. "She's never gone away. Here she is, still trying to protect her children from you!"

Tau shouted, "Objection! Argumentative!" and Rosa says, "Objection sustained." Elodie smiles at me.

Tau al-Gorz continues: "My father raised my people up to be great traders and sailors, artisans, helmsmen, and businessmen, wouldn't you agree?"

"Oh, yes," says Elodie. "The Minos I knew was a *grand homme* a great man."

"He made Keftiu," pronounced Tau al-Gorz.

"The Minos brought riches and knowledge from overseas, yes, but the island was sustained by the love and respect the people had for the land, and their belief in the wind, the water, the earth, the sun, the bees, the flowers. The people knew this one lesson down to their very bone marrow – respect the land. You know that, too."

"I knew that then, but I've moved on! I'm making this world without the goddess!"

"Objection!" barks Caiman.

"You really want to object to that, godmother?" Rosa warns. "He said in evidence: *I knew that then, but I've moved on*. Tau al-Gorz has just admitted to *wilful* ignorance."

"Ha! Egg! You are right. Objection withdrawn." Caiman laughs and sits down with a thump and cracks the bench slightly. Personally, I wince when Caiman called Rosa, "Egg", but no-one else, including Rosa, seems to mind.

Tau al-Gorz started to expand in bulk.

"This court is rigged," he bellows. "Rigged and rotten!" Rosa's wig blows off in the smelly gusting of his roaring breath, while objects fall from the shelf behind her. She bangs the hammer. "Order," she shouts back. "Those were your own words, Tau al-Gorz. *I've moved on*. Where have you moved on? You come from an ancient culture where there was a balance between nature and humans. Where are you now?"

Rosa starts to expand and grow bulky as well. A larger, fiercer Rosa, but certainly not as large as Tau al-Gorz. Elodie, sensing her cross-examination is finished, hurries over and sits down on my bench, and grabs my hand.

"I think I'm done, *cheri*," she says. We both watch Rosa in awe.

Rosa reached behind her and jammed her pink vegan wig back on her head.

"Where are your witnesses, Tau al-Gorz?" Rosa asks.

"I don't need any," he says.

"Why not?" asks Rosa. "Is that because not one of your minions dares come into the Hall of Justice, because they actually have to tell the truth here? About what you've been doing? About your plans? About the risk?"

"My plans are none of this court's business. I have many international projects underway and I must attend to them," Tau al-Gorz yells. His head almost bumps the roof now as he fills the space with his musty bulk and smelly, soiled robes. Both Siddley and Giddley, I can see, are stunned. Siddley just didn't have the moves any more. Giddley is in fact crying, her tears bubbling out and down the front of Tau al-Gorz's hairy chest.

"Your plans are everyone's business, TAU AL-GORZ!" Rosa bellows back, and a number of objects on the shelves behind Tau al-Gorz tumble off, including a pot plant which landed on the Old Man of the Forest's head which wakes him up.

Then Rosa pulls a bunch of papers out, and a big stamp.

"Your drilling in the Antarctic is denied. Too risky!" STAMP.

"Your farms in the Amazon basin, denied! Too risky!" STAMP.

"Your oil pipes through Alaska, denied! Too risky!" STAMP.

Each stamp is a body blow to Tau, who starts to lurch back into the crowd. People leap to either side as the ogre crashes into the rows of chairs behind.

Rosa hands the stamped documents to the friarbird who clamped them in its beak and hops across to serve them to Tau al-Gorz. Tau raises his huge palm to slam it down on the bird in front of him. I could see the friarbird quaking, but Rosa bellows: "DON'T YOU DARE SQUASH MY BAILIFF!" and her shout blows the green door shutters in the walls opposite open and draws in a gust of fresh wind.

Rosa's eyes are now a licking orange flame.

"For the capital crime of wilful ignorance, I hereby sentence you to live for five solar years in Keftiu in the year 2000 BC to relearn the principles of your culture. Furthermore, this court orders that you will not approach your younger self, the prince of Keftiu, or your father, the Minos, which will warrant PAIN of BANISHMENT to 10,000 BC for TEN years! You will be a traveling beggar for the term of your sentence."

She bangs the gavel while Tau al-Gorz has regained his composure and looks mildly amused.

"I'm not taking punishment from a sprat like you," he laughs, dismissing Rosa with the wave of a flabby hand.

But then Rosa pulls off her pink coconut fiber wig, unfolds it, and pulls out Heloise Simply's black tau from where it was hidden, and throws the little black object directly to Siddley who catches it without thinking. Siddley looks suddenly stricken, and then Tau al-Gorz, Giddley and Siddley disappear in a huge blue burst of sparks which fill the Hall of Justice with the smell of electricity and thyme, and then fall like petals onto the crowd.

AFTER PARTY

"I met the old ogre in Phaistos, another beautiful palace town in Keftiu ..." Elodie says but trails off because she's ultra-tired. The effort to tell her tale is a feat of endurance after her bubble travel followed by the big court showdown. Dark rings cloud her beautiful eyes, and she looks pale.

Still, all ears are on the key witness. All ears want the backstory. My urbex crew, minus poor Yusif, are crowded around. Sukki has her arm round Elodie, Chaz and Heloise tight beside them. Madam Cimbalom's here along with a couple of penguins who want to stay and party with the Judge. We are settled on stools around the ample kitchen island. Rosa, still wearing her stupid pink wig, and Lionel sit at the end of the bench sipping lemonade sherbets through paper straws. I have furnished the crowd with giant bowls of potato chips. Must be 2 a.m., but we are wide awake. Miloš, the dog, sits on Mrs Cimbalom's lap, sniffing the air.

Most attendees at the trial – Caiman, and other Elementals and projections – have faded to wherever they fade. Fearful of Tau al-Gorz, they were satisfied with the five year banishment, so no need to party for them.

But the crew assembled want the whole story. We knew the beginning and the middle, but how did Elodie become the star witness at the end? We crunch our chips and listen.

"As I said, I met the old ogre in Phaistos, another beautiful palace town in Keftiu on a hot lovely afternoon, yesterday, 4000 years ago," Elodie says, holding the floor with her strange time-twist tale. "I'd been hunting everywhere for Sukki ..." she hugs Sukki round her shoulders, "and *mon ami* Yusif. I was frightened for them because they'd disappeared without goodbyes. I looked and looked but instead of them, in the main square of Phaistos, I find the young prince hideously old and bloated with his strange moving tattoos – Giddley and Siddley – who I recognize from your descriptions, Benjee.

"Tau al-Gorz was doing okay, pretending to be a seer. Locals were bringing him food where he sat in the town square, because they felt sorry for him. They didn't recognize their handsome young prince. The old ogre's schtick was to call people over, ask questions, and get Siddley to tell them their fortunes."

Mrs Cimbalom says: "An honorable profession, unless you are Siddley."

"Giddley and Siddley were bobbing on his chest, being busy. I was walking through the palace square with young Althea, a senior priestess who was teaching me how to barter provisions from the Phaistos Palace stores. Remember Althea – she has the best ringlets, curling down to her *derriere*, and the smoothest complexion of all the girls – she may have even been elementalish, in my view. Strange, but pleasing vibes from her ... but I digress.

"The ogre sees us and immediately tries a crude seduction, with rude sex suggestions – he must have imagined, in his mind, he was still the hunky prince – so we laugh at the horrible old ogre and pretend he's joking. I knew who he was, but strangely, no power emanated from him, as you would find in any other Elemental. So Althea walks up to him and asks where he is from. He clammed up, but horrible Siddley said, *The future. We are the future,* a tone of menace is in his voice."

Everyone around the kitchen island is enthralled with Elodie's tale, including me, but I'm the drinks guy. While Elodie talks, I pour soda waters or expresso martinis, a red wine for Madam Cimbalom, and more lemonade sherbets for Rosa and Lionel. I make sardine shakes for the birds, while everyone listens in silence.

"So, sweet Althea and I, as guardians of the goddess, went to work on this great rude ogre, and told him about the net of nature of which everyone is a part – a net that isn't a trap, but a life support: the earth, wind, rivers, oceans that bring us fish ..."

A penguin honks.

"... and we seduce him with honeyed words, fine wine, and food from our bags, which he ate avidly. Then, when he'd had his fill he looked up and said, 'I know you,' pointing, staring at me with his beady eyes. 'You were a key witness at my trial. Before the Judge banished me here, throwing my lost toy bull into Siddley's hands, and forced me to become a mendicant.'

"Well, sir, I can honestly say I have never met you, I replied, and this ogre knew it to be true, but still the ogre looked very curiously at me, and I felt odd all the way to my fingertips, wondering how this could happen, as I knew of no trial, while I do indeed know The Judge. Even Althea, there in the glorious sunshine, observed me strangely. The ogre tried to stand up, but slumped back onto his giant cushion on the paved courtyard, then said to me, in a more angry tone, 'Just the other month. You tricked me into admitting my crime.'

"Althea again looked oddly at me and asked the ogre: 'What crime was that?'

"'Ha ha ha,' said horrible Tau al-Gorz. 'You two luscious lovelies are trying to trick me again. Get me into trouble.'

"Instead, his dear little good conscience, who couldn't help herself, spoke.

"'The crime was ignoring the goddess,' admitted Giddley. 'We've been sentenced by the Judge to five years in Keftiu, as a beggar, for ignoring the goddess for four whole millennia.'

"Althea laughed her tinkling laugh and said: 'Ahhh, well! The Great Goddess is everywhere here.'

"And Tau al-Gorz grumbled: 'Don't I know it.'

"And that was the moment when I knew I should leave. I had a *très important* trial to attend! We went back to the palace at Phaistos and I said *au revoir* to the lovely ladies of the goddess – hugs all round. The High Priestess Aria wept and gave me the triton shell, with carvings of the dancing dolphins, as my sacred talisman, and I arrived at the Court of Last Resort just in time for the trial and my cross-examination. And now I am very tired."

And she is, trying to blink sleep away.

Tau al-Gorz was right – the trial was rigged in a strange and backward way. Elodie had known the sentence and the punishment before she ever became the witness.

Only one other thing perplexes me.

"Also," I turn to Rosa, "how on earth did you have Heloise's black tau handy to throw at Siddley?"

"So," says Rosa, looking pleased with herself, "when we arrived on Keftiu, the little statue was sitting among the seaweed and driftwood. The little bull guided us from this dining room all the way to that place on the beach as it knew ancient Minoa very well. You guys were groggy or asleep, so I went exploring and just found it. 'Hello, tau,' I said, and I wrapped it in my beanie and put it in my pocket, just in case."

"You've had it all this time?" asks Chaz.

"Of course. When we returned to the house, I locked it in the safe, but right at the back like Mr Dawson Kennedy did, so no-one would find it. If it was Tau al-Gorz's emblem of power when he was a child – his toy – then that tau is very potent."

Heloise says: "Absolutely, it is."

Chaz laughs.

And Miloš finally speaks. He lifts his tired little nose and half-closed ogo-pogo eyes and in a squeaky, world-weary Eastern European accent, says: *"I zink it's time we all vent to bed!"*

*

I help tired Elodie up the stairs, and find some nice silk pajamas for her, and I tuck her into bed and then slide in beside her, with a warm kiss. I was so happy to see her.

"Tau al-Gorz visited the Hall of Justice, Elodie, and told me you'd died in an earthquake many, many years later, crushed by a falling temple. He looked so sorry. He looked like he meant it. I thought you would never come back."

Elodie, not yet asleep, opens her weary eyes to me, puzzled.

"Maybe he mistook me for my dear friend, the senior priestess Althea, from long ago – after all, my Benji, memories fade after 4000 years. Althea was preordained to be guardian of the temple in Malia, and Tau al-Gorz found her very attractive, and she and I were together a lot," murmurs Elodie with a sleepy smile. "Althea was very special with fabulous hair. She will be with the goddess now."

And with this explanation she falls asleep, a smile still on her lips.

I lie beside Elodie and stare up at the dark for ages until, through cracks in the drapes, dawn licks the ceiling with light.

By dawn, I'd filled myself with hopes.

I'd hoped Rosa was sleeping happy, knowing that she had been so boss in the conduct of her first really important trial.

I'd hoped Lionel had sneaked into his home like a wraith, way past 2 a.m., without disrupting his household and getting caught. He was very good at sneaking out these days through the secret conduit.

I'd hoped Tau al-Gorz would learn to accept his obligations to the natural world in the paradise that was ancient Keftiu, or what people these days call Minoa or Crete. I knew from the myths and history, that when his father died, the young prince became the famous, cruel King Minos, a ruthless and merciless leader who went on to make war with the other Mediterranean countries. This seemingly immortal ogre had been sent back to his origins to learn a big lesson. I hoped he would.

I'd also hoped that Yusif's health would get better – it was good to see Sukki laughing at the after party – and I hoped all of us crew would stick together even if we drifted apart.

And I dearly hoped that when Elodie woke up, there'd be some room for me in her heart next to her goddess, who was, when you think about it, a pretty wild old roomie anyway.

And then after two sleepless hours of heavy-duty hoping, I dozed and dreamed a quiet, ordinary dream that I was a clerk in the transport department, in charge of ordering the tram tickets for my city.

***

AUTHOR'S NOTE

Incredible Ancient Minoa is shrouded by crazy bull myths and archaeological arguments including the name of Minoa itself.

Egypt, the Mediterranean superpower of the time, called the place Keftiu, because the word exists in the hieroglyphics at Ancient Thebes. Early civilisations in Anatolia also knew the island state as Kaphtor.

Knossos, the great palace city was possibly pronounced Co-no-sos.

So the Minoans that Judge Rosa meets refer to themselves as something else because its most likely they didn't call themselves Minoans.

Greek scholar, Minos Kalokairinos, discovered the ruins of Knossos and did the initial dig but was stopped by his then Turkish overlords. British archaeologist Sir Arthur Evans later excavated and interpreted the findings and did a dodgy rebuild of the palace. Evans linked the palace complex to the legend of King Minos and the Minotaur, which was a reasonable assumption on his part, due to the bull frescoes. Through him we call the culture *Minoan*.

He also, unfortunately, took the credit for the discovery of the palace.

I've applied some writerly speculation, that the Minos – a word which emerges through Greek myths, was a word for "King" or "Chief" and that the Kings has a lineage. The art and other Minoan artefacts that have survived 4000 years of war, tidal wave, earthquake and theft point to an organised and highly ceremonial culture.

Remember – 4000 years is a long time for any truth to remain intact, and the mysterious Linear A writing of the Minoan civilisation, which would help explain the early phase of the Minoan Empire – before the mainland Greeks conquered Crete, has yet to be decrypted – although Mrs Heloise Simply made a good start when she lived at the palace.

Perhaps one day she'll publish her findings.

ACKNOWLEDGEMENTS

Thanks to all who have read and commented on Judge Rosa's various drafts – my writers' group, including Phil Kirby with his learned Jungian analysis on Chapter One, which arrived as a dream. I especially value the comments from young readers, especially Narayan and Naomi. Also wonderful - the advice on Young Adult fiction from childrens' author Emily Gale. Thanks to Steph Smith for the editing, and proof editing by my darling Alice Roughley. Red Tally Studios rock with the cover design, and Liquorice Light Publishing made the manuscript sing.

Ciara Somberly references a line from the song *Woodstock* by the blessed Joni Mitchell in the introduction to Ciara's masterpiece, *The Gods in the Machine.*

ABOUT THE AUTHOR

Colly Campbell is the author of the speculative cli-fi thrillers, *The Capricorn Sky* and *The Kyoto Bell*, exploring a future Australia battling a hostile climate.

By the time he was twelve, Colly had attended schools on four different continents, the last being Australia where he grew up in beautiful tropical North Queensland with his family. He later worked as a journalist, as senior advisor to Labor Ministers in the Australian Parliament, and as Communications Director of the Australian Institute of Criminology.

Although he's now a full-time member of the fiction faction, over the years he's written, published and produced plays, pantomimes, speeches, songs, feature articles, poems and childrens' stories.

Currently Colly is deep in Canberra's urban forest writing a new Judge Rosa case and the third book in the *Capricorn Sky* trilogy. You can find him as @collyology on Instagram and on Facebook as Colly Campbell Writer.

www.collycampbell.com.au